Jerry Hammersmith

LETTERS TO MARY SUSAN

From Her Outlaw Father

JERRY HAMMERSMITH

tellwell

Tellwell Talent
www.tellwell.ca

ISBN
978-1-77370-281-0 (Paperback)
978-1-77370-282-7 (eBook)

Table of Contents

DEDICATION

With love to my father, Allie Hammersmith (1910-2010). His boyhood memories of Jim Howard, shared with me in his senior years before his passing, made me determined to write this story.

INTRODUCTORY EXPLANATION

THIS IS A WORK OF FICTION. NAMES, CHARACTERS, PLACES AND INCIdents are products of the author's recollections of anecdotes and are used fictitiously.

My father, Allie Hammersmith, originally took me to the site of the Jim Howard homestead. It was one-half mile north of the one-room Teddington School first attended by my father. Jim Howard, one of that school's founders and first chairman of the school board, was one of my father's boyhood heroes. Dad told me many stories of Howard's homestead life, ones that Jim Howard had told my dad's maternal uncle, Roy Gaylord, (only 11 years older than my dad), who, after getting assurances of confidentiality, repeated them to his nephew. My father maintained that confidentiality over seventy years. Once disclosed to me, those stories inspired my commitment to fashion a historical fiction novel within which the Jim Howard stories would have a significant role.

Meredith Campbell in *Righteous Warriors* (2000), states that:

> "In the historical fiction genre, history is more than facts, dates, wars, battles, and political fortune. It

> weaves a fictionalized human story through actual historical events and eras. History, rather than being window dressing, drives the story."

Lee Paul, in Outlaws and Gunslinger Legends, says:

> "Whoever claimed that history cannot be changed was all wrong. The controversy surrounding Jesse James proves it. For more than one hundred years, researchers have done their best to lay him to rest, and for more than one hundred years they have failed. Since that day in 1882 when Tom Howard was gunned down in the parlor of his home, Jesse James has been an enigma. Eyewitnesses came forth to swear the dead man was the notorious outlaw, yet reports circulated almost immediately that Jesse James still lived.
>
> In the annals of western lore, there is no name more symbolic with western banditry than that of Jesse James. A product of the American Civil War, he rode into legend while still a young man. Many tales paint him as an American Robin Hood, with a gentle side filled with family love and compassion for the poor; that it was only incidental that he was a killer and an outlaw. It is a fact that his family and friends shielded him from the law for sixteen years. Was Jesse a misunderstood man betrayed by a friend and foully murdered, as many claimed? Or was he a desperate desperado, allowing another to be deceitfully killed in his place, so he could escape justice? Is there any way to prove who really lies buried in that grave in Missouri? No one has yet answered those questions to everyone's satisfaction."

This novel begins with Jim Howard recalling his life story from his Saskatchewan Penitentiary cell in the in Prince Albert in 1924. Sentenced to fifteen years, he reflects on the 78 years that brought him there. Each chapter describes his recollection of a period in his life. Following each chapter is the text of a prison-permitted one-page letter written to a daughter Mary Susan. She's in Missouri and he hasn't communicated with her for 42 years. A prison chaplain has encouraged him to renew contact.

This novel adds a fifth to four of the many options identified in the Jesse James enigma. A first option is the James Legend as most people know it. Second is the story of J. Frank Dalton who claimed on his deathbed to be the real Jesse James. Third is the story of James L. Courtney. Fourth is the story by Max McCoy in *Jesse, A Novel of The Outlaw Jesse James.* This novel's fifth option has Jesse, following his fraudulent killing, travelling from Missouri under the alias John Allen. He crosses the Great Plains in a Cattle drive to north western Montana. Employed as a ranch hand under a second alias, he soon finds himself unable to resist a return to his outlaw ways. Eventually, seeking escape from these ways, he heads to Canada's Carrot River Valley to homestead. Thirteen years later, one quick relapse to his old ways lands him in the Saskatchewan Penitentiary. At 83, arthritic and aged, he is eventually paroled by deportation to Montana in the care of his daughter. Readers are invited to draw their own conclusions on the continuing *James* enigma.

The main character in this novel is identified first as Jesse James, then as John Allen and finally, assuming the name of James Marion (Jim) Howard, a black cowboy and outlaw partner who was later killed in Montana. This novel's Jim Howard was, in real life, born in an area of Missouri close to where Jesse James had been born (Clay County) at about the same time. James, besides having relatives with the Howard surname, is known to have used the name Thomas Howard as an alias at times, including at the time of his alleged assassination.

These facts, when converged with the possibilities described by Max McCoy in *Jesse, A Novel of the Outlaw Jesse James,* (1999) *Bantam Books,* and this book's Sources, place this novel in the category of, '*while it may not have happened, it could have.*'

This novel's final focus, between 1911 and 1930, is based on some of the events in the post middle age life of a man known as Jim Howard in North Eastern Saskatchewan's Carrot River Valley. It weaves a fictionalized human story before, around and through actual historical events in an era of Saskatchewan history. Had it not been for the recollections of my father, Allie Hammersmith, the research assistance of the Melfort Public Library, newspaper collections of the Melfort Journal, the assistance of Saskatoon's Western Development Museum and the Prince Albert Historical Society, the Jim Howard story and some of Saskatchewan's connections with Missouri and Montana Big Muddy outlaw history would be incomplete.

Evidence discovered by Penny Markland of the Melfort Public Library in searches of old Melfort Journal newspapers was key to finding and telling this story.

Timely assistance was provided by Cliff Moore, the Chief of Education at Saskatchewan Penitentiary, who discovered and made available the journal of former Protestant Chaplain J.I. Strong, (the Anglican Protestant Chaplain at Saskatchewan Penitentiary, Prince Albert, SK in 1930) whose original Register is the only credible evidence that Jim Howard had been at that Penitentiary from 1924 until 1930.

Very patient, persistent and helpful Saskatchewan Archives staff in Regina, led by Carilyn Schwartz, supported by Catherine Holmes as well as Saskatoon staff, located some of the little Jim Howard and Birt Enders homestead evidence that remains. This was supported by the research work of Celeste Hannant at Information Services Corporation in Prince Albert, SK.

While officially-resourced agencies of the Canadian government assured me that no record of James Marion Howard exists within the records of any of their agencies, departments or institutions, the following page, including Howard's prisoner number, birth place, Baptist identity, penitentiary admission and parole release dates, copied verbatim directly from Rev. J.I. Strong's journal, tell us something different and make us wonder why, nine decades later, the Government continues to deny the facts. What really stimulated the 1930 parole of Jim Howard and why is the presence of a record of it denied to this day?

PAGE REPRODUCED VERBATIM

from Chaplain J.I. Strong's Journal

James Marion Howard	
Inmate No. 1133	
Date Received	Nov. 6th 1924
Date of Sentence	Nov. 5th 1924
Where Sentenced	Melfort, Sask.
Crime	Manslaughter
Term	Fifteen years
Previous Convictions	None known
Age	73
Nationality	Canadian
Where from:	Missouri
Calling	Farmer
Home Address	/
Married	/
Single	/
Widower	Yes
Temperate	Yes
Intemperate	/
Total Abstainer	/
Do you use dope and if so what	/
Cause of Crime	/
Creed	Baptist
Are you baptized	Yes
Are you confirmed	No
Are you a Communicant	No
Have you always been a Protestant	Yes
Knowledge of Parents	Deceased
Date of and how Discharged	10.11.30. Paroled

CHAPTER I

A FIRST LETTER TO MARY SUSAN

THIS IS A LOT FURTHER FROM CLAY COUNTY, MISSOURI THAN I EVER thought I'd get, thought Jim Howard as he speculated on his situation at Saskatchewan Penitentiary. He sat on his narrow bunk, a simple plank of pine with a thin pad of mattress. It hung from the rough cement wall by two chains and had to be folded up in the day time because the cell was only six feet by nine. A grown man could reach out both ways and touch the walls on either side of him. Across from the bed was a small wooden table that served as a desk to write his letters, or to hold a cup of warm water in the evening.

Silently, Howard reflected on the 77 years that had led him here. He looked younger than his age. He was five feet, eight inches tall and, despite his use of crutches and his crippled left forearm, he was fit. A reporter at his trial had said that. It had made it easy to convince Melfort's Saskatchewan Provincial Police and the court that he was only 73. He didn't know why that was important. He had always lived privately and his age was nobody's business. Now, he knew that would be the only way to survive this place.

He laid his chin on his hands, trying to remember how long he had been in this hell hole. The trial had ended November 5th, 1924 and the provincial police had deposited him in the Penitentiary in Prince Albert the next day. As he had shuffled through those big wooden gates dragging the heavy iron shackles behind him, he had heard them slam behind him; Jim felt a chill go through him that lingered, even later, during the hot summers when this place was like a Dukhabour oven.

The inmates were required to remain silent, not talking to another person unless it was to a guard. He also no longer had a name. Jim was not *'Jim'* or *'Howard;'* he was now '1133,' and he'd better respond to that. He hadn't minded the rule of silence as much as having his name replaced by his new prison number. On the outside he hadn't been much of a talker anyway; more of a listener. He had only talked when he had something to say; not when he'd just wanted to say something. This habit would benefit him well where silence was the rule.

At 77, he was one of the oldest inmates in the prison. However, he was immediately informed that this place offered no special treatment for the old. "You might be an old man, 1133, but you'd better be up and at it at the same time and the same pace as the rest," the keeper had declared on the first day.

The first month had been an orientation to the routines that would frame his life in this place, all in silence: up at 5:30 AM. 'Stand for the count', have a sponge bath and maybe a shave before marching to the Mess Hall for a fifteen minute breakfast of gray gruel flecked with husk, followed by tepid tea. Line up to wash his bowl, spoon and cup and put it back in a little grub bag to take back to his cell. Then, 'stand for the count' again, and off to work until he went back to his cell until 11:45 when it was 'stand for the count' and march to the Mess Hall for a fifteen minute lunch of a bowl of soup and one slice of bread; wash his 'tools' again and go back to cell on his range for lockdown. At 12:45, 'stand for the count' and then off to work until

4:00; back to cells to lie down until 4:45 and 'Stand for the Count' before marching to Mess Hall for a fifteen minute supper of a small boiled potato, bread and tea and sometimes a piece of boiled meat; back to the cells to lie back and think or read the bible or maybe a book from the little library off the dome if you'd managed to get one. Sometimes the Salvation Army people came to minister or leave pamphlets and sometimes the Chaplain came. At eight o'clock, the last 'stand for count' was followed by the water boy who came by to hand out a little jug of warm water to clean up with or save a little for drinking at night.

One night shortly after arriving, during his search for sleep, fatigue had unfettered Jim's thoughts and betrayed him as he began wondering about Missouri and his children. He hadn't seen or spoken to them since 1882 and yet, in here at night, thoughts of them wouldn't leave his mind. Was it guilt? Was he feeling sorry for himself? Even though Birt Enders, Don Willey, Bert Jobson and many others in the Teddington and Ratner districts had been good friends, he no longer thought about them in the same way. Is this what happened to new inmates? Or just to old, new inmates? Or just to him? He couldn't recall ever lying awake like this - even during lonely, cold nights, sleeping on the ground during the war.

Every day here was the same except Sunday, when there was no work and the prisoners could choose to go to church. Born to a Baptist pastor-father and an evangelizing Baptist mother, Jim had been baptized in their faith. But there was no Baptist Chaplain in this place. An Anglican Priest, J.I. Strong, welcomed all Protestant inmates to a service he held each Sunday. Rev. Strong also found a bit of time for short visits after service or in their cells with inmates who wanted to talk with him.

Chaplain Strong had a good relationship with the warden and staff of the penitentiary. What mattered to Jim was that the Chaplain agreed to have an evening visit with him once a week. Jim began to talk to him about feeling lonely. On the second Sunday that Jim was there, he disclosed to Chaplain Strong, "I've always been called a loner, but it's never been because I enjoyed being alone. Whenever I've tried to join the world, people always disappointed me so I don't go out of my way to make friends. It just leads to disappointment. My family is far away in Missouri and the people in Teddington and Ratner who haven't disappointed me can't come here. The only people around here that I can call friends are you and the Salvation Army folks," he concluded.

Rev. Strong smiled softly and said, "The loneliest moment in someone's life is when they are watching their whole world fall apart, and all they can do is stare helplessly. Convicted and sentenced at trial, then coming to this place and trying to adjust must be like that for you. I know you've been thinking of the way things were when you left your family years ago. The worst part of remembering the memories is the loneliness. Memories need to be shared by you and by the ones you love."

Holding back tears, Jim had responded, "All I ever wanted was to reach out and touch them, not just with my hands but with my heart. Sometimes being alone felt safe, but it never felt right. The fact is that I'm real lonely and likely to stay that way."

"The best you'll ever do is to understand yourself, know what you want, and not let anybody discourage you. Memories of your family are part of being lonely. Who you used to be is like a big black hole. You find yourself walking around it in the daytime, and falling in it at night, missing your family terribly. Loneliness is like being poor and unloved," the Chaplain responded sadly.

"Maybe I feel too dang much; maybe that's what's going on." Jim said.

"If you really want to feel better, you need to start writing to your daughter." The Chaplain smiled kindly. "You get to write one letter every month and you could use it to write to her."

"I can't do that. It'll just make her angry. She hasn't heard from or about me for all these years. A letter all of a sudden will just be an insult." Jim's reaction was quick and defensive.

"Remember what I said about the worst part of memories being the loneliness? I advised you before, and I advise you now, to remember that your kin have likely been going through this same loneliness as you. They haven't been able to contact you or know where you are. I said memories need to be shared - by you and by them," the Chaplain sat back and waited for Jim to speak.

"That might be true, but I left them; they didn't leave me. I'm sure they'll never forgive me when they find out I'm alive and in a jail in Canada," was Jim's final comment.

"Everything you've told me about your wife Zee and the love you shared makes me certain that she would have painted a loving picture of you to your children and insisted that, even though you were gone, they, like their mother, must love you forever." Rev. Strong's words carried a smile. "Come on, give it a try; she's not writing to you now. It can't get any worse."

Jim was finally convinced that even though one letter a month would be the most difficult thing he would ever do, he would write to Mary Susan. If he didn't, he knew he wouldn't last the winter in this place. His fifteen year sentence, with no outside contact, would kill him.

Like every other Sunday, this Sunday was spent alone in his cell. He began his first letter.

December 21st, 1924:

My dearest Daughter, Mary Susan.

Please share this letter with your brother, as, in the past, your Uncle Frank has written me that he is often away on business, and I would be unable to reach him.

I know this letter will be a shock to you and your brother. I am your father, Jesse James, or Thomas Howard, as you knew me, and I am alive and living in Canada, though I have taken another name. I was not assassinated, as you were surely told by your mother, but made a planned escape from our home, leaving my family to bury my half-brother in my stead. Your mother thought it would be best if I disappeared to escape my persecutors, so we arranged for a false assassination by my cousin, Robert Ford, and I fled with a new name and identity.

From the time your mother, Zee nursed me back to health from a gunshot wound in my chest, I loved her and swore I would never put her or our children at risk because of my reputation. My mother lost her arm and my little brother, his life to the bomb the Pinkertons meant for Frank and me and ever since, I feel great anger and shame when I think about how I had vowed to get revenge, but never did. Running away and taking my reputation with me seemed to be the only way to spare you all.

There were many stories about me and how I had died. They said I was a robber and a killer. Yes, I did kill, but those were times of war and fear. I stole to survive while we were on the run. But that is not the sum total of my story. I hope you will give me a chance to tell you about it.

Today I am in a prison, in a place you've never heard of and likely won't ever see, but it is time for you to learn where I have been and what I've done, in my own words. Because I was supposed to be dead, I could never tell you that I missed you and loved you. Here, I am allowed me one letter a month, so I am going to write you my story bit by bit. I need you to hear my truth. I will likely never get out of here, so there may not be another chance to tell you. Even if I never see you again, I will have told it with love. May this coming Christmas fill you with joy and happiness and a gentle spirit of forgiveness.

Your Papa,

Inmate James Marion Howard, #1133

Box 166, Saskatchewan Penitentiary, Prince Albert, Saskatchewan, Canada

CHAPTER II

MISSOURI ROOTS

JIM'S PRISON MEMORIES OFTEN WANDERED BACK TO WHERE HIS story had begun. Sometimes they were a melding of what he actually remembered and what he'd been told over the years. There were so many stories he wanted to tell Mary Susan that he thought were important and he didn't think she would care whether he actually remembered or had just been told.

He remembered when his name was Jesse James; his mother, Zerelda Elizabeth Cole, used to tell him that she had been born the older of two children in Woodford County, Kentucky in 1825. Her parents were James Cole and Sarah "Sallie" Lindsay Cole. She said that her family tree went to John Cole in Virginia. Jim remembered her as a beautiful, blonde woman, six feet tall with blue eyes. She had been told she got her domineering disposition from her father who had no fear of anyone or anything.

"Never show fear and never back down from any man or any woman," was her father's advice. Jim remembered how she'd insisted on passing these values on to her sons.

Her daddy died in a horse accident when she was two, and she lived with a relative until she turned fourteen and was sent to an Academy for Women in Lexington, Kentucky. "You'll learn to be a proper Southern lady," she'd been told. Shortly, she met the Academy's Baptist Pastor Robert Sallee James. In December 1841, she and the considerably shorter and older Robert were married in her guardian's home.

Although inheriting from his parents' estate, Robert decided that he wasn't going to be a farmer all his life and chose the ministry as his life's work. After arriving in Clay County, Missouri in 1842, he bought a small farm close to the town of Centerville and lived there, but soon set about organizing Baptist churches in the county. He was an eloquent minister and founded three churches in Clay County.

Robert and Zerelda James had four children: Alexander Franklin, born in 1843; Robert, born in 1845, (suspected of dying of cholera thirty-three days later); Jesse Woodson, born in 1847 and Susan Lavinia, in 1849.

Not long after moving to Clay County, Robert had grown tired of his strong-willed wife and they separated after the death of their baby son, Robert. They later reunited in 1846. The beautiful Zerelda was rumored to have taken a Clay County physician as a lover that year who was suspected by neighbors to be Jesse's biological father.

During the 1849 California Gold Rush, Robert James saw a way to abandon his family and informed Zerelda, "Willeyam and I are leaving for the gold fields of California."

"What makes you think that you're going to get rich there?"

"I'm not going to get rich," he replied, "but those greedy souls chasing gold need someone to preach the gospel to them." Zerelda never saw him again. She later learned that he had died of cholera at the age of thirty-two in a place now known as Placerville.

In 1852, Zerelda remarried a widower named Benjamin Simms, who had children of his own. He and Zerelda didn't have a happy marriage and they separated several months after marrying. Benjamin died a few months later in a horse accident. Jim recalled that he hadn't been very sorry about his departure or his death.

Again, Zerelda remarried in 1855 for the last time. Her marriage to Dr. Reuben Samuel lasted over fifty years and produced four children. He was a quiet, loving man, four years younger than Zerelda and he loved spending much of his time with his family. He accepted and loved Zerelda's children as his own, and in turn, young Jesse adored and worshipped him. They settled on the James farm and raised Sarah Louisa, born in 1858, John Thomas, born in 1861, Fannie Quantrill, born in 1863, and Archie Peyton, born in 1866. Neighbors whispered that Dr. Samuel had also fathered Perry Samuel, a mulatto boy born in 1865 to one of his slaves. Perry was raised as part of the Samuel family and was often included as one of the Samuel children.

One old slave, Uncle Alphonse was loved by the James and Samuel children. They went to him for comfort when they were sick or upset and he helped raise them almost as much as their mother did. He was likely only 40 years old, but to the children, he was an old man. Alphonse would often give one of them a silent hug when their spirits were down. Jesse recalled him as a strong, calm and quiet man who helped the children cope with the family tension over their mulatto half-brother, Perry.

While growing up, Frank and Jesse spent hours learning to ride and shoot and playing in the woods where they could disappear silently from sight. They had no fear of anything, something they learned from their mother, Zerelda insisted that her boys always stand up for their beliefs. She took the family to church and Sunday school regularly. Jim thought of his and Frank's early childhood as very normal. They were part of a loving and happy family living a peaceful existence. They were not any better or any worse than other boys of their time and circumstance.

But these were crucial times politically. Events of the nation that were happening on their doorstep would leave their indelible mark on the James boys. In 1854, Congress ruled that Kansas and Nebraska citizens should determine for themselves whether slavery should be permitted or not, and vicious border fighting resulted, followed by the Civil War.

Thus began the decline of life as they knew it, because the Samuel family farm home was located in dangerous Missouri territory, close to the Kansas border. While the Civil War lasted five years in other places, it lasted ten years in Missouri. Kansas Jayhawkers, from the anti-slavery side, began a series of slave-stealing raids into Missouri. Sometimes these slaves were sold back to their original owners at a tidy profit. The marauders left so much destruction behind that Missouri residents retaliated by taking matters into their own hands and became Guerrilla Bushwhackers.

In 1860, South Carolina seceded from the Union, followed by Mississippi, Florida, Alabama, Georgia, and Louisiana and Texas, Virginia, Arkansas, North Carolina, and Tennessee followed the next year. Missouri was split because slavery was such a divisive issue; some supporting the South and some the Union. Jesse's family had been slave owners for generations so they sided with the South and were soon subject to raids by the Kansas raiders who stole their livestock and burned their houses. Some Clay County farmers, wishing to avoid Bushwhacker/ Jayhawker fights, moved north to Iowa where they could farm peacefully and find strength with slave-owning friends in Missouri.

Several months later, Missouri's provisional government ordered all adult men to enlist in the state militia to fight for the Union. Frank James had no such intentions so he enlisted with Willeyam Clark Quantrill's Confederate Partisan Rangers. They wore only the uniforms they took from dead Yankee bodies and recognized none of the conventional rules of war, but they fought for the Southern cause. Every man knew that if he was taken alive, he would be shot. In turn, the Partisan Rangers showed little mercy to their captives. Yankees soon learned to fear and respect this band of guerrillas.

It wasn't long before the Missouri anti-slavery militia found out about Frank's connection to the Rangers. In May, 1863, a squad of Yankee soldiers rode into the farm yard looking for Frank. During the raid they hung Dr Samuel from a tree by his neck until he told them about Frank.

In his cell, Jim remembered them running him, an undersized 15-year-old boy, down in a field and whipping him until his back was torn and bloody. They also beat his mother, who was pregnant. Later, after crawling home, young Jesse found his mother trying to save her husband. She'd succeeded in cutting him down from the tree, but he was badly injured and would later be institutionalized due to a brain injury.

As soon as he was well enough, Jesse determined to strike back. He asked Frank, "Get me into Quantrill's Rangers with you." But Quantrill turned him down as too young. Word got around that Jesse had been to see the enemy leader and the militia returned to the farm. Neither Jesse nor Dr. Samuel was home, but Zerelda and the other children were. They were arrested and hauled to jail in St. Joseph for several weeks where they were accused of being Confederate sympathizers and they were starved and abused.

Consumed with hatred, Jesse sought Frank's assistance in trying another approach to Quantrill to beg to be allowed to ride with the Rangers.

January 25th, 1925

Dear Mary Susan,

I hope this finds you and yours in good health. I am healthy but I miss you terribly. I have so much to tell you about my life and hope you will try to understand how it all happened. How did I end up in this part of Canada and in jail? I'll tell it to you in the one letter per month that I'm permitted to send out.

I do not blame anyone for my circumstances. Any problems I have are my own, but I am still trying to understand, after seventy-eight years, how I got here and what led me down such a lonely path. My absence from your life has been selfish so I wouldn't be surprised if you were still angry at me. but all I can do is try to make some sense of it for you.

My parents were very young when Frank and I were born. Our father took off chasing gold while we were little lads, leaving our mother alone to raise us. Learning of his death, she remarried to Benjamin Simms, but it wasn't a good match so they both agreed to part. Mother married again and this time it was to last. Having Dr. Rueben Samuel for a step-father was good for us children, just as he was a good husband for our mother. We were a happy family in the early years, before the war and strife began. Together, they raised four more children and as we all grew up, she was a loving mother to us all, teaching us about her Baptist faith and the commandments and the difference between right and wrong. It often pains me to think of how things changed so much in later years.

I am reminded of one of the things she taught us when she said, "Don't ever believe that the James family or the State of Missouri will determine where you can go or what you can do – they've merely determined where you start. The rest is up to you." Those words of advice have given me great courage to seek my fortune and have lasted me a lifetime. Sometimes the path was steep and sometimes it was difficult, but it was always my own path.

Life changes things. I got an old newspaper from the library here and read that this past October 9th, the United States of America, having once engaged in a civil war over race, has announced that the they enjoyed the first Negro Baseball League World Series: 'KC Monarchs shuts out Hilldales, 5-0'. I guess Mother's advice was true.

Love, Papa

Inmate James Marion Howard. #1133

Box 166, Saskatchewan Penitentiary, Prince Albert, Saskatchewan, Canada

CHAPTER III

UNDER QUANTRILL'S BLACK FLAG

THIS PRISON JUST GETS COLDER AND COLDER, JIM THOUGHT, AS HE lay back on his bunk and tried to ease his aching bones. He'd only been in Saskatchewan Penitentiary for four months, but it seemed like forever. The horse hair mattress and the harsh wool cover on top felt like he was lying on the ground in a patch of poison ivy.

My poor old bones can feel every injury I've ever had, especially in my chest, where I took a bullet, a-running from those Union soldiers. The cold just makes it worse. That and no good, healthy food in here like the food I grew on the homestead will surely speed up my passing on.

To get his mind off his painful joints, which sometimes felt like punishment for all his old sins, Jim began to think of the days of his youth as one of Quantrill's Rangers. He was back in 1862 again, young and restless and angry.

• • •

"Quantrill's stubborn and doesn't like being second guessed. If he said you were too young, he'll still think that," Frank replied, going on, "How about we talk to Bloody Bill Anderson? He said he liked your spunk." Because the James family had always owned slaves, they had supported the Confederate Army from the time the war started so it was no surprise when Jesse's brother, Frank joined the Rangers in 1862. Jesse wanted to join as well, but when approached, Quantrill had said he thought the boy was too young and inexperienced.

One of Quantrill's lieutenants, Bloody Bill Anderson, had some influence with the leader, and Frank knew that if he offered to look out for Jesse, Bill might be swayed to convince Quantrill to accept him. Just as Frank thought, Quantrill agreed and from then on, Jesse considered Bloody Bill as a brother. The James brothers' cousins, Cole and James Younger eventually became Rangers themselves.

Willyam Quantrill had only been 24 years old when he and his Partisan Rangers, a wild troop of several hundred men, offered to join the Confederacy. They were sworn in in 1861, and became a major force of the Southern Missouri Cause. The Quantrill Rangers were known for robbing mail coaches, attacking Lincoln's supporters and persecuting any communities that Quantrill considered anti-Confederate. The Rangers were also accused of murdering Union Army prisoners.

Jesse was an experienced guerilla warrior by the time he was seventeen years old. He was a trim five feet, eight inches, lithe and youthful-looking with an oval face and his father's blue eyes. He had a hot temper and rode his horse like the wind, holding the reins in his mouth and shooting his guns with either hand, hitting his target dead on. He never missed. He used to say, "If it is a crime to love the South, its cause and its President, then I'm a criminal." He bragged that he would rather lie down and die in prison than pay allegiance to a Yankee government.

Bloody Bill Anderson's sister had been killed by the anti-slavers and his one goal in life was to kill Yankees. She had been one of a group of women who supported Quantrill and who had been arrested by Union forces. They were detained in an old building in Kansas that was so overcrowded, it collapsed. Anderson's sister was one of several women killed. Anderson was filled with anger and grief and vowed to get revenge for her death. He became a savage, chopping off his enemies' heads with his sword and carrying the scalps of many of his victims on his saddle bags. Nonetheless, Jesse worshiped him and tried to be just like him, though he could never force himself to be as brutal as Anderson.

Quantrill had been born in 1837 in Ohio. He was a schoolteacher for several years until he was charged with horse theft, and moved to Utah where he earned his living as a gambler. A year later, he moved again to Lawrence, Kansas and worked as a teacher until his criminal past followed him. By then, he was wanted for murder and horse theft, and decided that it would be wise to run off to Missouri in 1860 where he entered the Civil War on the Confederate side.

By late 1861, he had become the leader of the Partisan Rangers, a unit within Quantrill's forces; at first, his band was no more than a dozen men. They attacked Union soldiers and sympathizers along the Kansas-Missouri border and battled with Jayhawkers, who were pro-Union guerrillas. Jayhawkers staged raids on Quantrill's men from Kansas into Missouri and Quantrill was often heard to say that the Jayhawkers were just Yankees without uniforms. He ordered that his men show them no mercy.

Quantrill liked to appear gentle and innocent but, through his kindly smile, he often pronounced a death sentence on anyone he thought deserved it. Sometimes he even sang a tune softly as he shot his victims. Jesse was surprised when he learned that, at times wearing a disguise, Quantrill would go through small counties, proclaiming his own infamy, and declaring himself to be the greatest of all the Rangers. Jesse came to believe, as his mother had once told him, that "a lie repeated often enough is much stronger than the truth". Lie or not, it served its purpose and terrified Yankees and citizens alike. It was a lesson Jesse would long remember.

Quantrill's was the most savage fighting unit in the Civil War, using a style of guerrilla warfare that terrorized civilians and soldiers alike. Union forces soon declared him an outlaw, but to his supporters in Missouri, he was a hero. It wasn't long before the Confederacy made him a Captain.

As Jesse soon learned, both the Southern Guerrillas and the Federal troops were guilty of terrible cruelty that they inflicted upon both Missouri residents and opposing soldiers. There seemed little room to point fingers of guilt, unless they were pointed right back at themselves. As angry as he was about the cruelties he had experienced back home with his family, Jesse had a hard time keeping the bloodshed and brutality out of his dreams. Yet he soldiered on. It was during one of his days as a guerrilla Jesse received his nickname. He had been cleaning his pistol and it accidentally discharged, taking off the tip of the middle finger on his left hand. He'd shouted, "That's the dingest, darndest thing," and the others had quickly given him the name 'Jesse Dingus.' After he became a hunted outlaw, he always wore gloves to keep from being recognized by his lost finger.

There were other features that were harder to hide. When he was little, he got an inflammation on his eyelids. When it flared up, he looked as if he had pink-eye, and it caused him to blink repeatedly. Later, folks would say his stare was glassy and evil and he became known as a cold blooded killer, partly because of his appearance.

In April 1865 near the end of the war, Bloody Bill Anderson was killed in an ambush, and many of his men ran to safer ground in Louisiana and Texas. Quantrill had been killed in Kentucky. Jesse's brother, Frank, along with other Raiders, had surrendered and were paroled to go home.

Jesse and a party of stragglers, planning to surrender, had been riding to an official surrender station, when they came across some Union soldiers. Someone opened fire and Jesse was shot in the right side of his chest. He was able to crawl into some bushes as two Yankee soldiers followed him; he killed the first Yankee's horse, and then hid near a stream. The soldiers searched briefly, and then ran off, leaving

Jesse to find refuge. He'd been wearing a flannel shirt and the bullet tore through it before entering his flesh. It carried a ball of shirt with it and likely saved him from bleeding to death. When he was finally rescued, the wound was so severe he wasn't expected to live. Because he'd been shot in front of them, the rest of his unit thought he was dead and his name wasn't listed as one of those who surrendered. Ever after, Jesse was harassed by Federal troops looking for him. Technically, he hadn't surrendered so he was considered an outlaw. His fate was cast because he couldn't get to that surrender station.

Once able to move about, he sailed up the Missouri River on a steamboat and joined his mother and Dr. Samuel in Nebraska where they had fled to avoid the war. His wound was so serious that no one thought he'd survive. Dr. Samuel cared for him for about two months but Jesse didn't get much better. Sometimes he coughed up small bits of the flannel shirt he'd worn the day he got shot. He was sure he was going to die and begged his mother to take him home to Missouri, so they travelled to Kansas City where they stayed at a boarding house run by Jesse's Aunt Mary James Mimms. His cousin, Zerelda (Zee) Mimms, named after Jesse's mother, nursed him tenderly and during the next four months, he gained back his health, although that bullet remained in his right chest the rest of his life. Over time, Jesse fell in love with Zee, and they became engaged. They were married nine years later. For many of those years, Jesse was on the run.

Jesse, a good student of his mentors Quantrill and Anderson, had soon earned fame as a rebel guerrilla, a bank robber, a hijacker of trains and stage coaches and a merciless killer. But to those who still believed in the cause of the South, he was a hero to many in Missouri. After the war, he and his brother, Frank, along with the Younger brothers, applied what they had learned and for a decade, they robbed banks, stage coach and trains as they carried on their 'anti-reconstruction insurgency' against the Yankees.

• • •

I'm getting old, Jim Howard thought, as he lay upon his bunk. *I just feel like I'm readin' a book when I recall those days with Quantrill and Anderson. It hardly feels like it happened to me. And one thing's for sure. I never ever saw Quantrill's Black flag, or took an oath, nor did anyone else I knew. Maybe I imagined that part.*

February 22nd, 1925

Dear Mary Susan,

It's still winter up here in Canada, and I am chilled to my old bones most of the time. Back home in Missouri, the sun would be warming the earth a little but I sit here in this stone cell, picturing you out on the veranda with a cup of tea, taking a few minutes to read my letters. I hope you are well and that the children thrive.

I have much time to reflect on my life these days. I remember the convictions of my youth and I have many regrets about some of my actions as a soldier for the Confederacy, but it seemed to be the only way to protect our way of life and families. I think I am trying to forgive myself and be forgiven by the souls of those I have hurt. You've no doubt heard many stories of the war, of the actions of the Quantrill Rangers, of Bloody Bill Anderson and so many other military men. As in any war, both sides did some ugly things that we're not proud of during that time. Dr. Samuel once told me that the problem with history is that it is always written by the side that wins the war. I ask you, when you hear my war stories, to understand that I am only telling it from my perspective, but also to remember that our whole lives were being torn apart from anger and fear. I only know what my family and I went through, and have a tough time imagining how my enemies felt.

I am and always will be a Confederate. I saw brother fighting against brother, and innocent people killed over a war we didn't need to have, but we felt that we needed to protect our own kith and kin. Now that I am older, I see that the Yankees likely felt the same way. There was a lot of anger on both sides that sometime, somehow, I hope we can get over. If we're going to manage that, we'll all have to swallow our pride. I don't think that my generation - Yankee or Confederate - is ready to do that. Your generation will have to lead.

Forgiveness is one of the things I must seek, both for myself and from my enemies. I hope your generation can do that too, in the South as well as in the North, because I don't know if my generation ever will. Dr. Samuel once told me, 'Anger is an acid that can do more harm where it is stored than to where it is poured'. I fear that anger is still too deep on both sides for my generation to ever get over. I pray that yours will be able to.

Love, Papa.

Jim Howard, Inmate # 1133

Saskatchewan Penitentiary, Box 166, Prince Albert, Saskatchewan

CHAPTER IV

INSURGENT GUERILLAS

THE SNOW HAD PILED HIGH ALONG THE LEDGE OF THE TALL, narrow, barred windows that looked onto Jim's cell.

At least that snow will help to insulate this ice box of a prison against the north wind. I used to pile snow up around my farm house on the homestead to do the same thing. Surely do miss those days. I never thought I would end my life in prison, especially after escaping jail all those years after the war.

Jim laid down on his cot and looked up at the grey ceiling as his mind wandered back to the past. It was Sunday, the last Sunday of the month, and he intended to write his letter to Mary Susan soon, but he was tired and slipped into a lonely reverie about days lost. It was just over forty three years ago since he had been 'assassinated' back in St Joseph, Missouri, and had made his get-away out west. Maybe he would tell Mary Susan about those days. But he needed a few moments to rest his old, sore bones.

• • •

The years following the civil war were tough for Jesse and Frank, along with most of the Missouri guerillas. The new provisional government, via state constitution, had made everyone who had anything to do with the Confederacy, second-class citizens with little or no rights. When a former Ranger was arrested in nearby Clay County, the James brothers had gone on the run in case the captive ex guerilla, under interrogation, might reveal their whereabouts. It wasn't an easy life, living on the lam.

Politics and economic hard times had resulted in a difficult recovery after the war, especially for those who'd fought as irregulars or guerillas. The new constitution didn't allow them to vote, practice law, medicine, or other professions. They weren't allowed to have jobs or serve as officers of a church; they weren't allowed to take on mortgages, so they couldn't buy farmland, although the banks provided mortgages on the land to Yankees and non-Confederate southerners. Ex-Union soldiers were pardoned for all wartime activities committed after January 1st, 1861, but Confederate veterans didn't receive the same pardons. Confederates were ambushed and lynched, so many took up weapons once again, believing that the only way to earn a living was with guns. The James brothers thought they had no choice but to do the same.

At first, they had gone back home to Missouri where Jesse and Frank had hunkered down, kept quiet, tended their family farm and tried to live peaceful lives. Jesse even joined a Baptist church and was baptized to please his mother. They lived at their mother's farm for a while, but the Yankee occupation of the state was too much for them. Southern wealth was grabbed up by the banks who had taken advantage of the state constitution. Jesse and Frank saw that the banks' strategy was to use Southern wealth to finance farmland purchases, and call it 'reconstruction'.

Soon, the brothers formed a band of like-minded, tough ex-guerillas, survivors of the war. Frank and Jesse, their cousins, the four Younger brothers, and a dozen or so other veterans, all of them expert shots, became known as the James/Younger Gang. In Clay County, their home base, they were immune from the law, and like other Quantrill Rangers, they had friends all over Missouri, Oklahoma, Texas, Tennessee, and Kentucky.

On February 13, 1866, the James gang robbed a bank at the Liberty, Missouri Clay County Savings Association. It raised sixty thousand dollars. The plan, initiated by Jesse in their first bank robbery, was to send one man into the bank, go to the cashier and ask him to change a one hundred dollar bill. When the cashier went to the safe, a second man would enter the bank. He would go to another cashier and calmly say, "If you will write out a receipt, I'll do my banking", then sit down as if about to make a deposit.

When the cashier started to write out the receipt, both men would show their guns and ask for the contents of the safe, then back out of the bank and leave on waiting horses. This strategy, with several variations to suit different banks, became the signature of the James/Younger gang in bank robberies throughout the 1860s and 70s.

The James/Younger gang committed most of the raids on banks, trains and stagecoaches attributed to Jesse James in those years throughout Missouri, Kentucky and Iowa, but sometimes Jesse was blamed for crimes that he didn't actually commit. Two robberies might be committed at the same time hundreds of miles apart, yet witnesses at both scenes swore they saw Jesse James. To throw off detection and create confusion, different gang members would use the alias of Jesse James. It became a real chore to determine who did which crime.

Frank and Jesses believed that not only banks, but also stagecoach companies, were thriving on ill-gotten gains from the Confederacy. They began robbing stagecoaches in early 1874. In January of that year, the gang stopped a stagecoach on its way to Hot Springs, Arkansas and ordered the passengers to line up and kneel with their hands in the air. They were frisked for weapons, and ordered to give up their money and jewelry. Whenever a passenger was asked if he had fought for the Confederacy and replied he had, his possessions were given back.

"We only want to rob Unionists. In and since the war, Unionists robbed the South and this is just fair return," was Cole Younger's comment.

The men took the express bags from the coach and went through the mail, taking anything worth money. Their final act was to unhitch the horses from the coach, stealing them to sweeten the deal. The first stagecoach robberies, like the bank robberies, became the pattern for the gang to follow.

• • •

Jim paused his wool gathering and brought himself slowly to the present. *This everlasting winter keeps me chilled as a corpse,* he thought, covering himself with the wool blanket from his cot. The inmates weren't supposed to pull their covers over their heads so the guards could see them when they passed for the count, always afraid that one of the prisoners might have made a dummy and found a way to escape. *I'm an old man. Surely they'll take pity on me and not write me up for trying to find some warmth on a chilly, windy day. I think Mr. Peters is the boss today; he's kindly to me most times.*

He shivered as he waited for the wool blanket to warm him a bit, and wondered if Mary Susan would ever be able to understand how the people of Missouri had become so determined to keep their southern values and resist the oppression of the government. Even now, as he watched the pictures of the past move through his memory, it seemed impossible that he could ever be able to explain to her how scarred they all had been, after surviving the brutality and poverty and helplessness of those days.

• • •

Missouri became known as "The Robber State." The rest of America couldn't understand why the Gang had never been captured because they didn't understand the conditions in Missouri at that time.

Railroads had been given government bonds to buy up land and charge higher shipping fees, even though the voters of the state had voted against it and farmers, already in debt from the Civil War, could not afford the high fees. Property taxes were also raised to pay interest on railroad bonds. So when the James-Younger gang decided to deal out a little justice to the railroads who had chased farmers off their lands, many Missourians cheered them on. These self-identified insurgents called the railways 'the arteries of the Union', carrying the blood of Southern wealth and they intended to stop the bleeding.

They first held up the Chicago, Rock Island and Pacific train near Adair, Iowa, having heard that seventy five thousand dollars in gold was going to be transported on it. They broke into one of the railway's handcar houses to steal track tools, and rode to a curve in the tracks, where they removed bars and spikes from a length of rail. Next, they tied ropes to the rail and waited for the train. When it was past the point of being able to stop, they pulled the rail out. The engine turned over on its side, injuring the fireman and several passengers. When they found the baggage car empty, the gang robbed all the passengers. Jesse perfected this technique to such a high degree that other gangs imitated this style in their robberies.

• • •

Jim rolled over and turned his back to the cold wall of his cell. It radiated cold and dampness in this endless winter, just as it generated its own heat and humidity in the unbearable, hot summer. He was reminded of those days he and Frank slept on the ground when they were on the run after the Pinkertons began their merciless hunt for them. Suddenly, he felt a flush of anger and shame crawl up his back and onto his face as he recalled that day so long ago, when he learned that his little brother had been killed and his mother wounded because he couldn't protect them from the Pinkertons. The fire of his hatred flamed as high now as it had the day he learned of his family's persecution in his stead. It would never die until he did.

• • •

Back home in Missouri, the railroads, stagecoach companies and banks had hired the Chicago-based Pinkerton Detective Agency to put a stop to the James gang. On the night of January 25th, 1874, Pinkerton detectives surrounded the James farmhouse and tossed a thirty-two-pound iron bomb, wrapped in kerosene-soaked rags, through a window. They had just tossed one in a moment earlier, which had not exploded and Zerelda had been able to maneuver it into the fireplace to keep it from burning the house down. When the second bomb landed in the parlor, nine-year-old Archie picked it up to toss it into the fireplace as well. This time the bomb went off and he died a few minutes later. Zerelda's right arm was mangled and had to be amputated below the elbow. Dr. Samuel was also injured. This atrocity at the James farmhouse did much to sway Missouri sentiment in favor of Jesse and Frank and against the Pinkerton detectives.

On January 31, 1874, in defiance of their family's maltreatment, the brothers and their gang robbed the Mountain Railroad Train at Gad's Hill, Missouri, south of St. Louis. Witnesses said that five to seven members of the gang made a haul of twenty-two thousand dollars plus passengers' personal possessions. Jesse decided that they would hide out at Rob Willey's ranch, family friend who lived near Cedar Falls, Iowa. He was sure that no one knew about this place. He also knew that during the war, Rob Willey had been a member of the 'Copperheads', a group that had secretly raised money for guns and other supplies to be sent to the south. They were called 'Copperheads' because the Union people thought they were as deadly as the copperhead snake. The Willey-James friendship would last for many years with Willey providing food and money to them when needed.

By that time, the James brothers had become living legends. They had been ferocious guerrillas fighting along the border for the South, and Jesse had survived dreadful wounds which would have killed a less extraordinary man. Both brothers were known to fight at any hour, in any way, using many names and disguises, and they would not be driven from their home. Because of loyal friends, they were able to come and go like Robin Hood. They gave holdup money to friends, neighbors, and relatives to help pay their debts, and their family and friends never forgot. So when the James Gang needed to hole up, they had no problem finding a safe place.

Jesse once heard of the wife of a Quantrill Ranger who had been killed in the war. She feared that she would lose her home and land to the tax man if she didn't pay the high taxes he said were due. When Jesse rode into her yard asking for food and shelter, she told him of her troubles. He asked her, "When's the rent due"? and "What road is he coming on"? He gave her enough money to pay the taxes and purchase her farm back, but before he and the gang rode off, Jesse told her, "Be sure you get a receipt for the taxes and make sure it includes everything needed to give you free title to the farm."

Soon, the tax man showed up and the widow paid him everything, demanding her receipts. The tax man reluctantly gave them to her. On his way back to town, he was robbed of all the money by a gang of unidentified highwaymen. No one said who they were.

• • •

Clang, clang, clang. The guard came down the range, slapping his riot stick against the bars of every cell. Jim jerked out of his reverie and thought, *I'll never get used to that racket. This place is as silent as a tomb because nobody can talk out loud, yet they have to call us to count with that rude sound. It's not civilized.* Then he had to chuckle. *Who expected to find civilization in this place?* Jim had never sworn in his life, but he had been sent to prison to be 'corrected' of his crime where profanity by his keepers came with every breath. Oh, well, time to stand for count and wait to have his cell bars opened so his range could line up for the slop they called food.

Upon his return to his cell, a task that was slower coming back than going down for him because of the two flights of stairs that that had to be navigated by his old and arthritic back and legs, Jim sat back down on the cot and, dipping his pen in the ink, he began to write his letter to Mary Susan. *Dear Mary Susan.* When he closed his eyes for a moment, her childhood face appeared just as he last remembered seeing her. He laid the pen down and sat back on the cot. The memory hit him hard in the chest, like the bullet he had been shot with while escaping the Union soldiers. He still carried it inside of him, just like he carried the memory of those days.

* * *

By 1874, the James brothers had a ten thousand dollar reward offered for them "dead or alive" but still, they continued their robbing ways. The times and politics had begun to change, and Jesse knew that the beginning of the end might be hastened a few years later, with the election of Thomas Crittenden, the Democratic candidate for governor, and popular choice for the railroads.

The robbery that crippled the James- Gang had occurred on September 7th, 1876 when they attempted to rob the First National Bank at Northfield, Minnesota. Besides Frank and Jesse, the gang that day included three Younger brothers along with several others. In the shoot-out that followed, Bob and Cole Younger were wounded and two others were killed. The Younger group rode out of town in one direction and the James brothers in another without getting any money. The Younger brothers were soon caught by a posse. Only Frank and Jesse managed to escape. They evaded the law for several years by assuming the aliases of J.B. Howard and B.J. Howard, but the James gang lost favor among robbers because of that failure, and it became difficult for them to attract new members.

An associate of Jesse and Frank, Dick Liddel, had introduced Charlie Ford and his brother, Bob, small time outlaws, to Tom Howard (aka Jesse James) in late 1881. Liddel knew that the Ford brothers wanted to become part of the James gang, but he warned Ford that Howard's true identity had to be kept secret as he was on the run.

In early 1882, Missouri's Governor Thomas Crittenden, seeking re-election, had promised to bring gang members to justice. As a part of this strategy, Sheriff Timberlake of Clay County, Missouri approached Bob Ford and they settled on a plan to put the James Gang out of business for a fee. Jesse had been an outlaw for sixteen years by the time Bob Ford and Sheriff Timberlake had conspired and Bob Ford made his move at the first opportunity. He told the sheriff that he and Charlie were hoping to go with Jesse to rob a bank in Platte City, Missouri.

By the spring of 1882, Charlie Ford had moved in with the quiet Howard family in St Joseph, Missouri, keeping his knowledge of the James family's true identity secret. He often brought his younger brother, Bob, also sworn to secrecy, to visit with and get to know the family. The Ford brothers said they still wanted to go along on the Platte County bank robbery Jesse and Frank were planning. Jesse trusted very few people so he was cautious about the newcomers, but the Fords were able to get Jesse's confidence and he finally agreed that they could come along.

When Jesse had moved his family to St. Joseph, they'd settled under the name of Tom Howard, and he still had a ten thousand dollar reward on his head. Zee begged Jesse to assume a safer lifestyle and Jesse finally agreed that he would - right after the last bank robbery in Platte County, Missouri. A meeting to plan the robbery was held with Charlie and Bob Ford at Jesse's home in late March, 1882.

Jesse's younger half-brother, John Thomas Samuel had turned out to be another victim of the James brother's reputation. Carousing at a late New Year's Eve party east of Kearny in Greenville, he found himself defending his outlaw brothers, and began a battle royal with the defamers. Someone shot a rifle and John Thomas was shot in the chest. Although the partiers quickly sobered up and took John home to his father, Dr Samuel, the wound was serious and it didn't seem likely that he would survive for long. The family quickly sent a slave with a message for Jesse and Zee to come home to see John, before it was too late.

As Zee sat through the long night beside John's bedside, she stared at his young face. Until he had grown a beard, she hadn't realized how much he and Jesse looked alike, but in the lamp light, it was very obvious the two brothers were kin. She looked over at a sleeping Jesse who had taken his turn at the bedside earlier and now lay upon a nearby sofa, taking the opportunity to rest before they had to leave in the morning. Zee thought of what it had been like when Jesse himself had suffered that almost fatal gunshot so long ago. She shivered as she realized that she could lose Jesse to a posse or bounty hunter again, and become a widow in a heartbeat.

As the morning sun peeked into the dark bedroom window, Zee was filled with fear at the prospect of Jesse's arrest or death. Though it caused her great grief, because she knew she might never see her husband again, she fantasized about his escape and let ideas run through her mind, beginning to form a plan. If it was to work, Jesse would have to leave her and their young children in Missouri forever. Her love for him and fear for his safety was so great that she was ready to make that sacrifice.

She wondered what it would be like for Jesse to give up the outlaw life and their roots in Missouri and leave her and the children behind. But she believed that if the world could be convinced that he had been killed, Jesse would be able to escape beyond the reaches of politicians and their lawmen. Could she bear being separated from the love of her life forever?"

But she began that night to plot a way to make it all happen.

April 26th, 1925

Dear Mary Susan,

I'm happy to say that spring is coming, and I will soon be working in the prison gardens. I will see the sunshine again, and I know it will raise my spirits after a long, cold winter the likes I haven't seen since my first winter in Canada in 1911. I hope you and the children are healthy and enjoying the spring flowers back home. The garden was your mother's greatest pleasure.

You will recall that, in my last letter, I wrote about how I fought in the civil war for the side of the south, and later became a loyal defender of the rights of my people. That required me to become a kind of Robin Hood, by stealing from the banks and railroads and helping out the families who suffered under the outrageous new constitution. I earned a reputation for being an 'outlaw' when Frank and formed the James gang and worked at creating justice. That reputation was often worse than we really were, but, as I confessed to you in my last letter, we, as insurgents, were forced by the times to do some awful things. I seek forgiveness every day.

The Yankees fought us back by recruiting so-called lawmen to hunt us down. In our youth, we believed that obstacles couldn't stop us; those lawmen couldn't stop us and most of all, Yankees couldn't stop us. The Pinkerton detective agency, hired by the state, started a campaign to find us, or harass anyone we cared about. Your grandmother, Zeralda and my little brother Archie became their targets and as I said in another letter, my inability to protect them haunts me even now, in this prison.

Your mother was worried that you and your brother would also be targeted, so she began to make a plan to save us all. The price was terrible, but it worked. We knew it meant that I would never see you all again and that she could never tell you that I was still alive. I will tell you more about it in my next letter.

Love, Papa.

Inmate Jim Howard, #1133,

Saskatchewan Penitentiary

Box 166, Prince Albert, Saskatchewan

CHAPTER V

JESSE'S FAREWELL

IT WAS ALMOST SPRING IN SASKATCHEWAN, AND JIM HOWARD could feel the sun warm his bones as he worked outside the cell block; after much debate about what jobs might be available in the prison for a crippled old man, he had been allowed to work in the small garden hidden inside the forty foot brick wall of the prison.

I feel like Brer Rabbit when Brer Fox tried to catch him for dinner. Jim smiled to himself as he remembered the story. *'I don't keer w'at you do wid me, Brer Fox, 'sez ee', 'jes so you don't fling me in dat briar-patch."* Of course, Brer Fox did just that, and Brer Rabbit ran away safely, because the briar patch was his home. Uncle Alphonse had told the Uncle Tom stories to the James children when he taught them lessons about life and how to deal with people. Jim never forgot a single one of them, and they had come in very handy over his long life.

Jim had first argued against being sent out to hoe, plant and water the flowers the warden wanted raised for his wife. "I'm an old man, Boss. I can't bend over, and work like a lad. The sun gives me a rash, and I feel sick when I get too much heat. You should find a young fella to do this work." But the keeper, Mr. Peters, didn't like to be argued with, and he was determined to win his way. Jim chuckled to himself, remembering how he had put on a miserable face when Mr. Peters had ordered him to pick up a hoe and get out there. So every day he hoed, raked, tended to the little plants and waited for them to produce, just as he had once done on the homestead. And as he worked, he thought of his days with Zee and the children before he had gone on the run.

• • •

Initially, Zee hadn't trusted the Ford brothers, but now that Jesse had moved them into their St Joseph home, she saw the possibility of how they might be useful to her. The Fords had clearly wanted to become part of a renewed James gang, but from the beginning, when she had heard the gossip about a reward Sherriff Timberlake said the Governor was offering, Zee had suspected that Bob Ford might be greedy enough to do anything to get it. As well, flashing through her mind was the thought that when Jesse's half-brother John Thomas died, as they all expected him to, she and Frank could bribe the Ford brothers to lie that they had shot Jesse.

If they used John Thomas's body in place of his, Jesse could disappear safely, Bob Ford could tell everyone that he'd killed Jesse James, and could safely collect the reward from Missouri Governor Crittenden. Zee figured that two thousand dollars from the recent Glendale robbery could help her and the children move away and get a new start. The Fords would still get the ten thousand dollar reward and they would be public heroes. The more she thought about it, the more certain she was sure it would work. She and Frank talked about the plan well into one night.

First, they would have to set the scene. That would mean convincing Jesse's mother that it wouldn't be disrespectful to use John Thomas's body. He looked so much like Jesse, Zee knew she would understand. One son could save another by his death. For the whole time Jesse and Zee had been in St. Joseph, Frank had kept Zerelda, his mother, living in nearby Kearney, informed of their whereabouts. For weeks, John Thomas had been near death. His fever raged, and he was barely conscious. Then, in February, he got pneumonia and by March he fell into a coma. John Thomas Samuel wasn't going to make it.

On the 1st of April, during a secret, late night visit to Zerelda's home, Zee, Frank and Jesse had been sitting beside John Thomas's death bed, listening to him struggling to breath. An exhausted Zerelda was finally sleeping nearby so Frank and Jesse whispered softly, and talked about the details of the plan after Jesse had disappeared. "I'll take the new name, John Allen after I leave. I've never used that alias before. Once in a while, John Allen will send Frank a message by Pony Express about where 'he' is in case you need to send me a family message. If this is going to work, we have to stay careful." Neither Frank nor Jesse could bear to look over at Zee, now awake, who stared resolutely out the window into the lonely, moonless night sky. She had no words to offer and Frank went silent too; he just clasped his younger brother's shoulder, they both nodded and looked into each other's eyes. Zee's plan was underway.

Bob Ford and his brother Charlie had been visiting at the home of the quiet Thomas Howard and his family on April 3rd. The Howard family had lived peacefully in St. Joseph, Missouri for a few years and no one suspected that he was anything other than an upstanding, law-abiding, church- going citizen raising a nice family. They had no idea that their neighbor was really the infamous outlaw, Jesse James. Soon they would learn differently.

John Thomas died very early on the morning of April 3rd. One of Zerelda's slaves came to St Joseph to tell Jesse and Frank right away. Frank and the Fords quickly headed over to Kearney, picked up the body, covered it in a cart and brought it back to the Howard home. They then implemented the plan that would end the law's constant search for Jesse.

As they waited for John Thomas's body to arrive, Zee told Jesse, "I know that the longer you stay with us, the more danger you're in. You need to leave us behind and get out of Missouri to stay alive. I want you to know that I'll wait for you as long as it takes, even if it's until forever. I don't want you waiting around here with us and ending up dead", Zee whispered. Tears filled her eyes, and she vowed, "I'll love you always."

"You're a beautiful, clever woman and you shouldn't ever have to live alone to raise our children." Jesse took her hands in his and kissed them smiled softly. Zee smiled sadly.

"Even if you have to go away, I'll still be your wife and your lover forever and I know there will never be another woman for you either."

Jesse took Zee in his arms and gently kissed her, touching her hair and face with such passion that they both felt the other's tears wash any doubts away. It was clear that, even apart, their love was an unbreakable partnership forever. "Since you nursed me back from the edge of death all those years ago, there's never been and there never could be another woman for me, no matter what."

Once Frank and the body of John arrived in St. Joseph, they set the death scene, placing Jesse's guns on a table in the parlor. Frank and Charlie propped John Thomas's dead body up with a chair, facing a picture on the wall close to where Jesse might have been dusting off a picture hanging above his head. Bob Ford then took one of Jesse's pearl-handled pistols from the table and shot John Thomas's dead body in the back of the head.

Zee and her children had been in the kitchen when the shooting occurred. At the deafening sound of the gun blast, young Jesse Jr. ran into the living room to find who he assumed was his father on the floor with something oozing from his head. Zee began to scream and little Mary Susan started crying. Though Zee appeared to try desperately to stop the oozing, they all knew it was too late. The man appearing to be her husband was already dead. The Fords ran out of the house with Bob shouting for all to hear, "I just shot Jesse James! I killed Jesse James!"

A crowd of curious thrill-seekers gathered outside the home. In a few hours, as word of the shooting spread, crowds began gathering around the home, talking about the killing of the notorious outlaw,

Jesse James. Jesse Jr., who was only six at the time, didn't even know who the outlaw Jesse James was, believing that his father's name was 'Tom Davis Howard' and his own name was 'Tim Howard'.

When Zerelda Samuel (James) came from nearby Kearney, and saw the body, she proceeded to wail and weep and made positive identification, without naming him as Jesse, that it was her son. The good Baptist woman could not bring herself to tell a lie, so she simply failed to give name to the slain son, and allowed everyone to believe it was Jesse rather than John Thomas. The body was packed on ice and taken by train to Kearney where it was displayed and viewed by hundreds of friends, admirers and curiosity seekers. Later it was taken back to the James farm and buried in a plot near the house. This allowed Zerelda to keep an eye out for trespassers, souvenir hunters and anyone who might plunder the tombstone. It was hoped that burying her son at the farm would keep doubters from exhuming the body for further examination.

• • •

Jim slowed his gardening and wiped his sweaty forehead. The prison soil wasn't nearly as rich and loamy as the land back on the old Missouri farm. He wondered if 'Jesse James' grave was still lying untouched after all these years. He hoped his brother John Thomas had been left in peace to await for the Rapture the good book promised.

May 24th, 1925

Dear Mary Susan

I've been working in the flower garden lately and it's put me in mind of the days just before I left you all. It's been on my heart to tell you about how your mother and Uncle Frank helped me get away from the threat of the Yankee governor and escape to the West. The price on my head had made it impossible to live a family life so your mother came up with a plan for me to escape.

My half-brother, John Thomas Samuel, who looked a lot like me and had grown a beard like mine, had just suffered a fatal gunshot wound and was dying. Your mother thought that when he died we could convince a couple of bounty hunters to shoot his body and pretend it was mine. I could escape, having the bounty hunters collect the reward for my death. Your mother felt that she, Jesse junior and you could live a normal life without the Reconstruction Forces continually bothering you. I never saw her or you children again.

I felt guilty about using John Thomas's body, but he was going to die and even your grandmother, Zerelda, agreed with the plan. We thought you were too young to know about it, but I always hoped you'd find out I when you grew up. After I escaped, we thought everything was finished. It has taken over forty years to realize that it was just beginning.

I guess none of us ever figured out how to tell you. I believe your mother was afraid that if anyone outside our family ever learned that I wasn't dead, they might desecrate John's grave, burn our farm or take revenge out on her or you children.

I'm sure my first letter to you must have been a shock and for that, I am truly sorry. Perhaps I should have remained silent, but I hoped we might still develop a relationship, even just by post, if I could let you know that I was still alive and never wanted to abandon you. Like your mother, I've been true to our marriage and the love that she and I shared so long ago.

You and your brother never left my heart during all those years, and I love you still

Your Papa

Inmate Jim Howard, #1133

Saskatchewan Penitentiary,

Box 166, Prince Albert, Saskatchewan, Canada

CHAPTER VI

OUT OF MISSOURI INTO MONTANA

JIM HOWARD HAD BEEN SICK FOR TWO MONTHS BY THE TIME JULY of 1925 had rolled around. He'd had bad lungs since he was just a young man, when he had taken a Yankee bullet in the chest and nearly died. It was sheer determination on Zee's part that had kept him alive then. She stayed with him day and night, through fevers and chills and setbacks until he was finally deemed fit to work again, but he had spent his lifetime worried that the next influenza would take him or something as simple as a common cold might bring back the pneumonia again. And it had, several times, but youth and general good health had saved him.

Now, in prison, where it was either hot and humid in summer or damp and cold in winter and with food that he wouldn't have fed his dogs in the old days, Jim had no resistance to the illnesses that floated around in a large group of men who were forced to live in close contact. He had come down with galloping pneumonia in both lungs just after his last letter to Mary Susan, and had been taken to the prison infirmary by the old croaker who came in once a week to provide medical care, such as it was, to the prisoners. Many of them had died, and Jim considered himself lucky to have made it.

He was moved back to his cell in the middle of July, and finally had access to his belongings again. He sat on his bunk and laughed at himself. He was actually glad to be 'home' in his own cell on F 3 range. Carefully, he pulled out a sheet of writing paper and his pencil and thought of what he could tell Mary Susan about why he hadn't written in so long. On his sickbed, he had had lots of time to while away the hours thinking his past, but with the paper in front of him, his mind spun, trying to decide where to start. The last thing he had written to Mary Susan was about leaving Zee and the children after the phony assassination and heading west. Maybe it was time to tell her about his cowboy days wrangling herds and driving them north from Texas to Montana.

• • •

During and after the civil war, Jesse'd become functional in some of the tribal languages, and a few Indians in Indian Territory spoke a little English so he got by. Other than the tribes, the barren Territory was sparsely populated. During the escape-planning, Frank had assured him that "Indian Territory's a good hiding place for bandits on the run. You know most of those outlaws there and most of them know you. You'll have to be careful, but they won't squeal on you. The rest are Indians and they aren't going to help any white lawman get you."

Jesse agreed. "That's right, and most lawmen and bounty-hunting posses stay out of there anyway. It's not safe for them. That will make for a good escape and a new beginning."

In the second week of April, 1882, the quiet but determined Jesse James, now calling himself John Allen, entered Indian Territory. It was the home of Osage, Kiowa, and Apache, Cherokee and Comanche tribes. Members of these tribes and other bandit-insurgents on the run had welcomed the arrival of John Allen.

Immediately after learning of John Thomas Samuel's death, Jesse, as John Allen, had begun his escape-ride. He and Frank had chosen this route, recalling that many tribes, who had also been slave owners, were also Confederate supporters. Most whites in the Territory had been Confederates. Quantrill and his gang were heroes to them. Now many of them were outlaw insurgents on the run. He knew that, among both friends and foe, he must keep uppermost in his mind that he was now neither Jesse James nor Thomas Howard. He was on his way to becoming a full-time cowboy-drover. To avoid people who might recall the war days, he wanted to stay out of eastern Kansas. He'd go through Indian Territory, across western and central Kansas north to Nebraska. He would look for a cattle drive northbound from Texas to hook up with.

Now, on the east side of Indian Territory, he happened upon a cattle drive heading north through Nebraska from Texas. In an attempt to hire on, he found the trail boss of a group of Texas drovers, taking cattle north to the railheads.

After the war, the market for Texas cattle shrunk, leaving Texas ranchers with several million surplus head, so ranchers began to drive herds northward around 1866. There had also been a major shift in the choice of meat consumption, which had once been pork, and had become that of beef. Cattle worth four dollars a head in Texas might be sold for four times that in Missouri or Kansas.

A new workforce was also available. Ex Confederate cavalry, freed slaves who became black cowboys and Mexican gauchos filled a ready supply of skilled horsemen. John Allen fit right in with this new workforce, but it didn't come without debate. In his first attempt to get work, John met with Sheff Sot, a Drover trail boss. "Need drovers?"

"Got any experience? You own that horse?"

"That's my brand on his arse and I'm from Missouri. Farmed and raised cattle there and I rode with Quantrill for the Confederates."

"You were on the right side. Guess you know cattle and you can ride. How many horses you got?" Sheff was a man who didn't waste words.

"Just this one. How much you payin? Should be able to save and buy another, if yer payin enough." John was used to bargaining and shrewd enough not to give away too much information; lessons learned well as a guerrilla on the run.

"We're payin thirty bucks a month plus food to start. Do all right on your first drive and stay with us for anothern, we'll make it forty."

"Sounds good enough. But I have a couple questions."

"Shoot."

"You use any of those black cowboys on this drive?"

"Sure do!" Sheff looked up from under his bushy eyebrows and frowned, waiting for the next comment.

"Am I going to have to ride with any of them? My family used to own some slaves and I'm not comfortable riding beside them. They were one of the reasons for the big war." John felt indignant at the thought of being treated as an equal to a slave.

"Nope. Don't haff ta. You can go north by yourself. We got black, white, brown and red cowboys. They eat the same food; sleep on the same ground; do the same jobs; face the same dangers. You're welcome to join us, but if you can't be one of us, you can keep goin wherever you were goin when you stopped here."

"You're real straight, Sheff. I'll have to get used to that. Just a couple more questions."

"Let's have it. Spit it out."

"Will it be rough goin' on these drives? What'll the weather be like? I just like to know what I'm facing."

"Lots of rough goin'; some we can predict and lots of it we cain't. We ride a lot of different trails. Startin' in Texas, sometimes we're on the Chisholm, the Western, the Goodnight-Loving and other Trails on drives to Kansas, the Dakotas, Colorado, Wyoming and Montana. We've lost cowboys in stampedes, some froze to death in winter; some had heat strokes in summer and some drowned in the wild rivers we got to cross."

"Just thinking. It's good to know the risks. What if I want to quit down the line?"

"That's up to you son. Cowboys come an go. Some stay on the northern plains. Some ride back south an either catch another drive or stay there. Some stop in towns along the way, find a woman an stay there. Most are honest an hard-workin. Some are runnin' from the law when we take 'em on and some become outlaws after they leave us. It's your life and you decide, but on the drive, you're either with us or agin us." That was the longest thing Shepp had said so far.

"Sounds like we've got a deal. I'm going to join up with you. When do I start?" John could feel the excitement begin to build as he thought about being part of the drive north.

"Go over yonder with Bill. He'll show ya how to catch up to strays and get 'em back into the herd. Tonight it's his turn to have his crew patrol outside the herd and keep strays from gittin' away from us. Then tomorrow you can follow his lead and he'll show how we start by movin the cattle in a zigzag to keep 'em in a loose herd, workin from the rear of the herd."

Early the next day, the lead cowboy, Bill, began his instructions with a serious nod. "We need to make sure we're not circlin' roun' the herd. Keepin' pressure from the outside keeps pressure on what all the cattle figure is the 'scape zone for 'em all. We get the rear animals to start moving by givin' 'em a stare like a wolf would if he was sizin' 'em up. Ya need to make sure you don't spend too much time in an animal's blind spot. If ya do, he'll turn around and look at ya. Take yer time. You an' yer horse may need to make wide movements accordin' to how far the cattle are spread out."

John was amazed at how complicated just getting the cattle to move was. But Bill wasn't done yet. "Don't go after loose stragglers. Jes' watch 'em. If they're off to one side, they'll know it and they'll work their own way back into the herd. An' be careful not to bunch up the herd too quick. You only want 'em to be a little bit worried 'bout you bein' there. Don' want them to take off in a rush, cause they're ascaird. For a herd of cattle, worry always comes ahead of fear and runnin'.

That's how stampedes start and we don't want that. Cattle will always try to start circlin' away from where ya want 'em to go, just so's they can tell where you're at. That's their natural way to avoid wolves and other critters tryin to kill 'em. They always want ta know where the wolf is and what he's tryin' to do. That'll happen if you or the wolf is in their blind spot. So, if you want to make sure they don't start circlin', or if you need to keep 'em goin' in the same direction they need to go, don't stay – even for a little while – in any cow's blind spot.

Bill continued the lesson. "To keep 'em from startin to worry, change the way they're goin. This can take off the pressure and give them a reward for moving forward."

John Allen smiled to himself. Being a drover was going to be a lot like being the leader of an outlaw gang; always one step ahead of trouble. But he'd been out of the outlaw life for the most part, over the past few years since he 'retired' in St Joseph. He knew he could pick up the skills of the drive quickly though; he would have to if he was going to survive on the drive, let alone actually earn his living at it.

Most of the cowboys were younger than John, in their late teens or early twenties, and single. It seemed at first that a cowboy could be anybody with guts and a horse. But they also needed to be strong and smart to survive the harsh conditions of trail life. Despite his age, the very fit John soon learned the ropes.

Once they left White Deer, Texas in April or May of each year, the drives followed the Texas Trail through supply towns along the way. It took almost two and a half months, usually arriving at the N bar N ranch in Montana in midsummer. Occasionally a few drovers with portions of a herd continued west. Saloonkeepers, gamblers, and painted ladies were always waiting in supply towns and at the end of the trail to take drovers' hard-earned money.

Careful with his pay as he had always been, John managed to add a horse or two to his personal string each year, and by 1885, he owned five nice working horses. He would ride these horses in rotation, allowing some to rest and eat along the way while the others worked.

Rodeos had first grown out of the skills cowboys needed to learn and practice in their daily routine. Informal shows of bronc riding, calf roping, and steer wrestling were often held after the semi-annual round-up, and those grew into popular contests local folks loved to attend.

Although exceptional at all those skills, the near middle-aged John Allen had no intention of staying with the cowboy life long enough to become a Rodeo Cowboy. He especially didn't like the idea of being part of such a public activity where he might be recognized by some travelling rancher from Kansas.

When he became a drover in 1882, John had been told that he was lucky to get work on any cattle drive. Back in late 1870, a series of blizzards had struck the southern plains, and cattle either smothered under a crush of snow, or froze to death in their tracks within a short while. It had taken years to grow the herds again and get them ready for the long Texas drive north. John had been a drover for three years, even though the drives were not as frequent as they had been earlier. He had thought for a year now that it'd be good to settle down and get a job as a ranch hand. Three years in the physically and mentally harsh cowboy-drover life had toughened him up as much as his outlaw past had. He talked to his trail boss toward the end of an '85 drive.

"Look, we've stuck together since '82, doin' drives every year, but I'm wondering about settling down and being a ranch hand. Do you know the Beaverhead County rancher that's buying these cattle after we take them west from the N bar N?" The boss paused to light a cigarette he had just rolled with one hand.

"Yep. Name's Dave Vold. Good guy. Think he's Norwegian an' family's been there since '70. I'll introduce you an tell him you'll do a good job for him." John liked that response as he was pretty sure the odds for maintaining his job as a drover wouldn't stay great forever. The trail boss inhaled, then added, "Course, if you want to stay on, I can make sure you stay hired to go back down to Texas and back up again for at least the next couple drives. I hate to lose a good hand."

"Thanks, Boss, but I'm getting too old for any more killer drives. Now, introduce me to the Norwegian." So they headed over to a tall, red-headed rancher near the pens.

When John had shaken hands with the rancher, Vold agreed to hire him right away. He had said, "I like yer grip, lad. I'll valk yew 'n yer bedroll over to da bunkhouse 'n yew can find a bunk. Yew'll eat in da main house wit da family and da rest a da hands. Yew keep yure horses in da barn. Ve'll supply da feed an ve'll shoe 'em, but yew feed 'em and clean up after 'em."

John, always ready to earn his living, smiled. "Thanks a lot. What's my job?"

Vold said nothing while he slowly rolled a cigarette and licked it shot. Then, cigarette lit, he inhaled slowly, and drawled,

"Ranchin's not jes a yobb. It's a vay a life. Ve're a team. Allus verk needs doin." Another long pause and the drawl began again. "Fixin' fences; movin' cows from pasture to pasture; checkin' cows' health all a time; feedin' 'em in vinter; calvin' in February and March; brandin' from late April to de end of May; makin' sure der's nuff drinkin vatter for 'em; fixin' 'quipment; gadderin' horses and lookin' after 'em, 'n a lot of oder supprises dat I can't tell you 'bout 'cause they'll be supprises. Alvays lots to do. My foreman, he'll tell ya more 'bout it when it's time to do each yobb. More 'bout fall 'n spring roundups, 'n shippin' in the fall 'n all."

It took John a few days to understand the big Norwegian's English, but in time, he picked it up and soon, he felt at home on the big ranch with its endless pastures and herds of cattle as far as you could see. The work was hard, but the food was good and he even started to fit in with the other hands working there. Never a day went by that he didn't think of Zee and the children, but he knew it would be a long time before he might ever be able to sneak back home. Maybe never.

August 25th, 1925

Dear Mary Susan,

I am so sorry I haven't been able to write you sooner. I got sick and spent a long time in the hospital here, but I am better now. I didn't want to worry you, but I didn't have my belongings with me there, so couldn't write you. I trust you are all healthy and enjoying the summer time.

It wasn't long after the flowers bloomed in my little garden in the prison yard that I took sick, so I wasn't able to get a job on the prison farm as I had hoped. The keeper tells me that I might be able to work the big garden harvest if I am up to it. It will remind me of the harvests on my old homestead when I grew and prepared vegetables for the long winter. Your mother would have been so proud of me, doing women's work.

More of my story. After everybody thought I was dead, I made my way through Indian Territory, where I joined up with a Texas cattle drive that was driving cattle north to Montana to sell. It was tough but honest work and the pay was good enough. On my fourth cattle drive in 1885, I hired on to a ranch in Beaver Head county, in northwestern Montana that was looking for ranch hands. I'd had enough of cattle drives. It was exciting at first, but I was just getting too old for the hard work and weather. Living in one place was nice and the Vold family reminded me of my own back home. Lots of children, dogs and hardworking people who loved each other and lived a fair, Christian life. I began to feel safe.

An important lessons that I'd learned in the war helped me, both on the cattle drives and as a ranch hand and I would like to pass one on to you and yours. Fear defeats more people than any other thing in the world. if you do not conquer yourself, you will be conquered by yourself. I can't remember where I heard that, but it came to my mind often during the worst times of my life, and maybe you will think of it when you struggle with yours.

There are so many things I want to tell you, and I fear I won't have enough time or paper to write it all. I will write again soon.

Love, Papa

Inmate Jim Howard, # 1133

Saskatchewan Penitentiary, Box 166, Prince Albert, Saskatchewan

CHAPTER VII

BEAVERHEAD COUNTY – IT STARTS AGAIN

JIM RECALLED HOW, LATE ON AN EARLY SEPTEMBER SUNDAY AFTERnoon in 1885, he'd first met tall and lanky Dave Vold and was struck by the red shock of hair and an equally red handle bar moustache. Dave had huge hands and wore tired denim pants with a big, round rodeo buckle on the belt. He was about four inches taller than John Allen. Though he had a smile on his face, his penetrating, blue eyes looked right through a man, almost to the person behind. Dave's first language, like his parents, who had been immigrants from Norway, was Norwegian. He claimed to have shed the Scandinavian accent, but his neighbors, knowing better, smirked at that claim. Vold had walked John over to the bunkhouse to introduce him to the other hands. In his deep bass voice, Dave said, "Yu'll meet my foreman first und den da udder hands. Fall roundup's startin' tumurra' 'n dey can take yew out der. Soon's da roundup's done, ve'll get ready fer shippin'." Vold turned and headed back up to the main house, then turned slowly and nodded with his head. "Yew come up to da ranch house first ting in the morning with da resta' da crew fer breakfas'. But first, we go see Foreman Sam. He's got his own cabin und ve'll start der".

Dave led him to the foreman's cabin. Sam Hunter, balding and about John's age, was as tall as Dave. He was sitting on a bench outside a small log cabin. "Sam, dis here's Yawn Allen, nu han' I yest hired. I vant yew to take him over to da bunkhouse an' introduce him to da crew." Sam stood up, looked John in the eyes and shook his hand in a firm, strong handshake. "Howdy. Good ta meecha. Okay, less git over there."

The bunkhouse, home to the ranch hands, was only twenty yards away. It was a solid log building with four small widows along the side John could see. The roof was made of cedar shakes and a small stone chimney peeked over the top. John and Sam entered the low, Dutch door to the cabin. A Dutch door was likely useful in the summer when it was hot and you didn't want critters or snakes crawling in, but wanted a breeze to help circulate the smoke from the smokers. Inside, five single wooden beds, each with a mattress and pillow, lined two walls, three on one side and two on the other. The smell of man's sweat and horse manure drifted above the beds, and the room felt cramped.

In the corner to the right of the door hunched a cast iron wood-burning stove and a wood-box with kindling and chopped logs. Next to that, a water pail sat on a wooden apple crate with a dipper hooked on one side; a wash stand with a basin and bar of soap filled the rest of the corner. Two large lanterns hung from the low log ceiling beams, and a tall man could find himself with a headache if he forgot to duck down when he got out of bed.

Four cowboys were relaxing on their bunks after their evening meal. John immediately noticed that one of the men was black. At first, he was surprised that the black man was in the same bunkhouse as the white ranch hands. But recollections of black cowboys on cattle drives soon mellowed that surprise. Sam did the introductions.

"These here are the hands. Hank Burroughs, Clyde Evans, Jim Duvall and Black Jim Howard. We call him Black Jim 'cause we have two Jims, and nobody'd know which'n we're talkin' to. Boys, this is John Allen, new han', startin' tamorra.'"

There was a chorus of: "Howdy." A friendly voice rose out of the smoky air. It was Hank, one of the older men. "Where ya from, John?"

"I'm from Missouri. Where you fellas from," John replied. The men, one by one, began to answer. They were all former drovers who'd arrived at different times at the ranch. One was from Kansas and two from Texas. Last to speak, Black Jim responded, "I'm Jim Howard from Gladstone area in Jackson County, Missouri".

"That's just southa where I'm from," John replied, but he avoided being too specific. Old habits die hard, and wasn't ready to trust anyone yet.

That night, in the dim bunkhouse lamplight, John wrote his first letter since leaving home and deciding to settle down on a ranch. Over the years while he was on the cattle drives, he had sent telegrams about once a year, saying John Allen could be contacted at a certain supply town along the way, and he had never had a reply. Now, he wanted to let Frank know where a Pony Express letter could be delivered to a more permanent location if there was an urgent family message. It was short and revealed almost nothing about its sender.

> *I've been enjoying the countryside for the past four years, travelling from the south to the north and working on cattle drives. I decided to settle down for a while in Montana, but I'll let you know if that changes. You can send news to the Pony Express office in Beaver County if you need to, and I'll pick it up when I go to town. I'm enjoying the dry air out here.*
>
> *Bye*

The next day, Sam, already sitting atop his big chestnut mare, shouted out to the hands, "Okay boys, breakfast's over. On yer horses and let's get roundin' 'em up!" Already dressed and ready to go, John and the other four headed at a jog to the barn. Like Sam, they wore jackets over long sleeved flannel shirts. Head gear was a working Stetson stained with sweat and weather. A good hat was crucial to a cowboy. It kept the rain and snow off, and sheltered heads from the sun. Heavy leather chaps were an essential part of the uniform too; and just in case of rain or snow, rolled oilskin slickers were tied to the backs of their saddles. Once they'd saddled up and mounted, Sam's sharp orders shot across the yard.

"John, you and Black Jim come over here and ride 'side me. Hank, you take Clyde an' the other Jim with you. We're goin' up in the hills to start gatherin' yearlins an' start the fall drive taday. Jest gittin' ya used ta one of our fall jobs taday John. Black Jim and I'll tell ya a bit of what the rest of the year'll be like as we ride 'long. I want Black Jim with us 'cause he's the most 'sperienced hand 'n he's done all the jobs lotsa times. Any questions, jest ask him."

After they'd ridden for about an hour, Sam said, "Jim, I'll take John fer awhile. Later, you can tell him 'bout what a year on the ranch's like fer ranch hands. John, this first week will be a weeka gatherin' an' trailin'. That's jest part of May 'til September life here. We'll be gatherin' yearlin's from pastures up in the hills. When we git em in a herd we bring 'em to the feedlot at the ranch. Bringin' em down's a lot like things wuz on cattle drives. Ya need patience gettin' 'em to move in a circle an' knowin' what they think their 'scape zone is. Make sure yer smarter'n they are when yer herdin' 'em. Each cow has a certain distance it wants ya to keep away from. If ya git inside their 'scape zone, they'll move 'way from ya. If yer outside their 'scape zone, they won't move. 'Scape zones have a point a balance where the cow'll move 'cordin' to pressure – usually at the shoulder, but could be at the eye or neck er even the side. Every cow's different an' there's no 'average 'scape zone or point a balance.

As the day went on, Sam continued to talk to John over the mewling of the calves and cows. John thought he knew a lot about driving cattle, but it turned out that it was even more difficult to handle them when they were not being driven long distances. That dang escape zone was crucial when they were bringing them down from the hills where they had been grazing over the summer.

"Depends on how calm or how excited the animal is. 'Scape zone's usually biggest roun' the head and smallest 'roun, the arse. We don't want them to git scared and stampede on us." Then, like turning a page in a book, Sam started to trot his horse and shouted back at John, "That's nuff talkin' fer now. Let's start gatherin' an' trailin'. Fer this week, all six of us'll be gatherin' a small herd every day an' takin' it back to the feedlot. There we'll sort 'em out.

By the end of the first day of gathering and trailing, the six man crew had gathered a small herd that was big enough to drive back to the ranch and put in the feedlot. They would continue this daily routine for the rest of the week.

On the way back with the last herd, Sam and Black Jim took turns riding beside John and talking to him. Sam leaned in and said, "Soon's we get back to the ranch, we're gonna' start gettin' these cattle sorted out, some fer shippin,' some heifers for breedin' 'n some fer winter feedin'. That'll keep us busy every day this week. Better rest up tonight, cause we'll be up and at it with the sunrise."

Later that evening, as John and Black Jim sat alone on the bench outside the bunkhouse, John was moved to begin a discussion. "Both of us are from Missouri, grew up not far from each other either. Being as I'm white and you're black, we aren't likely gonna be friends, but who knows how long we're gonna work together so we better be civil. My family owned slaves and I thought they had a right to, so I fought for the Confederacy. I'm not apologizing for any of that. You come from a slave family and you're free now, so let's get used to it."

Black Jim sat straight and looked John square in the eye. "Glad you brought it up. All day, I wuz thinkin' we better figger out how we're gonna git along. I've heard it said that if ya can't get over something, the best you can do is get through it. I think it's time for us to git through it. We don' have to be friends, but we need to keep workin' together. Today wuz a good start. Let's keep it up."

"When you talk like that, you remind me a lot of an ol' slave we called Uncle Alphonse. When we were kids, he had as much to do with bringing us up as our mother did. Whenever we thought we were in trouble, we'd run to Uncle Alphonse and he'd give us a hug, talk gentle and make us feel better. He'd just take us in his big old arms and tell us it'd be okay. In those days we thought he was pretty old but he likely was my age." The two cowboys sat back and lit a smoke, finally relaxing around each other as they laughed. Despite their vows that they couldn't be friends, a relationship built on grudging admiration and respect gradually led to a trust that would last a lifetime.

That first day of gathering and trailing foreshadowed the beginning of John's annual ranch routine of roundups. Just as Dave Vold had predicted, they moved cows from pasture to pasture; shipped them, checked their health. Then there was feeding in winter, calving in February and March, branding from late April to the end of May. Most important, John had to look after his own horses because they were how he got his work done. There was always a lot to do and John and the other hands worked well together. John was a real teamworker and his bond with Black Jim continued to grow. Each knew that, without speaking, he could depend on the other and over time this unspoken trust was to lead to adventures beyond their time at the ranch. As a ranch hand, John knew his decision to leave the drives had been the right one at the right time.

However, the ranch hand's life meant long, miserable and boring hours in the saddle for low pay. Ranch hands were still faced with a high-risk potential for injury, making this a short term career for most. The cowboy life was working everyday with only occasional hour or two of freedom in town.

John began to hear about a new outlaw culture repeated in stories that other ranch hands picked up in nearby towns and in the newspapers Vold had at the ranch. Besides flourishing in northwestern Montana, the new, easy-money culture was also popping up in Montana's northeast. At times John thought that re-entering the outlaw lifestyle might lead to the kind of haven he was getting an itch to return to.

This emerging, exciting Montana outlaw culture thrived on cattle rustling, stealing horses and robbing stage-coaches, trains and banks. These were all activities in which John, as Jesse James, had had a lot of experience. Many recently unemployed cowboys had entered the outlaw culture. Some joined existing gangs and others started up on their own. Ranch hands were among them, as they couldn't tell how long their jobs on any ranch would last.

To the still trim and muscular John Allen, the excitement of the high-risk, high- reward life of an outlaw began to feel irresistible. The bond between him and Black Jim Howard seemed to have the makings of a good partnership. Although Black Jim was dependable and tough, John needed to find out his attitude toward the outlaw lifestyle. John had come to depend on Black Jim, but did he want him watching his back in a robbery? For sure, Black Jim didn't talk too much and didn't brag. That would be important in any action they might undertake.

At the end of a day one late July evening during haying, the crew pondered the rumors that outlaws were working in Montana. They were all tired and their bellies were full, so they were just spinning tales. Sam drawled, "This ain't all so new. I've been told that way back in 1865, over in Portneuf Canyon, a stagecoach goin from Virginia City to Pocatello wuz robbed and the loot from that has never been found."

"How much loot was there? I wonder what happened to it," John asked. He noticed Black Jim listening quietly with a curious look on his face.

Sam didn't seem at all excited by the story. He just said, "I wuz tol by a hand at the ranch from back in those days, he just heard that three guys, hidin' in the willows in Portneuf Canyon, wuz waitin' for the stage. His story wuz that 'bout mid-day, when the coach crossed the stream, it had to stop at a rock barrier the bandits had laid across the road. When the coach stopped, the three guys, all masked, came out and held it up. They had an inside man, Jim Willeyams from Boise, ridin' the stage as a passenger."

"How much did they get?" John repeated.

"Heard they got $86,000 in gold dust and bullion,"

"What'd they do with it?" This time John was a little louder.

"Heard they cached the loot somewhere close by."

"Many people on that stage?" Black Jim wondered.

"Quite an assortment of people - seems like lotsa people wuz interested in Beaverhead County. Musta bin around the gold rush days."

"Who else would know about this story?" John wondered aloud.

"Jess Whitmore, the new hand Vold had jus' hired from Boise, Idaho. Seemed ta know lots about Idaho and Montana bandits."

"Wonder why they used that Portneuf Canyon over in Idaho? Did your Idaho guy have any idea?" One of the other hands added.

"Perfect place. Canyon's narrow, with lotsa trees and brush. Perfect place to hold up a stage. 'Specially on the Virginia City–Pocatello route."

"Why was that such a good spot on the route?" Now Black Jim was getting interested.

"On its first day on the road, that stage used ta cross Ruby Mountains and stop near Dillon. Next three days it would folla the Union Pacific Railroad tracks from Dillon to Pocatello. Evening of fourth day, the coach'd pull into the Sod house Station. After supper, that Willeyams guy slipped out and went right to where the other bandits were hidin'. When he got there, his information was music to their ears. He told them there wuz two full strongboxes fulla gold dust and bullion on the stage. Then Willeyams snuck back to Sod house Station 'fore anybody noticed he was gone."

John and Black Jim, without any further comment silently stored all the information from Sam. Sometime, it might be useful. In one of their private evening discussions, John finally started to feel out Black Jim.

"What did you think about Sam's story of those guys robbing a stagecoach over in Portneuf Canyon twenty years ago?"

"Real interesting. Guess somma them gotta way. Good for them! Wonder what happened to the hidden loot?"

"I imagine the gold bars were pretty heavy. They couldn't have carried them too far on horseback. Have to keep our ears open 'bout them ever bein' sold or recovered. It might even be buried there in Portneuf Canyon."

"I'd sure like to hear some more of Sam's tall tales. Might find out about other things that used to happen around here in the old days." John suggested. "Ol' Uncle Alphonse used to tell us we'd learn a lot more listening than talking and I think maybe he was right."

A few evenings later, John again brought up the topic of outlaws and their shenanigans. "Got any more tall tales about outlaws who robbed in Beaverhead County?"

With an all-knowing, sly grin, Sam again drawling, replied, "Matter of fact, in Bannack in January, 1864, a group of Vigilantes hung Sheriff Henry Plummer and his two deputies."

"Hung the Sheriff? How'd that happen?"

"'Parently they found out that even though he was duly elected, Sheriff Plummer was the leader of a gang that had not only carried out more robberies than they could count, but also the murder of over a hunnert people. Group a' citizens banded together as part of the secret Montana Vigilante organization. In one month they captured and hung over 20 outlaws. Rest a' the gang left this part a' Montana for their own health!" The men all laughed but John and Jim looked a little uncomfortable. Didn't seem to think that was funny.

Over the rest of the summer of the '87 haying season, John and Jim took advantage of every opportunity they had to listen to Sam spin stories of the growing Montana outlaw culture. Like cowboys everywhere, they enjoyed a good story, and Sam was the one to tell it. One evening, John and Black Jim began to openly discuss what they might do if they left the ranch. "Way things are going it's hard to tell how long Vold's ranch's is goin' to keep all hands on. We better be thinking about what we can do next."

"If this ranch can't keep us on, not likely any other's goin to." Jim sounded down.

"Maybe we'll have to start doing the same as a lot of other cowboys are doing. Gotta make some money somehow. You game for something a little outside the law?" John waited while Jim thought about that.

"You mean like we should find a gang to join up with or just start up on our own?" Jim looked over his shoulder as he spoke.

"I tried robbing banks and trains and stagecoaches down south before I came up here. I'd sooner just be with one partner than a gang. There's too many of those Plummer-type Vigilantes around here. They put me in mind of the Pinkerton Detective Agency back home. Makes me nervous. I been hearing about easier money in places like Valley and Sheridan Counties just a few days ride to the northeast a here. There are a few lawmen around there, but I don't hear much about Montana Vigilantes. How about we head over there and try things?" John asked.

So right after the fall round up two unlikely friends, one white and one black saddled up and headed out for greener pastures.

October 24th, 1926

Dear Mary Susan,

Harvest is over and I finally have some time to write you. I got your letters but only just sat down to read them again. They bring me great joy, and I picture all of you in my dreams at night. So, now I will tell you more about the adventures of your old father.

When I left Missouri, I thought I could leave the past behind. I tried, but after being a drover on cattle drives and a ranch hands in Montana, another cowboy, Jim Howard and I thought we'd move on. Jim's from Missouri and the Howard name is one that I had used from time to time. In fact, you were born to it. Jim's one of those "black cowboys," so we called him "Black Jim." At first I wasn't happy about working with a black cowboy because my family had owned slaves for generations. Once they were freed after the war, some slaves became cowboys. Their lives were just as hard as any other cowboy's, but out on the plains they didn't have to put up with the same laws that other ex-slaves faced, like staying separate from whites. Black Jim Howard, like me, used the cattle drives to ride north.

He was escaping the South and I was escaping my past and we ended up as ranch hands together. How did this ex-Confederate guerilla from a slave-owning family end up with an ex-slave as a partner? Our old slave, Uncle Alphonse, who had passed before you were born, helped raise us and we always went to him when we were sick or hurting. With Alphonse, we never felt the divide between slaves and whites that was so important to adults. When I met Black Jim, he was a lot like Uncle Alphonse; strong, calm and quiet and I grew to trust him over time. Together, we became outlaws again, and took up life on the run. This time, there was nobody to protect, because your daddy didn't exist anymore. I'll tell you more in the next letter.

Love, Papa

Inmate Jim Howard, #1133

Box 166, Prince Albert, Saskatchewan

CHAPTER VIII

VALLEY COUNTY

THAT NIGHT, WITH THE ARTHRITIS PAIN ONCE AGAIN KEEPING HIM awake, Jim's jailhouse thoughts drifted back to 1897 and the Lone Star, a favorite saloon in Culbertson. He contemplated the ten years after he and Black Jim left Beaverhead County.

• • •

They had worked their way over to northeastern Montana and had made quite a reputation before reaching Valley and Sheridan Counties, though they hadn't wanted that. Unlike many Wild Bunch outlaws, they were friendly and generous with most people, trying not to earn bad reputations. John had had enough of that as Jesse James and Black Jim had been on the receiving end of it as a slave, but a bad reputation was hard to avoid when you were a robber and thief.

By the late 1890s, with the Canadian West opening up for homesteading, there was a great demand for horses and cattle and it created a ready market for Valley and Sheridan County bandits to serve.

Once a herd of horses had been stolen, outlaws often sold them again back to the original owners. They might even steal them a second time and make even more profit. Many ranchers had unregistered brands and brand inspectors had to travel from Glasgow. By the time they got there, animals had often been re-stolen and re-branded. The Big Muddy and Wood Mountain canyons and gulches that lay over the border in Canada, offered good concealment and hiding places. Outlaws sometimes even harbored the stolen horses in huge caves until it was safe to drive them out again.

To get to know that terrain, John and Black Jim had secured jobs at the famous N bar N ranch, south of Glasgow. They'd heard that the ranch didn't ask too many questions before hiring and many Valley County outlaws would spend time laying low at the N bar N. John even got the ranch to agree that he could drop in from time to time to see whether any Pony Express mail had arrived for him. He had sent a Pony Express letter to his brother, Frank, so, just as before, on the cattle drives and the Vold ranch, he'd know where urgent family message letters could be sent.

Between its main ranch and its northern base camp up at Wood Mountain in Canada, the N bar N was an important stopping place in cross-border horse and cattle trading. It offered a mutual and beneficial relationship between the ranch and the Montana bandit culture, and sometimes outlaws stayed over for a few weeks, earning their way by doing a little cowboy work before moving on. They felt safe there.

Even though slaves had been legally freed, Jim Crow attitudes still prevailed in the north as well as the south. Blacks still weren't permitted to go into bars, cafes, hotels and other businesses used by whites, so Black Jim always had to wait outside while John went inside. John had been leaning on the bar in the Lone Star Saloon one day when a wiry young cowboy walked slowly up beside him and said, "Hi, I'm Birt Enders. They shook hands and then Birt asked, "Can I buy you a beer?"

"Well, a sarsaparilla would sure be nice, I guess." Allen spoke carefully. "I don't make a habit out of talking with strangers, but I've seen you around Culbertson and Glasgow a few times. I didn't know who you were. What's on your mind?" The men drank their beer and chatted a bit before Enders leaned into Allen, speaking softly so no one could hear them.

"I've heard lots 'bout you n' your black partner. I'd like to talk 'bout joinin' up with ya sometime."

"Lots of things said roun' these parts." John responded. "Best not to believe what ya hear an' only half of what ya see. Right now, we ain't doin nuthin' and we don't ever join up with nobody," was Allen's sharp response.

"I ain't sayin' yer doin' anythin', but just supposin' somethin did come up, why don't ya let me show ya what I can do," Birt challenged after he'd slurped down half his second beer.

This young fella's got guts, thought John as he sipped his own drink. "Okay, if somethin' comes up, we'll lecha know. I'm in this saloon least once a week. If I see ya, maybe we can talk. We can take it from there."

He recalled wondering what this steely-eyed young cowboy had heard about him and he was worried. Ten years earlier, walking slowly into another Helena saloon for the first time, he had nodded to a young fellow standing up to the bar beside him. "I'm new in town and I'm wondering 'bout what's goin on here."

"New? Where ya from?" The young fellow had smiled and stuck out his hand. John made social chit chat, and the lone cowboy had offered to buy him a beer.

"Just came up from the Virginia City – Bannack country," was John's response as they shook hands.

"From the gold rush country? Heard 'bout lotsa action over there fer a few years. That the kind a 'goin-on' yer askin' 'bout?"

"Not really." John's natural caution warned him, so he reigned in his curiosity. "Jes wundern' what it's like roun' here."

"Well, there was lotsa action fer awhile around here, but it's all moved over to Glasgow, Culbertson, Valley County n' the Big Muddy now." The lad began to tell John about a famous outlaw of the day, Con Murphy. "Murphy was Helena's last outlaw to be hung by a mob". He passed along the Murphy gossip with some glee, elaborating greatly on the story that John had already heard from other outlaws. He watched John's face all the while, looking for some kind of reaction. John ended the conversation abruptly, worried that the young fellow might be working for a bounty hunter and trying to get information. He quickly left the bar and he and Black Jim moved on.

So John was cautious when young Birt Elders approached him in 1897 in the bar in Culbertson. Surely Enders hadn't picked up a story about him and Jim and their growing reputation. He didn't like being talked about, especially in a place like this saloon where he liked to drop by and have a quiet sarsaparilla without being recognized.

The kid looked to be maybe sixteen years old, about thirty years younger than either John Allen or Black Jim. Of course, John had only been sixteen when he'd started riding with Bloody Bill Anderson, under Quantrill, so he didn't worry about Enders' age. On the other hand, Enders had heard about John and Black Jim and seemed to want to get to know the silent and iron-fisted team of loners.

John had asked around about the lad after the first meeting, and John, first-rate horsemen himself, had been very impressed with what they'd heard about Enders' ability with horses. Cowboys drinking in the bar had observed that, '*Young Birt's forgotten more bout horses than most guys ever knew*'. The partners had been impressed by the lad from the beginning, and by the time they had met him a few times, they liked him, but they'd needed to have a closer look at him to make sure he was a good fit. They weren't about to initiate too much contact until they checked him out from all angles.

Enders said he was from White Owl, South Dakota, not far off the Outlaw Trail. He had wide shoulders, a small waist and narrow hips and, when they asked around, John and Black Jim heard that he was tough and quick and had that amazing ability to silently commune with horses. They'd also been told that, while Enders never started a fight, he never backed away from one and he could hit an opponent twice before the other could throw a punch. Apparently,

Enders' punches were so hard it seldom even took two of them to have an opponent flat on his back.

Two weeks later, having had a few discussions about the Enders option with Black Jim, John was back in the Culbertson saloon looking for Enders. They had decided to break their rule to work alone, and wanted to take young Enders on as a partner. He would prove to be a good one.

Leaning on the scarred wooden bar, John was soon again approached by Enders.

"Glad to see you again Mr. Allen. I was hopin' you'd drop by one of these days. Anythin' happenin?"

"Good to see you too, Birt. Matter of fact, may be somethin you'd be interested in."

"I'd be pleased if you'd tell be 'bout it."

My partner and I have been looking around and we are talking about an easy job in a little place called Saco, just northwest of here."

"I know the place. Go on." Young Enders had moved right up to John's side, so he could listen better and not be heard. His shone with a glint of excitement. John looked into Enders blue eyes cautiously for any reaction.

"Well, that place has a small bank. Usually only two clerks workin' there. One of us would go in first and ask a clerk for change for a $100 bill. As soon he turns to the safe in back for money, another one of us will come in an' say, "*If you'll write out a receipt, I'll deposit my own bill.*" Then he'll sit down like he's gettin ready to make a deposit. Soon's the clerk starts writing, both of 'em'll pull their guns and tell them to give you all the cash outa the safe. Soon's they do, Jim'll stuff it in a saddle bag. The two of ya'll then tie them hand n foot n gag them. Then you'll come out." Birt laughed as he realized that John had already planned that he and Jim were the first two partners going in.

"Where'll you be?" Birt asked.

"Waiting outside on my horse, holding the reins to both your horses, an watching in case somebody shows up. Soon as you're out and on your horses, we'll head west as fast as we can."

He listened calmly, assured by Birt's steady eye contact and statement, "Sounds good to me. Where'll we be headin'? To the west?"

John continued with the plan. We'll head towards Great Falls so anybody watching will think we're heading for the mountains further west. Once we're south of Great Falls, we'll turn back and head fer Culbertson. There's a ranch north of there that'll let us hide for awhile. It's called the N-Bar-N and we'll vouch for you."

"I'm in! When do we head out for Saco?"

"Jim'll meet us outside this bar before it opens early tomorrow morning and we'll head right out," replied a relieved and encouraged John Allen.

After Birt showed well on the Saco job, tactical variations of the approach continued from time to time, but throughout the 1890s and into the early 1900s, the threesome preferred bank, stage and train robberies, which had a lower priority than livestock for a number of reasons. There was lower risk for getting shot, and it was easier to steal and dispose of the horses and cattle to buyers because branding was done by ranches on a hit and miss basis.

The Big Muddy and Valley County, in addition to spawning the Wild Bunch and the Nelson (Sam Kelly) gangs, occasionally offered safe haunts to some of Butch Cassidy's gang. The independent, *we'll do-it-our-own-way,* traits of the Allen/Howard/Enders team suited the Big Muddy Outlaw Culture. They got along well with Sam Kelly based on a mutual respect. Through the Kelly connection, the three of them developed the same kind of relationships with both Leroy Parker (Butch Cassidy) and Harry Longbaugh (the Sundance Kid) and were often invited to participate in either a Cassidy or Sundance Kid job. Because their independence was well known and respected, they were never pushed.

Cassidy had previously set up the Outlaw Trail, a series of connecting routes that ran through the nearly barren states of the West. It wound south from the Big Beaver/Wood Mountain areas in Canada's Northwest Territories, down through Miles City, Montana, the Black Hills in the Dakotas, the Hole in the Wall in Wyoming, and then to Brown's Park, crossing over to Robbers' Roost, Utah. Winding through Arizona and New Mexico, it ended up at Cuidad, Juarez in Mexico. John Allen had heard about it often as he made the long south/north cattle drives years before. It had become a main route from Canada to Mexico; the trail, by following canyons, caves and gulches, offered hiding for horse thieves, rustlers and robbers alike. Arrangements had been made with ranchers about every 15 miles, where fresh horses could be traded for tired ones. Outlaws on the run could easily leave posses far behind.

For the next ten years, Birt joined John and Black Jim for horse and cattle stealing trips into and out of the Big Muddy. Sometimes they'd steal them on the Canadian side and bring them to Montana or North Dakota for sale.

They all loved the obscurity they could maintain as part-time cowhands at the N-Bar-N ranch in northeastern Montana between the Missouri and Yellowstone Rivers. John and Jim had introduced Birt and the N-Bar-N to each other after their first job together in Saco, as promised. Often, as outlaws on the run, they'd hide from the law at the N-Bar-N and as long as they did their jobs as cowhands, there were no questions asked.

Most often they'd steal horses in Montana or Dakota and take them north to sell. Sometimes, they holed up in the caves Sam Kelly (Dutch "Red" Henry) had set up in the Pilot Butte area. Even though the caves were just old, enlarged wolf dens, they made a safe hideout from Montana posses for the threesome and their horses. Between rustling escapades, they'd sometimes join up with a few other bandits on a bank or stagecoach robbery. Sam Kelly told them about Joseph Jasper or 'Troublesome' Huntley, who lived close to where the Canadian Royal North-West Mounted Police were establishing a new post near Big Beaver, just a few miles over the Canadian border.

"Be sure you get to know him and stay on the right side of Jasper Huntley," Sam had advised. *"If there's one a' them Mountie patrols nearby, and if he likes ya, he'll help ya out by tipping his rain barrel over as a signal not to come by."*

Following the establishment of the Royal Northwest Mounted Police in Canada, American bandits had become cautious of Canadian law enforcement when they sold stolen U.S. property in Canada. Many of the Big Muddy outlaws came to the Canadian side to lie low, not to settle disputes or rob. They didn't mess with local ranchers and the ranchers usually returned the favor. If they needed a meal, they were fed, but they were expected not to bother people. The need for caution was reduced in 1899 when two hundred forty five Mounties volunteered for service in the Boer War in South Africa. For the duration of that war, Big Muddy outlaws took full advantage of the smaller force on the Canadian side.

John, Jim and Birt had come to know Sam Kelly in Glasgow in 1898. Kelley was about six feet tall, a slim one hundred eighty pounds, red-haired, red-whiskered with sharp eyes, often described as '*cold-as-a-fish*.' Although Kelley was ten years younger than John and Black Jim, the three had sometimes thrown in with Kelly, known as the Nelson/Henry gang, on what looked like a good-paying job. Kelley and whatever crew he had at the time, was not averse to robbing the occasional trainload of Montana gold. As John, Jim and Birt had done with others in western Montana, they occasionally held up a stage coach, though the loners had most often done these kinds of jobs by themselves. John had taught Black Jim the very effective methods for train and stage robbery he'd developed years earlier as a James gang insurgent. Jim had been a quick learner. After they'd met Enders, they found him to be a partner they could trust. Like them, he seldom drank and he didn't talk much; he too was a quick learner.

Allen, Howard and Enders soon became too well-known in Sheridan County. With that infamy came posted 'Dead or Alive' rewards, and the interest of vigilantes and bounty-hunters, the very reason they'd tried to avoid notoriety.

Shortly after Christmas, 1900, John dropped in to N-Bar-N to ask whether there'd been any Pony Express deliveries for him. The foreman had said. "There's one letter fer you. It came in early December." John took it but couldn't bring himself to open it right away because it was the first letter he'd received from Frank. He was worried about what urgent family message it might contain.

• • •

Reflecting on years past from his prison cell, Jim realized that from the time he'd arrived in Montana, he had never dealt with the Confederacy's defeat or the war, so after a few years there, he'd committed to remaining an insurgent. The Republican state administration had branded him an 'outlaw', and in Montana, as John Allen, that label had been renewed because it was the most practical way to live. He'd known that he still had Union enemies in the south; carpetbagger-owned banks, stage lines, ranches and railroads. Up in Montana, he'd watched the same kinds of people with the same kinds of motives, carrying on the same kind of exploitation. He recalled how, when reading Frank's letter, the kind of anger he hadn't felt for years welled up. He felt the guilt he'd felt then for leaving Zee and their children alone, though he hadn't been angry at her for insisting on his escape. Neither of them had seen any other choice. It had been either stay and die or run and hide. The time on the Beaverhead County ranch had mellowed that anger and guilt somewhat, or maybe he'd just buried it, rotting away inside him.

December 15th, 1925

Dear Mary Susan:

The time goes by so slowly in here that I have lost track of when I last wrote to you. I continue to be reasonably well, despite my old age. I hope you and yours are the same. I think I will tell you about my adventures when I left the Beaver County ranch where I had been working as a ranch hand for a couple of years. I met a black cowboy there who became like a brother to me, in spite of our different colors. We talked a lot about how living out west wasn't much different than being in Kansas during and after the war. The same big businesses were robbing the same little people. Black Jim saw it too, just from a different angle. When he was a slave, he was looked down upon, and as a free man in Indian country, he saw the government doing the same kind of discrimination to the Indians. We both wanted to make things a little more equal, so we took to robbing the big businesses, like the banks and stage coach lines and such.

We moved on to greener pastures in Montana, the Dakotas and even Wyoming at times. We made a pretty good living stealing horses and cattle, and even did a train or two, until we got too well known, so we started going up into the Big Muddy area. We got into Canada once in a while too. We didn't consider ourselves outlaws, just men who were punishing the greedy carpetbaggers who were still exploiting the people and calling it business.

But I always remembered my family back home in Kansas and dreamed of a day when we could all be together again. That is, until I got a letter at the N-Bar-N ranch one day from your Uncle Frank, and it changed my life.

I will tell you about that in my next letter. Please be patient with me, but I don't get much paper to write on here, and I have run out of it. I also need to save up enough money to get a stamp. Remember how much I love you all.

Love Papa

Inmate Jim Howard, #1133

P.O. Box 166, Prince Albert, Saskatchewan Penitentiary

CHAPTER IX

ZEE'S PASSING

HOLDING HIS CHIN IN BOTH HANDS, JIM HOWARD SAT IN SILENCE, staring into the nothingness of his cell. It was Sunday again, and he hadn't written Mary Susan in many months; it was so easy to lose track of time in prison; one day bled into the next without meaning. But his daughter never left his mind or his heart, and before he slipped off into sleep, he had wanted to write her before the black depression overtook him again. His thoughts drifted back twenty-four years to Montana's N-Bar-N ranch. They began with the first time he had taken Black Jim to the N-Bar-N to find some work for the two of them.

• • •

It was winter and too cold to be 'working on the move', running from a posse. John and the ranch manager, Billy Patterson, had become good friends when they'd met on the Texas Trail cattle drives back in 1882, and John had long before made arrangements to have the ranch act as a silent recipient of any Pony Express mail that might come for him.

The ranch had a two-story log house with a big, open verandah. Long benches and large sun chairs lent themselves to private meetings and discussions among the residents. John had felt a chill come over him when the ranch foreman asked him to come by to pick up a letter that had arrived for him. No one knew where he could be found except Frank and he knew that his brother wouldn't send a letter unless it was very important. When the foreman handed it to him, tucked into its Pony Express bag, he had just held it for a while, frozen in silence; he hadn't been able to open it right away. *Will it be about Zee, or the kids? Maybe our mother, Zerelda?* Apprehension had stampeded through his mind. Finally, he took a deep breath, opened the packaging and tore open the envelope inside. His hands shook as he read Frank's words:

December 13th , 1900

Dear Jesse

Before you left, we agreed that I'd write only when there was an urgent family message, so here it is. I'm deeply sorry to have to tell you that your wife, Zee died Tuesday, November 13 at her home in Kansas City. She had never gotten over the death of your twin sons, Gould and Montgomery back in 1878, before you left, and she was subject to passing illnesses. Perhaps that is why she was so determined that you flee to save your life. In her weakened state, she took sick with the grippe last Christmas and never got better. She was a good woman and always spoke kindly of you to the children. They will be cared for by family until you see them again, so don't worry about them.

Zee didn't want to be buried where her grave might be a public spectacle due to your notoriety, so we placed her body in a vault at Elmwood cemetery in Kansas City. Later we'll take her to be buried beside the grave marked as yours in Kearney. She didn't want a public funeral, so it will be very private with only the family present.

I am very sorry to have to send this letter to you. I know your loss will be great...

He had read enough at that point and he set Frank's letter down on the veranda picnic table, intending to finish it later, but instead, he jammed it into his jacket. He had felt numb. He had gone about his daily chores of being a ranch hand, not trusting himself to even try to deal with the grief he knew would overwhelm him when he finally acknowledged that the only love of his life, mother of his children and best friend was gone. Zee had saved his life after he had been shot in the chest by a Union bullet, and it was she who planned his 'assassination' and escape into Indian Territory. In all their time together, he had never looked at or desired another woman, and he vowed he never would, even now, with the devastating news.

It was almost two days later before John could finally read the rest of Frank's letter that had lain crumpled in his pocket. He could hardly take in a breath as he stared at the words on the page.

...When people around home heard you'd been killed, they thought you must have left a wealthy widow. That was not the case. In fact, the only valuables that Zee could lay her hands on were a few weapons, a bit of stolen jewelry and assorted souvenirs. Soon, most everything in the house was put up for auction to pay her creditors. Zee and the children finally had to move in with her brother in Kansas City.

A few months after your staged death, Zee wrote to me. I know how proud she was, so it must have been very hard for her to ask for help. She said she was not in good circumstances and that a little money would greatly assist her, so when I could, I would take a little to her, but she still had to sell some family mementoes that were precious to her. She finally even had to sell your house. I would have helped her more, but by then, I had quit the outlaw business and was struggling to keep my own family going.

Your children were very sad after you left, but they were just too young to be told the truth of your escape. We always intended to tell them the truth, but as time went by, it seemed better to leave things the way they were. Zee suffered from terrible loneliness and worry about where you were and if you were in good health, but she knew any contact might put your new life in danger.

Zee started to wear black mourning clothing and did so until the day she died. She never remarried, living her life as a widow and looking after the children all alone. She was a very beautiful and brilliant woman. If she'd wanted to re-marry, she could have had her pick of men but she was true to you, even though she knew she might never see you again. She could have made a lot of money and become famous by telling stories about you, and our gang, but there too, she couldn't be bought.

Young Jesse Jr. is a good son; he still calls himself Tim Howard, his assumed name when you moved to Missouri as the Howards. You would be very proud of him. He started working at odd jobs when he was eleven so he could help support his mother and sister. When he grew up, he became a lawyer out in California. Mary Jane Susan became a beautiful woman, just like her mother. She married a local farmer, Henry Barr and they are good, hard working Christians.

Mother is still alive, though she is failing at nearly 76 years of age. We all miss you, Jesse, and pray that this letter finds you are safe and healthy, though I know it does not bring good news. I will write again when there is more news. Please let me know where to send future letters.

Your brother Frank

Thinking back from his Prince Albert cell in 1926, Jim realized that by the time he'd arrived in Montana, he still hadn't personally dealt with the Confederacy's defeat. After a few years there, he'd continued as an insurgent. At home, the Republican state administration had branded him an "outlaw" and in Montana, as John Allen, that label had been renewed as the most practical way to live. In the south, he'd known that he still had Union enemies: - carpetbagger- owned banks, stage lines, ranches and railroads. In Montana, he'd watched the same kinds of people with the same kinds of motives, carrying on the same kind of exploitation.

He recalled how, when learning of Zee's death, the kind of anger he hadn't felt for years welled up again. He'd felt guilty for leaving her and the kids alone, though he hadn't been angry at her for insisting on his escape. They'd seen no other choice. It had either been stay and die or run and hide. The time on the Beaverhead County ranch had permitted the anger to mellow somewhat.

That anger had returned with the news of Zee's death. He'd felt justified about the Montana attacks he'd led against carpetbagger-like banks, stage lines and ranches. The railroad companies had been bringing carpetbaggers west to exploit land and resources with the same attitude they had brought to the southern 'reconstruction' in 1885.

Zee's death had burned inside him since early 1901 and had made him realize that he wasn't finished with those railways. He knew how; it had just been a matter of figuring out when and where. Even in the midst of his anger, he knew he mustn't act without a plan. He'd talked with Black Jim and Birt Enders about his need to involve them in another focus beyond robbing banks and stage coaches; the trains were their next target. And having a new focus helped him put his grief back down inside his soul.

December 30th, 1926

Dear Mary Susan,

Again, I apologize for not writing you before now. What with the spring and summer farm work, and then harvest, I was just too tired to write and when winter fell once more up here, I was taken over by a black depression that I am only now returning from. I have had these spells all my life, and I hope you do not inherit them.

I have pondered long about why I couldn't leave the outlaw life behind me when I escaped from St Joseph, Missouri. I seemed to spend my whole life either running from anger or letting it explode in me, so after a few years of being a ranch hand I just returned to what I knew and what would make me feel better, God forgive me.

All that anger must have come to my early experience the Civil War visited on me and my family. It seemed that the worst damage came after the war was over and those rich Yankee carpetbaggers just kept robbing and punishing my people. When I got out West, things were not very different. I saw how banks, stage coach companies and railroads were doing the same kind of thing to the Indians as they had to us southerners. We had been called outlaws, so I found some friends of a similar mind, and we became a kind of Robin Hood band again. We gave to those who were poor and treated badly, and we punished those in power.

I finally figured all this out after I got a letter from your uncle Frank, telling me your mother had passed. I could feel myself get real cold and quit feeling anything but that anger. It's taken a jail sentence to give me the time to figure it all out.

There are so many things I would have shared with you if I had been able to be there for your growing up years. But among the many lessons that I learned from your mother, one seems appropriate to end this letter with. He would tell me often, "There will come a time when you think everything is finished. That will be the beginning".

I hope my letters will allow you to see that the stories you have heard about the outlaw Jesse James, the man who left his wife and children, has another side.

Love, Papa.

Inmate J Howard, #1133, Saskatchewan Penitentiary

Box 166, Prince Albert, SK

CHAPTER X

RENEWING INSURGENT TACTICS

AFTER FRANK'S LETTER ABOUT ZEE'S DEATH CAME, JOHN ALLEN had withdrawn into himself and tried to focus on being a ranch hand, so he, Howard and Enders just stayed there. That strategy worked for a year until, late one night, after a long day on the ranch, he lay in his bunk, and began to think about his past. His mind suddenly filled with thoughts of robbing trains as well as their crews and passengers. It seemed to come out of nowhere because he hadn't thought about train robberies for a while.

The next day the ranch hands got their one day a week off to spend some time on their own. John found his two partners and they decided to head into Culbertson to the Lone Star Saloon for a few beers and some distraction. When they'd first met up, John had brought up the suggestion that they should add trains to their list of robbery targets. Riding in to the little town was a good time to bring it up again. They ambled along, enjoying the slow, rolling pace of the horses, head down and slumping into their saddles, like all relaxed cowboys do. The dry earth muffled the sound of hooves and they released a gentle smell of manure and about-to-sprout pasture grasses.

They squinted into the sun as it shone down on them and they walked their horses at a nice gentle stride. Out of the blue, John said, "I've been thinking that maybe we should try robbing a few trains. What do you think?"

Birt looked up, curious but interested. "You got anything in mind?"

"I've been thinking a lot about how the same Yankees who were robbing the South after the civil war are now doing it here in Montana. Washington's been helping the railroads, the greedy bankers and land holders out here in the West, just like they did back home. Railroads have been getting lots of free land from that Washington deal and they've been selling it to big land companies who are bringing in homesteaders, raking in cash and stuffing it in their bank accounts. It's time they started paying something for all they're getting," John answered. His face had grown dark and stormy, like a thunder cloud.

"Agreed. What's your point? How do you propose we go about that? Robbing banks is one thing, but we never robbed a train before," Birt continued. John was silent for a long moment, then he began to recount how he and his brother had perfected their strategy.

"Well, we used to start by having one guy break into a railway handcar house to steal track tools. Then we'd ride ahead to a curve and remove a track bar from a length of rail. Next, we'd tie ropes to the rail, lay it back down and wait for the train. Soon's the train got past the point where it could stop, we'd pull the rail out. Once the engineer saw the missing track, he'd try to put the train into reverse, but the engine would be going so fast around the curve, it would turn over. That'd put the engineer, the fireman and several passengers out of commission. Then we could get into the express car and rob the passengers."

"Don't see any reason why that wouldn't work in Montana," was Black Jim's response. Birt quickly agreed. Both partners had stolen a quick look at each other to make sure they were both in agreement with John. They knew all three had to be in agreement to make the plan work flawlessly.

"In Missouri, it worked so good that other gangs copied us. The law even blamed us for robberies that happened when we were miles away. They just couldn't find us because they were too far behind our trail." John had paused as he rolled a cigarette paper with tobacco with one hand as he rode, licked it sealed and lit it. He took a long, grateful drag, and looked off into the dry grassland as his mind replayed the old scenarios of his glory days.

"But we'll need to have a hideout that's a long way from the places we've been running to in Valley County and in Canada," John finally continued. "Montana lawmen and those Canadian redcoats have experience chasing us and others in an out of Canada."

"What do ya have in mind?" Black Jim's brow furrowed. He didn't want to have to run from a posse again, as they had when there were a few close calls in the past.

"What about starting down Cassidy's Outlaw Trail?" Birt spoke for the first time. "Goes right past my old home territory of White Owl in Meade County, South Dakota. From there, we could head south-east over to Sioux Falls and into Iowa."

"I like that. For a young fella, you have a good mind." John was thoughtful as he considered. "I don't want to go all the way down Cassidy's trail and end up in Mexico though. When you get to Mexico, where are you? Why not end up in Iowa?" They all had a chuckle, because John was somebody who didn't like Mexicans much. The conversation took another turn as John pretended that he hadn't already thought of another place to hide out.

" I've got an old friend from Civil War days still living in Iowa. He's one of those 'copperheads' that hated the Yankees and used to give us a little cash, some supplies and a place to hide out when we needed it. He'd help an ex-Reb." He continued slowly. "I seem to recall Rob Willey having a nice piece of property about seventy miles southeast of Sioux City, up in north western Iowa. It was about fifty acres and brought him a nice living. It was in a good hunting area and he put part of it into warm season grasses and food plots for even better hunting. That Iowa red cedar bush has lots of deer and wild turkey, even a few pheasant and quail in it. Willey moved up there just after the war started. Smart man to get out when he could."

John was glad his friend had escaped all the misery that had rained down upon the enemies of the Union, but he didn't hesitate to look to him for help one more time. "Willey found good land on the west side of the Cedar River, with lots of wildlife, shelterbelts and good crop soil. We could camp and live off the land for a few days or even few weeks if we had to. We wouldn't even have to depend on Rob for any grub. 'Sac an' Fox' Indians have lived in that part of the country for hundreds of years, using plants and animals for food; we could do the same."

Black Jim had followed John's words with interest, but he was an impatient man, given to bouts of impulsiveness. He pulled his horse to a halt, causing the others stop as well. "Now that you two have a hiding place and getting us fed all figured out, are we gonna plan what train we're gonna hold up? We got to plan those details first 'fore we figure out our little holiday in the woods! Which train? Where do we hit it? When? And what about how we're going to get away first so we can get to the hideout with that copperhead?" Black Jim's questions were abrupt and rapid, but they made some sense.

"Good questions, Jim." Birt replied. "Got any ideas John?"

"You boys have been hanging out in Culbertson more often than me. Have you heard about any big hauls coming through by train?" Both Birt and Black Jim knew that John didn't drink alcohol and it annoyed John to have to remind them that Birt was the saloon goer, not him. If he went, it was always on business.

"Heard a few cowboys talking last week about coal mines that had been built along the Tongue River north of Sheridan. The Burlington Railroad moved into that route back in '92. There's lots a' new miners and their families livin' up there, and the mining companies pay 'em in cash. The best way for 'em to bring it in is from Billings by stage or train. They think it's too risky to send cash that far by stage, so it comes by the same train that brings mining company store supplies. Seems to me we need to find out when the cash'll be goin' in and figure out when, where and how to hit the train."

"Starting to look good to me" John responded. "When's a train carrying cash due through there?" They didn't know that yet, but they all agreed that they'd keep an ear to the ground to listen for any railway news.

One night, as they sat out on the ranch veranda, smoking and talking, Black Jim had some news. "Yesterday, I heard a few hands who came out of the Lone Star talking about pay day for five mines in two weeks. Nobody notices a black cowboy, so they talked right in front of me. Should be some cash on that Burlington Express due through Jordan about then." He smiled, happy to see that the train caper was actually moving ahead.

"Black Jim, you could join up with Indian Jack Dawson and Pascal Bonneau, break into the Jordan handcar house and then get set up on that downhill curve east of Jordan. The three of you can be waiting back in the bushes just around the curve. Once the train flips over, you can hit the express car." Clearly, John had already planned to add to their crew by two men.

"We know Indian Jack, but who's this Pascal guy," Black Jim was suspicious. He, like both John and Birt, was always cautious about involving a stranger, particularly in any new caper.

"He's a half-breed from a place called Willow Bunch, up in Canada. Met him at the N-Bar-N back a bit when Sam Kelly introduced him to me. He's worked with Sam and Indian Jack on a few horse, cattle and bank jobs. Both Sam and Indian Jack trust him and they'll vouch for him."

"Anybody that Sam Kelly trusts is ok with me." Black Jim sat back and relaxed. Birt nodded his agreement.

Two weeks later, early on a Wednesday morning, John, Black Jim, Indian Jack and Jack Pascal were set up in the bush just downhill from the curve, awaiting the train's approach. They had already readied the rail for extraction. As planned, when the train got past the point where the train couldn't stop in time, they pulled the rail out. As expected, the engineer tried to throw the engine into reverse, but was it was going so fast around the curve, the train turned over. With the engineer and the fireman badly injured, John, Black Jim and Birt attacked the Express car's strongbox. They had to dynamite it open; in the meantime, Pascal and Indian Jack got into the passenger car and robbed the startled passengers.

The five robbers met downhill far enough away from the wreckage to count and divide the take. There'd been payrolls for five mines totaling fifty thousand dollars in the strongbox, but the passengers' total had only been eighteen hundred dollars. "Let's split the fifty thousand five ways and leave the eighteen hundred for the two of you," John suggested. Birt and Black Jim just nodded. They didn't mind paying a little insurance to insure the two others wouldn't turn them in down the line somewhere.

"Thanks. Mighty kind of you. If you ever plan on doing another of these jobs, get in touch with us through Sam Kelly again. Pascal and I are going northwest to his home territory around Willow Bunch," Indian Jack replied, and they shook hands, mounted up and rode off. John, Black Jim and Birt headed southeast.

Five days later, John, Jim and Birt pulled up to Rob Willey's log cabin in an opening beside the Cedar River. Surrounded by tall, red cedar, it was almost invisible to passersby. Willey stepped out of the low cabin door with a wary smile that softened as he recognized John and uttered a surprised welcome. The visitors could hear the sound of a pistol safety being disarmed from behind Willey's back.

"Hello friend! How've you been? I didn't know whether you'd survived through the war or not. Heard you were shot, but it looks like you made it. Been up here long?"

"Got to northwestern Montana with the cattle drives in the late 80s. Been in the central states and the northeast since then. We've been 'liberating' northern Yankee horses, cattle and cash back like we did in the south after the war, and now we've started on their trains. Since you helped us out during the war, we're hoping to find a place to pitch our tent, hobble our horses and hideout from time-to-time. Whatcha think? Are you still up for that?"

John felt no need to provide any more detail about the robberies and Rob's inclination was to not intrude by asking. Their ground rules had been established long ago. As John sat down on the veranda for a chat, Black Jim and Birt unsaddled, watered and hobbled the horses so they could graze. They pitched the tent and gathered wood for a campfire. This gave John and Rob some time to start catching up on their post-war lives.

"Like I said, I've been doin' whatever I needed to do to make a living," John offered. My wife passed away in late 1900, and I've been moving around ever since." He waited for a few breaths and cleared his throat, swallowed the lump that always came when he thought of Zee and went on. "How've things been with you and the family?"

"My own wife died with the pneumonia about three winters ago and my boy and his wife went back to Missouri. They thought life was just too tough for them out here and they are still angry at me for bringing her out here. I haven't heard from them since. My grandson, Donnie, their boy, stayed with me for a couple years, but he headed up to Canada last year. Said he was going to get some free land by homesteading. Once he gets the land all cleared and proved up, the government'll give him freehold title and Canadian citizenship. It's okay for him to become a Canadian farmer, but it's not for an old guy like me. I'll just live out my days right here."

"Where did he go?" John thought for a moment, then added, "I've heard about the odd Montana cowboy doin the same kind of thing. Wonder what it's like up there."

"Said he was going east of a place called Prince Albert, along the Saskatchewan river, but who knows where the hell that is?" John sensed it was time to drop the subject of Rob's family which clearly made him feel lonely as he remembered the past. He stood up and started to head out to the tent to leave Rob alone, but turned around for another word.

"Sorry for the loss of your wife, but it's nice to catch up on the years, even if your son and grandson left." Another pause, then, "And it's good of you to let us camp here once in a while, like the old days. I'm glad we can still be friends. We'll, guess I better head over to the tent to see what the guys are doing for supper."

When he got there, John saw that Birt had killed a couple grouse and Black Jim had opened up some canned beans and put the coffee pot on. Black Jim was a good cook, and things had begun to smell pretty nice. They brought out their tin plates, cups and spoons and squatted around the fire, enjoying their supper. That night, the bedrolls felt mighty good.

For a few days, their daily routine involved shooting some small game and birds, berry picking and wood–gathering, with the odd trip down to the river for some fishing. Rob let them be, not bothering them at all. John enjoyed going up to the cabin in the evening for the occasional visit with Rob, where they reminisced about the war and the defeat of the South. Life was good, but the visitors soon found themselves longing for something more exciting to do.

One day, Birt thought out loud, "How long'r we going to keep sitting 'round? Must be somewhere we can make some money and have a little adventure."

"Got any ideas?" John asked.

Black Jim's response was quick. "Last time I was hanging around outside the Long Branch, a guy was telling me about a bank called the 'First State' over at Crosby, a little place in North Dakota not too far east of Valley County. Said he thought it'd be a pushover."

"Might give us some quick and easy cash while we're waiting here for the next train job we can hit," John hunched over his tin coffee cup and lowered his voice, even though he knew they were alone. "Every job can't be a train robbery, but we should be watchin' for the next good one."

On an April, 1904 morning, the three of them rode into an unsuspecting Crosby in North Dakota's Divide County. Using the method that John had taught them, they got away with ten thousand dollars.

They used two tellers as shields as they left the bank and cleared people off the street by shooting their pistols in the air as they exited. A quickly assembled posse tried to follow them, but soon lost their trail after Birt had used some rags to put 'socks' over their horses hooves to disguise their tracks. When they changed horses at a ranch along the Outlaw Trail, they left a note saying they'd gone to Moose Mountain up in Canada. The posse thought they'd gone north.

This ruse became something that they would use often in the future. Once Mounties had returned to Canada's Big Muddy area at the end of the Boer War, where they had been sent as soldiers for the Canadian government, many Valley County outlaws had needed to find another escape route so they had gone east to the Souris River in North Dakota. They had followed it north into Canada, and made their way up into the Moose Mountain area. Sometimes outlaws, after escaping into the Big Muddy, ended up making a new life by homesteading around Moose Mountain. But they usually maintained intermittent contact with their old stomping ground across the border to the south and supplemented their farm income with a little horse or cattle rustling.

John, Black Jim and Birt had made good time and arrived back at Rob Willey's a few days after the Crosby bank job. John was ready to make new plans. "Well, we made a nice haul in Crosby, but now, after we take a good rest, we'll need to get back after those trains."

"Where's next?" asked Black Jim. "We keep hearing about lots of 'Wild Bunch' action in Wyoming. Should we maybe head over there?"

"You guys can head over there if you want, but I'm sticking to Montana. Know the territory much better. I'm hoping you'll both stick with me."

"Well, I don't want to break up our crew so I'll stick with you." Black Jim responded quickly, and Birt's assurance was, "Me too. You're both like brothers to me."

"How about you two going up to northeastern Valley County and scouting out the Great Northern and Soo Line railways for a chance at one of them? While you're at that, I'll send a message to Kelly see if

Indian Jack and Pascal Bonneau have come down from Willow Bunch to Glasgow or Culbertson. Bonneau told me about getting as much as two hundred dollars each from North Dakota farmers for rustled ten dollar Montana horses and he won't pass up chances like that for long, especially when some of those horses are free for the taking."

John stopped a moment, thinking about the opportunity for easy money with little risk. "Now, that might be a chance for quick and easy cash between train jobs for us." Looking up again at his two partners, he went on. "You check out the northeast for trains and I'll send the message to Sam; how about we meet up in the Lone Star in two weeks?"

Jim and Birt agreed and were soon headed off to Montana. John headed westerly of the other two. All expected that in two weeks they'd meet in Culbertson and be readying themselves for another train robbery.

Nearly three weeks later, Black Jim and Birt were sitting on the porch at the Lone Star's bar that had been their daily perches for a week, when John walked in.

"Took you an extra week," Black Jim said. "Hard to find those two half-breeds? What'd they have to say?"

"Arranged to meet them here in the Lone Star next week," John replied. "But more important, anything for us with the trains?"

"Maybe you remember Miles City from your cattle drive days. Fort Keogh, big army post's been there since'77," Black Jim explained. "It's been headquarters for the Montana Stock Growers since '84 and that and the Northern Pacific Railway, which came in '81, made it a leading cattle market. Each year, its home to a big rodeo. With so much livestock flowing in and out, there's lotsa money and lotsa moneyed folk flowing in and out too. Most of that money and most of them folks come in by train from the southwest.

Black Jim could hardly wait to tell John more about the information the two men had learned. "Birt found another good location, east of Jordan too, for a hit on the Northern Pacific. It'll be bringing in lotsa cash for Miles City next month too."

John's immediate response was, "Isn't that around the place where some guys killed the engineer on a train job in '02? I don't want to kill anybody. That would get the Pinkertons all riled up to hunt us down."

"That was six years ago' and we're not for planning to kill anybody either," said Black Jim defensively. "We're known as friendly and generous to most people, usin' our guns only when we have no choice. I don't even want ta rile up that Sheriff Costner, never mind the Pinkertons. In that new east-of-Jordan spot Birt's picked, we won't need to kill anybody, if they're smart."

"That spot'd be just right for Pascal and Indian Jack to help us," Birt added. "When we meet up with 'em at the Lone Star next week, and if they want in, they'll help make it work better. It's a pretty big job. So, are we all agreed?" Three cowboy hats nodded assent. "We just need to meet up with those two half-breeds. Are we ready for this?"

May 12th, 1927

Dear Mary Susan

I surely do think of you a lot. I can't imagine you being any older than that little girl I left behind so many years ago. But I know you are a grown woman now yourself, and maybe one day you will make me a grandfather.

I've been thinking about some of the lessons I learned from those Yankee crimes of Reconstruction. They left me so angry when they happened, and just as angry many years later. Some of us young Rebs back then had started to retaliate at the injustice by robbing banks, stage coaches and horse and cattle ranches. Yankees in Washington had started helping the crooked banks and land holders, so we gave away most of the proceeds of our robberies to folks who lost everything after the war and couldn't get their own land back, and then we started making the trains pay too. In the South, railroads had been getting cash and stuffing it in their bank accounts by getting lots of free land. The same thing had begun to happen up north too where they were selling stolen land to land companies that were bringing in homesteaders and ripping them off with high prices.

Some of us thought it was time Railroads, like the banks, started paying something for all they were getting, but most people were afraid to face down them down just as they'd been afraid of the banks and land companies. Some of us believed that while it's easy to sit up and take notice, that's not enough; what's difficult is getting up and taking action; there may be obstacles to taking action, but obstacles can't stop you; problems can't stop you; most of all, other people can't stop you. Only you can stop you, so we decided to take action against the Yankee railroads as well as the banks and land companies. Just like in the South, we were called bandits, but we knew we were just continuing our insurgency against those same Yankees and helping out those who were oppressed.

Maybe this letter will help you understand how your poor daddy had to leave you behind, and what my life has become in the years that followed. Just know that you were always in my heart.

Love, Papa.

Inmate Jim Howard, #1133Saskatchewan Penitentiary, Box 166, Prince Albert, Saskatchewan

CHAPTER XI

ZERELDA DIES IN OKLAHOMA

"WE THOUGHT YOU TWO MIGHT BE STUCK UP IN CANADA, BUT IT'S good to finally see you. We've got a job you might like," John greeted them. "You still travelling on Injun time? That what held you up?"

Pascal had a hot, French Canadian temper and shot back. "Forget dat smart talk 'bout time. We're here on de day we said we be here. We jus' didn't' agree what time dat would be. Whatcha got in mind?" Their wait, although it had seemed longer to John, had really only been about three hours before Indian Jack and Pascal had walked in.

"Birt found 'nother good spot for a Northern Pacific train-heist – somethin' like the first Jordan heist.

"Jordan?" Indian Jack queried. "Ain't that the place where they shot a train engineer?"

"That's the name of the place, but that was some years ago and the spot Birt's found is east, down the track from Jordan - in a deep canyon that's just right for us. No need to kill anybody long as they don't get careless and we don't – and there'll be no need to force the train engine off the track" John replied.

"Dat's good. Don' mind robbin trains, but we don' wanna come down here ta kill anybody. Lucky dat engineer didn' die after dat last Jordan job we did. What's da plan for dis job and de escape after?" The Métis went on, "an' later you can tell us 'bout any odder action you might wanna offer us a piece ah."

"Yup." John didn't waste words. "Birt thinks that, just before midnight, he and I should hideout in the engine's coal bin on the passenger train 'fore it leaves Jordan. Then, when the train stops to take on water at that depot just east of Jordan, we'll come out and order the engineer to keep the train goin' east. On the upside of the hill that Birt's picked out, we'll order him to stop. You, Indian Jack and Black Jim'll be waiting there with five horses. Black Jim'll bring some dynamite to the express car and dynamite the safe. You and Indian Jack can go through the passenger car and signal us when you've got all the loot you can grab, and you go wait outside with the horses. We'll warn the engineer to keep the train rolling east. Then we'll jump off and the three of you'll ride up, bringing our two horses. We'll all take off into the bush and by the time the posses are ready, we'll all be long gone. Once we're away and settled, we can start to talk about some other ideas we might have." For a man of few words, the plan was concise and detailed. Each man's role, the location of the heist, and the getaway was clear.

The train robbery had gone as planned; soon they were gathered in the *Hell Creek- Arm-Missouri Breaks* area about twenty five miles northeast of Jordan. They knew that area was a good place to hide out while they considered their next plan. It's location was another safe option for sanctuary from either the Montana or Canadian law when required, in addition to Willow Bunch, Sam Kelly's Pilot Butte Caves near Big Beaver, Moose Mountain and North West Iowa.

After a few days of resting both the men and horses, John was overcome with his old impatience to get on with other things, so he announced to the others, "This seems like a good time to talk about what we do next." He paused, took a long tug on a cigarette and went on his eyes were deep black holes, the only indication that he was excited.

"Must be a lot of spots up here in the northeast where we could find some easy-to-grab horses that could bring us good cash from your contacts up at Willow Bunch, Pascal. We should be able to hideout up there until the heat's off us, if we have to. What do you all think?" "Whacha got in mind?" Pascal was slow to answer; always a man who kept his business to himself, he wondered if he wanted to share his source of quick cash with his part time partners.

"Seems like you're as good at finding easy-to-grab horses as I am at finding trains to hit,"

Birt challenged, "but do we want to be a gang or just a crew? Seems we trust each other some and can work together pretty good, but do we need the reputation of a 'gang'?"

"Mebbe we don' need to always work togedder for every job. Indian Jack and me, we sometimes like to pull smaller jobs dat don' need so many partners." Pascal didn't want the attention a gang might bring, but he liked John and the guys. "Us, we can mebbe do some jobs togedder." They left it at that, promising to discuss a plan later.

* * *

In his Prince Albert cell, Jim sat back lazily on his cot, where he spent most Sundays, and he smiled as he recalled how the bunch of them had spent the rest of 1910 in small, mutually-supportive 'crews' of two to five, stealing horses, robbing little country stores and occasionally taking out a small town bank. Each of them kept his own personal 'stash' of ill-gotten proceeds in a small, easy-to-conceal saddlebag. Jim thought of how important he had thought that stash was, and how it had helped pay for his Canadian homestead a few years later. He even had a little of it still stashed away in a bank near the homestead. It was his '*just in case*' stash. He hadn't had time to get to it before the police had picked him up and took him to prison in '24.

Yup, he had made some big mistakes in those days before he left America. The biggest was not trying to slip back into Missouri years before, to have one more visit with Zee and the children. But the call of revenge on the Railroads and Banks and the excitement of the wild lifestyle were too great, and he had always told himself he would do it after the next robbery. Then, when he learned of Zee's death, he'd felt the need to distract himself from his grief.

Jim had tried to make excuses for his inability to get home by telling himself that it was too dangerous, too soon, and that he needed just a few more jobs so he could bring some money for his aging mother, Zeralda, and the children. Laying there on the hard cot, he knew he'd lied to himself for all those years, and that he'd just been giving in to his own selfish need for retaliation and, though he hated to admit it, even adventure. It was a bitter pill to swallow. He knew he would have to confess all of that to Mary Susan in his next letter.

• • •

The day after they got to Hell Creek, Pascal and Indian Jack said they were off for a week on a horse escapade of their own. Pascal's brother had told him of a Canadian rancher who had about two hundred fifty horses that had been pastured on some land that was rented from the Assiniboine Sioux on the Fort Peck Indian Reservation. Prairie fires had destroyed a lot of grass on the ranchers' side of the Canadian border, so the good grass on the reservation meant the horses wouldn't starve. Pascal and his brother knew of a Big Muddy hideout north of Redstone where, after they stole the horses, they could keep them until they had sold them for the fifty five hundred dollars that had been promised by a Redstone rancher.

"Wish we coulda cut you in, us," Pascal had said, "but ya know de deal we made. Mebbe we can do dat next time." John Allen had always had a lot of respect for Pascal's abilities with livestock. The Métis was reputed to have started with four horses and four cattle on his little piece of land near Willow Bunch in 1896 and by 1900, it was estimated that he had expanded it to about four hundred horses and the same of cattle. John wasn't likely to question Pascal's opinions on ranch stock.

"Thanks for mentioning it," John replied. "Black Jim, Birt and I have some small jobs that we've been thinking about. We'll see you when you're back in a week from today and we'll talk if anything else might have come up by then."

Shortly after Indian Jack and Pascal had left, John had pointed out to Birt and Black Jim that nearby Miles City, on the mouth of the Tongue River, was still '*a hundred miles from nowhere*' and still filled with saloons, brothels and gambling dens. It was an excellent jumping off spot for some of the action they hoped for. Not long after, on one of their visits to town to get supplies, their luck was looking up when a former Fort Keogh army post trader, who had recently become town merchant, told them of his plan to buy merchandise on a trip back East. The trader had told John that he was afraid of carrying cash on the first leg of a North Pacific train trip to Bismarck, North Dakota, so, by supplying some alcohol, he'd been able to convince some of his old army contacts to let him hitch a ride with an army ambulance. It was perfect because it was always guarded by fifteen soldiers on their way to pick up the Fort's payroll. The trader had seen to it that each soldier would receive his fair share of liquor.

John, Birt and Black Jim, armed with rifles, had waited on a plateau above a steep-walled valley for the ambulance that carried the trader and his escorts. They stopped the ambulance at a sharp corner in the bottom of the valley and the soldiers were robbed of a total of twenty five hundred dollars each from the Fort's payroll. The trader also lost the three thousand dollars he had intended the ambulance and guards to protect.

When they got back together at Hell Creek, the three had agreed to pool five thousand dollars from each of their two recent escapades before taking out their share of one thousand dollars each. For most of the next year, in any of Montana's towns, when one of them wanted to treat the others to a drink, he'd say, jokingly, "Come on, chum, have one on me; I've still got one of the old trader's army dollars left." John, Birt and Black Jim felt that they'd shown Pascal and Indian Jack that, even without them, they'd really pulled off a job that made them famous, even if no one knew who this new gang of bandits was.

When Pascal and Indian Jack returned the next week as promised, fresh off their own escapades, the Métis observed, "Mebbe de five of us should try our luck a li'l nort'wes' a here. Mebbe be some action near places like Fort Benton, Sun River, Missouri Breaks and Fort Shaw, to say nuttin' of places like Great Falls an' Helena."

"Yeah, that's right. Good thinking, Pascal. Montana Central laid tracks from Helena to Great Falls, Fort Assiniboine and Pacific Junction just a short time ago, joining that main east-west line. John added, "Those goldfields around Helena should be sending out something to Glasgow once in a while that we'd be interested in."

"Since those tracks bypass the old east/west crossing, that'ud give us a chance ta go after loaded coaches," Birt added in, "but we'll need temporary headquarters. It'll be too far to be ridin' there and back from any of our other spots. Too easy ta be seen."

"How 'bout Rocky Gap jus' east a Great Falls in dose Highwood Mountains," Pascal had asked.

"Sounds good. You Canadians know of a few good hiding places up there, too, don't you," had been John's response.

"Yeah. not so risky as goin' back an' fort' to Willow Bunch, wit Montana lawmen, Vigilantes an' Canadian Redcoats along da way," Pascal pondered.

Later that evening, John told Pascal and Indian Jack about his need to make occasional visits back to the N-Bar-N ranch. They were comfortably full of Black Jim's stew and biscuits and were sitting around the camp fire. He saw it as a good time to pull them aside for a chat.

"Can you and Pascal come sit over here for a minute?" he'd asked Indian Jack. "You both know where the N-Bar-N ranch is, right? Well, I'm going to go back there by myself for a few days. I check in there regular to see if any private Pony Express mail has come from the south for me. If you two wait here with Black Jim and Birt, I'll be gone for about a week. When I'm back, we can decide if we want to do another job." The weather was good, and the horses were tired, so everybody agree it was time for a little holiday while they waited for John to return.

• • •

In his cell, Jim recalled that, for the second time, a letter had been waiting for him at the N bar N. He'd opened it hesitantly. The letter had begun:

Dear Jesse

Remember how we agreed that I would write you only on matters of urgent family matters? That's what I did just before Christmas 1900 when Zee died. Now, the urgent family matter is about our dear and faithful mother, Zerelda, the woman that each of us has loved since the day we were born. She was with my wife, Annie when she fell dead on the afternoon of Dec. 10, 1910, in a state room of a northbound Pullman train near Oklahoma City on its way to San Francisco. She was 86 years old and was in exceptionally good health and in good possession of all her faculties. Surprisingly, heart disease was thought to have caused her death, though there had been no indication of that during her lifetime. Her long and healthy life, right up to her end, should be a good omen for both of us.

Both Mother and Zee are gone now, so you must stay away from our old family home. The children are good and well looked after. We all love you.

Your brother, Frank

Good Omen? What good could there be in the death of a mother? What do I do now? I can't go back to Missouri. This Montana outlaw life can only lead to being killed or jailed. Is that what I want? Do I just end it by finishing myself off? Nobody will miss me anyway. Maybe, this train job, then one more, should be the last one here. Maybe, Jim, Birt and Curt Thompson, (another bandit they had picked up for short jobs), *will all agree to come to Canada, become homesteaders and qualify for*

Canadian citizenship. Missouri, Black Jim's slave years, Banditry and the Confederacy can all be left to history.

He remembered wondering whether the others would agree. Having had enough of shooting, running and hiding, he was sure that Black Jim, Curt and Birt were willing to think about it, but they would want a firm plan. Pascal and Indian Jack had said that, from Poplar, they could just take their share of the horses and go northwest to Willow Bunch while John, Black Jim, Birt and Curt could head straight north to Big Beaver up in Canada, with their share.

When John returned to his crew, he brought up his thoughts on moving on up to Canada. As he had thought, Black Jim needed a good plan before he'd agree to anything. He'd brought up the sloppy planning they'd done for another job to rob the Fort Benton army payroll robbery from a paymaster's wagon, where the plan had been to lie in wait near Blackfoot Creek Canyon southwest of Great Falls. Somehow the army had heard of their plans and delayed the trip so they'd had to give up on that plan. Another one for an army payroll robbery was foiled and the disappointed gang, following Pascal Bonneau's example, decided that, after they'd pulled off a Montana Central train job, they'd go back to livestock stealing.

Birt and Black Jim had first met young Curt Armstrong when the newcomer had told them about a large livestock ranch near Glasgow and thinking about its possibilities led John to consider stealing some horses. Curt said it had stock of 350 horses, so the three of them, seeing a "ticket north," immediately overcame their resistance to new partners and agreed to try Curt for the train job and, if he did well, partnering with him for the ranch job.

"Birt's found a good spot to hit that Helena train about half-way between Great Falls and Fort Benton. Even if we don't get their payroll, we'll still get some of the Yankee's Army money" John had declared.

On the 5th of April, 1911, the northwest bound Montana Central from Helena made its regular stop in Great Falls at about 10:30 a.m. John Allen purchased a ticket and boarded the train as a passenger. Birt was already on the train and had his gun leveled on the engineer.

Black Jim had earlier boarded the train, crawled over the tender box into the engine cab and leveled his gun at the conductor before he could pull the emergency cord. John made his way back to the engine and gave an order to keep the train moving until it reached the bridge south of Fort Benton.

The train stopped at the bridge where Pascal, Indian Jack and Curt were waiting with escape horses and dynamite. Black Jim and Birt fired their guns along the passenger cars to keep the curious inside. John Allen ordered the engineer to disconnect the baggage and express cars and pull the engine away. He commanded that the mail clerk and the express messenger open the express car doors and jump out.

Using the dynamite brought by Pascal, Indian Jack and Curt, they blew the safe open and took out four bags of notes: ten- twenty-dollar bills and unsigned bank notes from the Bank of Montana on each. They also took a package containing American National Bank funds and a bag filled with silver coins.

When they got up to Rocky Gap, their hide-away, they counted out sixty thousand dollars to share. Birt, Black Jim, Curt and John had all agreed that they would have enough of the Big Muddy following the Poplar job and they wanted to find a way to settle down. They agreed that, like Sam Kelly planned to, they'd find places away from both American and Canadian law that, would make it possible for them to use their stashes to live normal lives.

"I hear that, under Canadian law, a person can select a quarter-section as a homestead and, over a few years, clear it, break it, improve it and, as long as you do everything required, you get title to the land and become a Canadian citizen. Sam Kelly told me that a few other outlaws have done it and he plans to, so why not us?"

"Count me in." was Black Jim's immediate reply. Birt and young Curt agreed. Although they were younger than John, they wanted a future that was more stable than that of being a Big Muddy outlaw.

"Pascal's already a Canadian citizen and he can look after Indian Jack so we don't have to worry about them." John had concluded.

Pascal and Indian Jack had already told them that, following the Poplar Ranch job, they would take their share of the stolen horses, hide them out with their Assiniboine friends on the Fort Peck Reservation and sell them off when the time was right. It was time for all of them to make the change from outlaw to homesteader.

October 23rd, 1927

Dear Mary Susan,

I am so sorry I haven't written for a few months. I haven't been well and my arthritis has been acting up, so getting down the stairs to the mess hall and back up to my cell has been a trial for me. I do hope you and the family are well and not affected by the bad drought Missouri had last year. I read in the old newspapers from the library here that it was the worst in the history of the state. Farmers must surely be hurting. Well, I'll write some more of how I got to Canada.

By early 1911, some of my partners and I had begun talking about taking off to Canada. I had been avoiding either the Yankee army or the Yankee-driven law for nearly fifty years and I was tired of it. Your mother was dead by then, and I hadn't seen you or Jesse Jr. for nearly thirty years. Missouri thought I was dead and it would have been big trouble for me and many others if I had tried to go back there. And, truth to tell, I had finally accepted that I had continued the outlaw lifestyle for my own selfish purposes as well, - greed, thrill and fame no longer seemed good reasons to take the risks that went along with them. By 1911, when I was still John Allen, Montana had put a price on my head too, so there was little left for me to do except keep up the insurgency against Yankee banks, railroads, land owners and others, and I no longer had the heart for that.

I knew of other insurgents who had escaped to Canada, applied for and taken out homesteads and earned freehold title, letting them obtain Canadian citizenship and putting them out of reach from American law. I began to recall some of the things my mother had taught me. One expression that helped me make my decision to move north was, "We can let situations rule us or we can take charge and rule our lives ourselves." I realized that by being an outlaw in both Montana and Missouri were situations that I had created, and they ruled me, so I decided that if I was going to take charge and rule myself, it would have to be in Canada. I headed up there with a few of my crew and started a new life. I had no idea how hard it would be.

Love, Papa.

Inmate Jim Howard, # 1133, Saskatchewan Penitentiary

Box 166, Prince Albert, Saskatchewan

CHAPTER XII

ESCAPE TO CANADA

AS THE FOUR HAD RACED TOWARD THE FAST-FLOWING MISSOURI River, one of the posse had shot Black Jim Howard in his saddle, wounding him seriously. In great pain, he kept riding and doing his part. The posse'd kept after them and the stolen horses as they'd tried to head across the Missouri River, north for Canada. As they started across the river, another sharpshooter killed the wounded Jim. With him dead, the posse closing quickly and the steady 'pop – pop – pop' of flashing guns spelling closing danger, the remaining three, intending to come back later, abandoned the stolen horses. They galloped their own horses across the Missouri and up the north bank. As they started across, Armstrong's horse was shot by another posse sharpshooter, and he fell into the rushing waters of the river leaving the two remaining horse thieves to continue trying to cross.

"That gun-happy posse that killed Black Jim just shot Curt's horse from under him! They missed him, but in this wild river, he'll never make it ta shore!" Birt Enders shouted ahead to John Allen, as their horses scrambled up the north bank of the Missouri River just southwest of Culbertson. Birt was looking back at the strong, young twenty-year-old Curt Armstrong as he struggled against the swift-flowing current. The bounty hunter who'd shot Curt's horse had stopped on the south bank and the guns of the whole posse were still popping and flashing as they continued shooting at Enders and Allen.

Only a few days ago, Curt had motioned to his partners in the early dawn and whispered, "It's right up on that butte just ahead." He was gesturing toward a large ranch, lying still asleep in the darkness. They were close to Poplar, a village on the south side of the Fort Peck Indian Reservation. John, Birt, Black Jim, Pascal and Indian Jack had ridden in slowly and silently, then herded three hundred fifty horses out of one of the ranch's main pastures. They were planning, as they'd done on so many other trips, to divide the horses by giving one hundred seventy five to Pascal and Indian Jim, leaving one hundred seventy five for the other three to sell north of the border. If they could keep the horses calm, they'd get away so no one'd know they'd been there until morning. But it hadn't worked out that way.

The ranchers had set out guards who had heard the horses moving around and, fearing a wolf attack, had gone out to settle them down. In an instant, an alarm was raised, and armed cowhands had begun a chase to catch the rustlers. Pascal and Indian Jack had managed to separate their horses from the herd and move them back towards the reservation, but John's crew headed theirs towards Culbertson, thinking that taking separate directions would confuse the posse and aid in their escape. They had been over and around these hills in other rustling jobs, going from rock pile to rock pile, their horses moving quickly and easily between bushes, rocks and gullies. Now, running the Poplar ranch horses in front of them, they'd again stayed concealed through canyons and gulches. As was their habit, they planned to rest a few hours only at night. Allen had known they were within one hundred miles of the Canadian border and he hoped to make it there before they were caught.

Their plan had started to fall apart when the Poplar ranch guards had met up with some nearby neighbors who were then joined by more vigilantes from the town of Poplar. A group of bounty-hunters who had been tracking John and his men for a week, joined the hunt the next day and made it a big posse, all eager to make the bounty that was offered on the rustlers' heads.

The chase continued for several days across northern Montana, both sides stopping only long enough to rest the horses before moving on. Within a mile of the Missouri River, one of the posse had wounded Black Jim and followed the crew and stolen horses through a series of gullies as they tried to head across the Missouri River and north for Canada.

The posse knew about the prices on the rustlers' heads, and stopped to shoot from high ground whenever they could catch sight of them. With the posse in close pursuit, John, Black Jim, Birt and Curt had abandoned the stolen herd, galloping their own horses into the Missouri and along the south bank before starting across. Just as they'd started across, Black Jim was killed, and Armstrong's horse was shot by a posse sharpshooter. The other two had continued across alone.

Birt stopped halfway across and turned back, shouting to John, "You keep going. I'm going back, I can pull him out!" He'd wanted to rescue young Curt from the swift and boiling waters of the Missouri, ignoring the gunfire.

"Birt, they just shot Black Jim and now Curt's horse. The horses we've been herding are scattered all over hell and those bounty-hunters will nail you if we don't keep moving," Allen shouted back. Birt spun his horse around and came back to John, angry but willing to listen to logic of John's words.

"Curt's gone and we can't do anything to save him. We've lost two good men, but once we're clear of here, we'll come back and round up the horses. We can't give up eighty-five hundred dollars' worth of horses. But we have to stay alive or we ain't gonna get back."

John Allen had some experience with being chased by Yankee soldiers during the war and by posses in both Missouri and Montana; he assured Birt that Curt was paying a price they'd all known could be extracted at any time. Birt was still trying to accept that Black Jim had just been killed as Allen had warned that two horses couldn't get three of them clear of the posse's guns. Calling on his Civil War Guerilla experience, Allen repeated that they had to either keep riding or die right there. He'd known the hurt of being helpless when he'd had to see young men die bloody deaths in the war and during his Missouri insurgent years, but he'd learned to hide his pain and though it was tough, he knew he'd have to hide it once more.

"Armstrong always knew that in this kind of fracas, those who are still up and running have to keep running. If we don't, we could all go down instead of just one. I know it's tough to do, especially when it's the youngest one down, but we have to let him go. Those bastards will either shoot him or wait for him to drown so they can fish him out of the water and take his body to the Sheriff in Glasgow and collect the bounty."

The posse had hoped to collect one hundred dollars for Armstrong's body to add to the hundred they expected for Black Jim. John growled, "If we don't keep moving, that bounty-hunting scum could be taking four bodies back. They'd collect the two hundred for you and the five hundred for me on top of that two hundred," he added. Allen thought the bounty-hunters would only get a hundred for Howard because he was a black cowboy and because Armstrong was a greenhorn with no rep, they'd be lucky to get a hundred for him dead or alive. If the pursuers thought they had a chance at the nine hundred dollars on all of them, they'd take it!

Finally across the river, John headed north toward Plentywood with Enders at his side along the east side of the Fort Peck Reservation. Pascal and Indian Jack had already headed west to the Reservation. Allen and Enders continued at full gallop to the sloped entrance of a hidden coulee gulch east of Plentywood known as the Outlaw Coulee. Besides the two of them, it had often served others as an escape route on desperate runs north to Canada. They pulled up their horses and rested under some scrub trees in a small, hidden hideaway. After the rush away from the river, it was time for talking and making some escape plans.

"We'll have to head onto the reservation, find Pascal and Indian Jack and then all of us can go find our share of the horses. They can keep theirs in their hideout on the reservation. When the time's right, they can sell them to their rancher contact at Redstone. We'll take ours north to Sam Kelly's caves and, in a while, ship them east on the railroad. That should bring us about two thousand dollars each to put in our stashes, along with the twelve thousand dollars each of us got from the train job before we left. It should be enough to set us up as Canadian homesteaders."

After a second crossing of the river, once they were sure the posse had given up on them, they rounded up the stolen horses and drove them back across a shallow spot on the river, finally arriving at the caves with one hundred seventy-five horses. The commanding Peake's Butte overlooked the caves and revealed a view of trails that were often frequented by Redcoats. John, still cautious, remarked to Birt, "How 'bout we take turns resting while the other one's looking out? That way, we'll know when Mounties might be showing up and, even if we have to leave the horses behind, we can get back across the border into Montana."

"Good plan," Birt replied, "but how long we gonna' stay here with these horses? Shouldn't we be gettin' rid of 'em?"

"I say we ride northwest over to Willow Bunch and see whether Pascal's sons have any ideas about how we might sell 'em. Pascal has a big ranch there and his boys run it when he's away." John and Birt set out to meet up with one of the Bonneau sons and, since Willow Bunch had rail service, the son and three other riders came back over to the Peake's Butte caves, paid a total of twenty five hundred dollars for the horses, and left John and Birt with three horses each; one pack horse and two to alternate for riding. The son took the rest back to Willow Bunch to ship out by rail.

John had been thinking a lot about Black Jim. They'd been partners for many years and, for a man like John, friendship and trust were hard to find. If he took Black Jim's birth name, James Marion Howard, he could honor Black Jim and his memory would live on. Besides, he had taken the name of Howard when he and Zee had hidden out in St Joseph's and it felt familiar to him. It would also give him a new identity he could use to enter Canada, leaving his past behind him. So the new Jim Howard and Birt Enders had contemplated their trip north into the unknown: a little town called Prince Albert near the Saskatchewan River.

"But, we'll be passing-up a lot of easy jobs in Valley County and we don't know the country north of Big Beaver and further north to Willow Bunch." Birt had warned.

"Well, with those Canadian Mounties spending so much time on the north side of the Big Muddy, the horse-stealing action back and forth 'tween Montana and Big Beaver has really slowed down," was John's reply. "These days, more Montana guys are heading further east over to the Souris River in North Dakota. Then they take their horses and other goods north to Moose Mountain. There are ranchers there who used to work the Big Muddy, too. They deal with the Montana guys and even put them up sometimes. Once we find a spot to settle, we can travel back and forth to Moose Mountain and, if we want, operate from there." John concluded. They'd heard Sam Kelly and others talk about taking out Canadian homesteads, and knew that, by becoming citizens of Canada, except for the odd quick-cash run, they could put Valley County and the Big Muddy behind them.

"Never thought you'd make me a homesteader," Birt replied, "but at one time I thought about homesteading in Meade County before I left South Dakota. Even got selected for a quarter, so why not in Canada? Once we get there, ya figure we should go northwest like Sam did?" Birt wondered.

"No, I reckon after we get up to that place called Prince Albert where people register for homesteads, we should pick out land east 'a there along that Saskatchewan River. Sam went northwest and settled near a place called 'Debden.' My old Iowa buddy, Rob Willey said that when his grandson, Don, left Iowa, he told him, after picking out land east of the Canadian Lands Office in Prince Albert, he was going to homestead there just on the south side of the river. We should be able to find out from the Canadian Lands Office just where Don Willey is. If there's homestead land near him, we can apply for it. For me, having a neighbor who is the grandson of someone I know will be like going home," John answered, then went on. "I'm gonna use Jim Howard's name to apply for a homestead. Those folks up there won't know any different. They probably never heard of any Howards, white or black, from Missouri. I bet they never even knew any black cowboys," John summed up, continuing, "If he's anything like his granddad, Don Willey won't even blink when he hears I have a new name."

• • •

Jim's jail-cell thoughts rolled back to whether, in 1847, Jesse's parents had ever wondered if their newborn son would someday end up in Canada. They couldn't have imagined the Guerilla warrior or Wild-West outlaw he would become, nor had they heard of Beaver Head County. Neither Montana nor Oklahoma had yet become states. His struggling mother, having lost two husbands, trying to get a farm started, had only seen her sons' future as farmers. Canada would not become a country until twenty years after Jesse's birth and there would be no Province of Saskatchewan until thirty eight years after that. The years and the events that had formed him rolled past in his memory.

How could they have even imagined that in seventy seven years this healthy, gentle and sweet-willed little baby would be sentenced to fifteen years in a far-off Penitentiary? It would have been inconceivable that it would happen under an assumed name that included John's mother's maiden name. Robert and Zerelda James could never have imagined how or why Jesse would first become John Allen and then James Marion Howard. They never would have believed the story of how he would escape St Joseph, live on a bountiful Montana ranch and then leave an outlaw life to become a homesteader in a place called Teddington, Saskatchewan.

But Jesse had been caught up in the '*Go West*' wisdom of his day. Many '*East-Coasters*' would have seen Clay County, Missouri as far enough west. Jesse, however, sharing in the dreams of many other Big Muddy outlaws, saw wealth further north and west. He had wanted a life with only self-imposed limitations, believing that without those imposed by society, he could achieve anything he set his mind to.

These thoughts led Jim to start a letter to Mary Susan:

January 3rd, 1928

Dear Mary Susan,

The winters are long and cold up here in Canada. I don't ever remember the chill lying in my bones like this when I lived on my homestead. But when it is too cold to go out and work, it gives me time to write to you, my dear. I hope you are all well.

It has been on my heart to tell you how I assumed my new name of James Howard. It's a long story, but at the time, it seemed the only way to begin a new life without fear of being chased by a posse. I still wanted everyone back home to think the man who was your father was assassinated back in St Joseph, Missouri.

From the time I left Missouri, I always thought I could leave yesterday behind. I tried, but after cattle drives, and later as a ranch hand as John Allen, another cowboy, Jim Howard and I thought we'd move on. Jim was from Missouri and the Howard name was one that I'd used as an alias when I was Jesse James. In fact, you were born to that name. Jim was the black cowboy I told you about. At first I wasn't happy about working with him. So how did I end up with an ex-slave as a partner? He was one of those slaves who'd become cowboys after the civil war, and had come north in 1877 and stayed around Dillon. He was hired on one of the new ranches, and I found a job at the same ranch in 1885.

When I met him, we were both around the same age as our family Slave, Alphonse, had been when I was a kid. Jim was strong, calm and quiet, much the same as Alphonse had been and, once I got to know him, I trusted him completely. I knew he always had my back covered. When two other partners and I decided to head for

Canada, he agreed to come along. Then, on the way, he was shot and killed by a posse of Montana Vigilantes. It was like losing part of my family and I grieved his loss for a long time.

Taking Black Jim's name seemed a natural way to keep his memory and make a new beginning in a new country, so I became Jim Howard and that is how I am known up here in Canada to this day. No one knows my real identity but you. I still think its best that way. Until next letter,

Love, Papa

Inmate 1133, Jim Howard, Saskatchewan Penitentiary,

Box 166, Prince Albert, Saskatchewan

CHAPTER XIII

HOMESTEAD ENTRY

JOHN AND BIRT HAD WAITED NEAR PEAKE'S BUTTE UNTIL, AS agreed, the Bonneau crew had arrived to take all but six of the stolen horses back to their ranch where they would be shipped east by rail. As soon as the herd was gone, Birt impatiently asked, "Are we gonna get goin' or we gonna jes' keep waitin' here? How far you figger Prince Albert is? Wonder how long it'll take?"

"I've bin told that it's a little over three hundred miles as the crow flies and should take somewhere's between five to seven days."

"But, how far is it an' how long will it take if it's two crows, each one riding between two horses and leading a pack horse?" Birt hadn't lost his sense of humor in spite of all the adventures over the past few days.

"Let's get goin an' we'll know we're there when we get there. First, we head northwest a' here 'til we get to a river called the South Saskatchewan. I heard there are two Saskatchewan Rivers – a North and a South. Once we're on the east bank of the South Saskatchewan, we'll just stay on it past a place called Saskatoon. Funny name, comes from an Injun name that I can't even say," were John's instructions. He'd gone on,

"About two days past Saskatoon, we'll get to a ferry at a little place called St. Louis. We'll cross over there on a ferry and in another half day we should see Prince Albert. The way its bin explained to me is that the two rivers – North and South Saskatchewan – meet up in a fork about a half-day's ride east of Prince Albert and, once they're joined up, they're just called the Saskatchewan River. That's the one that Rob Willey told me about – it runs just north of where his grandson, Don, is homesteading."

Birt had confidently responded, "Sounds to me like you have it figured out so that we ain't gonna get lost. Once we find Prince Albert and that Canadian Lands Office there, we otta have enough information to get to wherever we decide to homestead. you spent all that time as a drover on the old Texas cattle drives, so I'll jes' folla ya 'cross the prairies up here. Cain't be much different – jes' no cattle ta watch over."

"Right. Much the same as a cattle drive, without the cattle, but we only have three horses each to rotate to let the other two rest and eat grass along the way. Drovers always had five or ten to keep them going. And we don't have a chuck wagon so we're gonna have ta carry our bedrolls on the pack horses. And our stashes, guns, spare clothes, and whatever else we have room for. Since Black Jim's gone, we'll just have to take turns preparing chow. Should have enough beans, rice and canned goods along. Medicine too." Jim counted it all off on his fingers.

"And there won't be no payday", Birt had chuckled.

The first thing they'd had to do once they got to Prince Albert was to get a stranger to direct them to a livery barn where they could each register their extra horses while they made their way to the Lands Office. The livery barn attendant told them that the Lands Office was in the new Post Office on the corner of Church and Third Street and he gave them directions. They'd made their way there, tethered their riding horses at the hitching rail outside the impressive new red brick

Post Office that had just been officially opened and found their way inside to the Lands Office. The expressionless Homestead sub–agent responded to their request for information by first glumly asking, "Yer names please. Where ya from?"

"Jim Howard." John wasn't even surprised by how easily he'd lied. "From Missouri." Besides convincing the sub-agent, John had almost convinced himself.

The sub-agent led them over to a Homestead Map. "Any particular townships or quarter sections yer interested in? Want to have a look at the map?"

Jim had carefully scanned the map on the wall, looking for Don Willey's name. Finding it, he asked, "What about this section – seventeen- in township forty nine? Only one of four quarters has a name on it."

"Yep, yer right," came the reply "but that's a long way east a civilization. There are lotsa places closer to Prince Albert with merchants you can get to easier."

"But the name on the South East quarter just happens to be a grandson of an old friend in Iowa. We both wanna be close to him. He probably knows most of the nearby homesteaders round there and I'm sure there's a country store where we can get most of what we'll need. Can you put my name on the North East quarter and get the papers to sign?"

"An' will ya put me down fer the South West quarter an' git the papers for me?" Birt had already made up his mind.

"Okay, but there'll only be time to do yers today, Howard and, Enders, you'll hafta wait 'til tomorrow," came the impatient agent's reply, followed by, "An' yer address will hafta be *Lost River*, like ever'body else livin' out there.

After agreeing to the agent's conditions, the two of them had made arrangements with the livery barn attendant to let them sleep there in the hay loft that night. The young attendant, much more helpful than the sub-agent had been, explained how they could get out to the Teddington area.

"Jes' stay on the south bank a' the river an' head east. "Bout twenty, twenty five miles out, you'll come to a river fork where the South Saskatchewan River joins the North. Couple a years ago, the city of Prince Albert decided to build a hydroelectric dam there, thought it would create cheap electricity for the businesses. I figure it's too far from town to do much good. Named it after some trapper called John Cole, I think. We call the forks the La Cole Falls. From there on, its jes' called the Saskatchewan River. The area yer lookin' fer's another twenty-five, thirty miles."

"How'll we know when we get there?" Birt asked.

"Good fortune for ya, almos' like ya planned it. Last week a fella called Bert Jobson started up a small store in his Teddington house. He jes' happens to be in P.A. right now to pick up supplies fer his store. His team's right over there an' his buggy's outside. I'm sure he won't mind if ya ask if you can follow him out there. Little slower'n yer horses like to travel, but you'll be sure to get there. He'll be leaving in a day or two, soon's he's got his stuff loaded. That okay for ya?"

"Surely is. Sounds better than gettin' lost in some bush along a strange river," Jim quickly replied. "An' thank ya for all yer help. Tomorra's perfect. Birt's gotta finish up at the Lands Office today an' who knows how long that's gonna take?"

Jim had been pleasantly surprised when they met Bert Jobson the next morning. He was a tall, heavy-set man with an English accent. He, like Jim and Birt Enders, was an immigrant, but unlike them, he was from England and his 'Bert' was short for Bertram, while Enders' 'Birt', was short for Birthold. Jobson had a good, firm handshake to go with his ready smile. It was the kind of handshake that Jim had grown up trusting. He immediately liked a person with that kind of handshake.

They left the next morning and, as they departed, Bert Jobson said, "It's a two day trip for my team and wagon so we'll camp jest after the forks, a little more'n half way. When we get there, we'll cut a few spruce boughs ta lay our bed rolls on fer the night. If we get an early start the next morning, we'll be at Teddington before that day's over."

Jim settled back in his saddle and took in the strange, new surroundings in the forest east of Prince Albert. It was an opportunity to experience an exciting, new wilderness. He'd been awed by the tall stands of jack pine and spruce mixed with poplar and birch as he rode through the wildflower-strewn forest, alive with the song of warblers and the rat-a-tat of busy woodpeckers. Bert Jobson had told him that this area was the ancient haunt of beaver, moose, elk, wolf, black bear and red squirrel.

The trail had been rewarding yet challenging, requiring sturdy travelers for any extended trip. Jim had an almost seductive love for the Great Plains; for the silent relief of low-lying valleys and rolling hills stretching across the prairies of middle Saskatchewan, Montana, the Dakotas all the way south to Texas.

Jobson had told them, "Once we git past the forks and we're on the south bank a' the Saskatchewan River ta Teddington, this trail'll take us ta where there ain't no railways or telegraphs. Jest a few cart trails ta supply homesteads and trading posts. When settlement finally expands beyond homesteading, a system a' roads an'a population center will git built."

That first night, after they had tethered the horses and had a supper of beans, bacon and bread, they sat back over some strong camp coffee and Jim thought to himself, *I'm gonna be part of a new future that'll be starting right this minute. It's a long way from home.*

Jobson asked them about their reasons for coming in Canada. "We're all immigrants so I been wonderin' what brought you gents up here. I'm a Brit and I left my home 'cause I was sick a hearin' so much talk about war with Germany. Crikey, I wanted none of that an' I figured I might as well make a new start in a new country where good, unbroken land was available. I hear both of you're going to be homesteadin' near another Yankee neighbor of mine, Don Willey. What brings you up here?"

"Calling me a 'Yankee' is fightin' words. I jes' come through a war to free ourselves from 'Yankees' so I don't like being called one Yer from the country that we Americans had a revolt against, but I think we'll get along fine. I speak English and so do you, so I'm with you. I've seen enough warrin' in my life time. And Don's the grandson of a friend of mine back home."

Birt Enders, who had been listening in silence, suddenly spoke up. "If the two of ya have all the problems a' the world figured out, mebbe we can sleep fer a few hours so we can git that early start." With sunrise early the next morning, a cheery voice rang out over the campsite.

"Coffee's on an' pancakes are ready," Jim had heard Bert Jobson shout just before daylight the next morning.

They had busied themselves getting their own horses as well as Jobson's team and wagon ready to go. Jim and Enders shook off the morning dew, folded their bedrolls and went over to the campfire to warm up. Then they had breakfast and by mid-afternoon, were well on their way of the last stretch of their journey. Later that day, Jim was almost asleep on the back of his chestnut gelding when he rose straight up in the saddle to the sound of Bert Jobson's shout, "That's Don Willey's place down there."

Jim had been very impressed to see, just down the hill, a small valley with a slight height of land that could be a water divide at its base. Bert Jobson called it a 'hollow,' but Jim and Birt were used to referring to this kind of shallow valley as a 'holler.'

At its base was a small log cottage nestled in the trees, close to a clearing where Jim could imagine getting down to the Saskatchewan River for fishing. He could also imagine Don Willey hunting moose and other game not far from his door. Much of the property was treed with aspen, birch and all kinds of shrubs with berries. Jim knew that the homestead he'd selected bordered on the north side of Don Willey's, in the same section and the same township. The Homestead office in Prince Albert had explained that a township consists of thirty six sections; a section is a mile square, containing four quarter sections. Willey had the SE quarter, Jim the NE and Birt Enders the SW with the NW still unoccupied. Every six miles in a westerly and easterly direction was identified by increasing numbers known as the range line. Every six miles in a southerly and northerly direction was another line, known as the township line, again increasing in numbers. Then every sixth range line was numbered by a meridian line. The surveying crews had run a straight line at every mile, digging four holes in the form of a square, and throwing the dirt up as a mound in the center. There, they had driven a square pin, or iron, with the number of the section, the township, the range and meridian, cut in Roman numerals with a chisel. A homesteader was always able to tell his exact location when he found one of these corner mounds.

Excited to get located on his own homestead, Jim was happy to have Bert Jobson introduce him and Birt Enders to Don Willey who had just stepped out of his cabin. They exchanged pleasantries and Jim extended greetings from Don's grandfather before explaining that they had come to Saskatchewan looking for a homestead and would be Don's new neighbors.

"Let's go find that pin and the quarter section for each of you," Willey had said to Jim and Birt, leading them to locate their new homesteads.

◆ ◆ ◆

Jim Howard felt lonely that night as he lay back in the uncomfortable prison cot, thinking about those early years. It would feel good to write to Mary Susan about it. Almost like talking to her as if she was right beside him.

March 17th, 1928

Dear Mary Susan,

I have been thinking about how nice it would be to talk to you in person, instead of through letters, but even our relationship through the mail has given me great comfort. That is why I want to offer you some fatherly advice that might be useful to you sometime. It never meant much to me until I received Frank's letter about your mother's passing. It was a terribly sad and lonely time for me and the world seemed to be such a hopeless place, but then

I remembered it, and it lifted me up. I know I wrote about it to you once, before, but it bears repeating. It went like this: 'That time when you think everything is finished can sometimes be just the beginning. 'I learned that expression to be so true over the years that followed and I hope it will help you through life's struggles.

Before escaping to Canada, I remembered it again as I realized how much of my life had been running FROM something. I was running FROM Yankee rule in the civil war; we kept running FROM it in the Insurgency. I was running FROM the law when I left you all in St Josephs. I ran FROM the cattle drives. and then FROM working on a ranch to become an outlaw again in the Big Muddy; I even thought I was running FROM it all when I decided to hide myself up here in Canada.

But, after I started my homestead life, I realized that I had been given a new beginning. What seemed like another ending helped me make a brand new life here on the Canadian prairies. I made the decision I wouldn't run FROM anything again during any years I might have left. perhaps that is how I ended up here in prison, but I have no regrets. I will write more letters soon about how that all unfolded.

Love,

Papa

Inmate Jim Howard, #1133

Saskatchewan Penitentiary,

Box 166, Prince Albert, SK

CHAPTER XIV

A NEW CHALLENGE

BOTH THE NEW JIM HOWARD AND HIS SIDEKICK, BIRT ENDERS were excited to begin the adventure of finding their new homesteads. Looking to the south and west from the hill on the north of Jim's quarter, they could see a green sea of forest. As they gazed on it, and dreamed of the beginning of their new lives, they heard Don Wiley say, "Well, as ya' know, the homestead process only begins with entry. Ya already started that by goin' to the Dominion Lands office and filin' for claims fer yer parcels a land. These here are yer homesteads that yer looking at. Now, to prove 'em out and git ya title to the land, we need ta git ya started on meetin' the requirements. Besides lookin' at 'em, we better start talkin' 'bout those requirements an' how yer gonna do that."

South and west from the northern rise on what was to be Jim's property, the homesteaders' eyes were struck by tall groves of aspen poplars and spruce, interspersed with dense patches of shrubs. Even Jim's civil war scars and his outlaw- hardened heart were moved by the virginity of this soon-to-be-home forest, but his silent reverence was interrupted by Birt:

"Are we gonna jes stand here an' stare at the bushes or are we gonna find my quarter too?"

"Sorry Birt. Yers is jes' down there ta the right, on the west side of my quarter," Don Willey chuckled and they moved on.

Satisfied with having paced around both quarters, Willey declared, "Ya done yer applications an' ya already signed that ya intend to be a British subject once yer homestead is proved up. So let's talk about how ya need to do that." He went on, drawing out his words as he paused every now and again to ponder the vast vista in front of them. "Ya have ta cultivate an' live on the land fer three years. Or ya have ta live no farther'n nine miles from yer homestead. Long as ya share costs fer the grub and hep with the work in an' outa the house, yer both welcome ta stay at my place 'til yers are ready."

"Ya sure were right 'bout wantin' ta settle close ta Don's place," declared Birt.

Smiling, Jim nodded and answered for both he and Birt. "Thanks Don. Guess ya can tell from what Birt said that we accept your offer. Now, what else do we need to talk 'bout before we start to work?"

"Yup, ya hafta start buildin' a livable house in the second year, so if we start this summer, it should be easy fer each of ya ta finish by next summer. At the start a' the third year, ya hafta finish the house and start living on the homestead. Yer expected ta live on it fer at least six months of each year."

"An," Don Willey began again, "within the first year, ya gotta break at least five acres an' have it ready for crop. By the second year, ya hafta crop the first five acres, an' break an' prepare least five more. Then, in the third year, ya must crop the ten acres broken in the past two years, an' break an' prepare fifteen more acres for crop." That much talking required Don to stuff another ball of 'chewing tobacco into his cheek before he went on.

"Ya hafta fence yer whole quarter section with a good fence. Like me an' the other American homesteaders who haven't lived in Canada long enough for naturalization, ya'll be entitled ta receive 'letters patent' fer yer homestead as if you were a British subject, as long as the Canadian government says that in everything besides residence you're qualified to be a naturalized citizen."

"Also," he continued, "ya'll hafta give six months' notice in writing if ya intend ta apply for patent. Patent makes the land yers an' then, as a British subject, ya'll get freehold title to it."

"Sounds like a lot of dang government rules," Jim observed.

"Tha's right. Lotsa rules an' lotsa hard work, but in the end, ya'll git title ta a hunnert an' sixty acres a land that ya really only paid ten dollars fer. I got through all those rules an' all that hard work, so you can too. Ya already seen the land I got for it," were Don Willey's proud final words.

"Now that we know what the rules are and we know there'll be lots of work to do, how do we get started?" Jim was all business.

"Better start with clearin' yerself 'nough land an' collectin' 'nough logs on each quarter fer eacha ya ta build a house an' barn on. Yer also gonna need 'nough clear land right away fer a garden, too. Still time ta grow a few things this year. Too late for some, but ya'll be able ta git beans, peas an' 'tatoes an' there's still time to pick a few berries in the bush. Think I can talk young Roy Gaylord into doin' that fer ya at a low price. I got a few seeds I can give ya both for this year.

As the men walked back towards his homestead, Don chatted some more about life on a homestead. "I'll take ya ta meet young Roy's dad, George taday. They're up from Wisconsin an' George is a dang good blacksmith. Even built a blacksmith shop on his homestead. Havin' horses an' needin' ta break land, you'll wanna git to know him. His son's a good young fella' an' a real good worker too. He's only 'bout twelve year old, but he sure does know his way in the bush an' he's already a good shot an' a good hunter. Never wastes a bullet." Don stopped for a moment to look up at the sky, then finished up with, "That's 'nuff talkin' fer now. Where ya wanna start?"

"Let's start on Birt's place." Jim's considerate reply was typical of a Missouri gentleman.

"Oh no, ya led us here so we'll start with yer place. How do we go 'bout clearin' it?" a grateful Birt Enders insisted.

"Well, let's start with those five acre patches that have the smalles' and thinnes' bushes on 'em. They'll be easiest ta clear and ya can see where there'll be 'nuff room fer a small log shack, a barn an' a garden on each quarter. There'll even be five easy acres ta clear, break and plant enough crop fer the nex' year," Don observed

Jim thought for a moment, then, "An' it ain't far away from enough trees that'd make good building logs so, long as yer good enough to keep lettin' us stay with you, even if we can't get our houses finished before winter, we can get enough logs cut and hauled out to get a start so we could finish our own places the next summer, easy."

"Clearin' the underbrush, grubbin' an' pullin' out stumps, breakin' an' levelin' the land ain't easy. It'll be slow and hard," predicted Don Willey.

So, as promised, early that first summer, Don Willey introduced Jim and Birt to George Gaylord and his son, Roy, as well as some other Teddington homesteaders. Robert and Bill Thompson, Cornelius Reimer, Alf Jerrard, and Carl Hendricks were long time farmers, and knew the ropes well. Besides them, Howard and Enders met several other neighboring families as well as business and working people while on trips to the communities of Brooksby and Star City.

As with many rural communities of the day, people there had been thrown together into a harsh new environment where there were not yet many farms or roads. There were few amenities and no local government. They had to create all of that, and to do so, they had to work together, even though their languages, histories and customs differed.

Jim Howard, the Missouri outlaw, was finally fulfilling his dreams on his Northeastern Saskatchewan homestead. He had left behind a war and an outlaw past in his path. A rewarding future lay before him; one in which he no longer ruled with the force of his gun, but with the love of what promised to become his homestead. Jim would watch the land around him prosper and small, rural communities build up before his very eyes. Having no regrets, he faced each new day filled with the hard-won strength of his troubled past and his new will to succeed.

Early on, he'd pressed Don Willey to help them get the land ready. "Okay, that's how we get started and we know where we're goin,' but I always feel a lot better if I know the road I'm gonna' be takin to get to where I'm goin.' What steps do we take to get from the start to havin' the homestead ready fer patent?"

"Let me lay 'em out in the order that they'll happen an' we can talk about the details when we're doin' eacha them." The words rolled determinedly out of Don's mouth. He was the expert now, in spite of being the younger of the men.

"Farmin' a homestead takes a lotta different little jobs that need ta be done all year round. Most of 'em are hard work and some take a lot of strength by horses or by mules or oxen if you can find 'em. Whether it's seedin', discin', hayin', summerfallowin' or harvestin', the work's long an' hard an' yer gonna have some hardships. I know yer big, strong fellas an' ya done lotsa' hard work, but I don' think ya've done any of the things yer gonna' hafta do now," he emphasized. "Ya hafta look after little things like getting good drinkin water; travelin' a long way fer anythin'; makin' sure there's 'nuff firewood fer heatin' an' cookin' an' a whole long list a' things that ya won't know about until ya need ta'. Anythin else I can tell ya now?"

"Our horses ain't farm workin' horses." Birt interrupted.

"There are folks 'roun' here with good work horses an' you can mebbe pick some up in Star City fer a good price," Don offered, "They ain't purebred Clydesdales, Percherons or Belgians, but they are good. A team a' workin' draft horses would do the two of ya fer the first year or two. An' by the end a the third year, ya each have to be croppin' thirty acres. Between ya', that'll be breakin' sixty acres in the first three years. That's 'a lotta breakin' an' it'll take a lotta horsepower," Don finished.

"Maybe Birt an' I should make a little trip to have a look at this Brooksby place an' maybe even Star City," Jim interjected.

"Depends on how much time ya' wanna spend in Brooksby, but if the Livery Barn'll letcha sleep in the hay loft, ya could spend a day in each place an' get back here on the third day," Don offered, continuing, "Takes one day there an' one day back for each one. Might take two trips, one to each place. 'Bout a day's ride from here to Brooksby an' back; good day from here to Star City an' nother day back," Don Willey responded, adding, "Be happy to show ya the start a the trail an' tell ya' landmarks ta watch fer 'long the way."

"Okay, we'll head out first thing in the morning.'" Jim concluded the conversation.

They were awake and had an early breakfast before saddling up Jim's Chestnut and Birt's Paint the next morning. Conversation began once they were out of earshot of Don Willey. They'd liked and trusted him right away, but their years as Big Muddy outlaws had taught them to maintain confidentiality.

"Let's look Brooksby over today, but not dip into our stashes to buy anythin' 'til we've had a look at Star City tomorra," Jim began as they settle into a gentle canter into the prairie grasses.

The Brooksby Livery Barn operator said he knew of a few draft horses for sale, but he thought the sellers were asking over four hundred dollars each. The main business they found in Brooksby, besides the Livery Barn, was a General Store with a Post Office. It seemed to them that the store had little that Jobson didn't have in his store and they knew that Jobson had already applied to have a Teddington Post Office and had received word that it would be approved in 1913, so Brooksby wouldn't offer them much that they didn't already have at Teddington.

They ate some grub they'd brought in their saddle bags, made arrangements to sleep in the Livery Barn hay loft and went on to Star City the next day.

From the first moment of their arrival, they were very impressed with what they perceived as almost a cosmopolitan center in Star City, compared to Brooksby and Teddington. The railway had arrived in Star City in 1904 and, in the seven years since, many businesses had opened. Besides the railway station, there was a General Store, much larger than the stores in the other two locations; there was a bank and the Livery Barn that, besides selling work horses on consignment, had a harness shop; there was a hotel, a doctor's office, a lumber yard, a farm equipment dealer and even a barber shop.

Before they left Star City, they made arrangements with the Livery Barn owner to come back in a week to meet with a man who wanted to sell a team of work horses. The Barn owner agreed that they could finalize the purchase of harnesses at the same time. They also arranged with the equipment dealer to purchase a wagon, a well pump and a breaking plow at the same time. They agreed that, after the first breaking on their two quarters, they'd come back for the other machinery and equipment they'd need.

When they got back to his place, Don Willey was surprised and impressed to hear about their trip. "I figured when we met that you two were gonna' be all right and now it seems I was right. I'll know for sure when ya come back from your trip a week from now," he exclaimed.

A week later, in Star City, they bought a team of draft horses for three hundred dollars, and a double-horse harness for thirty five dollars. They bargained for a farm wagon for fifty dollars, a walking breaking plow for twenty dollars and a shallow well pump for eight dollars, agreeing to wait until summer to buy the haying and harvesting equipment.

When they'd met the horse vendor, he had shown them two draft horses he was selling, "These ain't Clydes," he began arrogantly, "but they're special and I otta be getting' at least five hunnert for the team."

Birt had briefly interrupted, "I know nuthin' 'bout workin' horses, but Jim grew up on a farm so talk with him." He turned and nodded at his stony-faced partner. "Whatcha think Jim?"

"Three hundred, take it or leave it," Jim insisted.

"Well, you guys're robbing me, but I'll take it," was the reluctant reply.

They decided to hitch the new team to the wagon, then load the plow and well pump into it for Birt to drive home, while Jim rode his horse and led Birt's. Knowing that Teddington folks might be suspicious of two supposedly 'poor,' green American homesteaders showing up with so much expensive farm equipment, they'd agreed to tell Don Willey that they had borrowed money from family before coming north to homestead.

Jim pondered aloud, "We better make a third trip to Star City pretty soon and put our stashes in the bank. I know neither of us likes banks, but I'm kinda worried about somebody sneaking into our saddle bags and taking our cash. I trust those Mennonites and Bert Jobson, but we need to get our money out of the reach of those foreigners from Europe. I don't trust them and since we're the only bank robbers around here, we ain't gonna rob the bank. Bankers ain't talkers so our stashes should be safe in there. I've got just about ten thousand dollars left in mine. What about you?"

"Not that much, mebbe seven thousand so I want to hide mine too," Birt agreed, adding, "Ain't it 'bout time we met that blacksmith and made sure that he can look after our horses and equipment? We got lottsa work fer him," he finished.

"Where does that George Gaylord and his son, Roy live?" Jim asked Don Willey after they were back.

"'Bout ten miles south," Don replied.

"Mebbe we can go there tamorra." Jim wanted to get his equipment ready as soon as possible.

"Let's git breakfast at sun up an' leave 'bout eight. I'll take my sulky and team. You guys follow on yer ponies," was Don's quick reaction, "Now, let's get ta bed. Mornin' comes early here."

May 15th, 1928

Dear Mary Susan:

Here it is May already, and spring is well on its way. We will soon be putting in the garden in the prison yard and planting some pretty flowers for the warden's wife. Puts me in mind of the excitement of us homesteaders, getting ready to get our first crop into the ground. I sit here and imagine you getting your garden ready for planting too, and enjoying that warm sun on your bonnet. How your mother loved to kneel on the fresh dug up dirt and plant her little seeds. Well, some more of my story.

Once we'd found our homesteads, with help from our new neighbors, we knew we had to do a lot of work in order to become owners of the land we were on. Of course, we were nervous about that. It was a new challenge that we'd never faced. We had farmed before, but in a territory that was very different from the one we were on in Saskatchewan. We'd never been homesteaders who had to clear and break forest land and turn it into farmland. Even with advice and help, I worried if we could do it. But we'd made up our minds that, no matter what, we were going to be successful, own our land, build on it and farm it

In the beginning, it was only a dream, but we were committed to it. We had to believe that commitment is what changes a hope into reality. Some call that being stubborn. I will be writing you more letters about how our commitment and our stubbornness helped us as homesteaders.

Love, Papa

Inmate #1133 Jim Howard,

Saskatchewan Penitentiary

Box 166, Prince Albert, Saskatchewan

CHAPTER XV

GENTLEMAN HOMESTEADER

THEY ARRIVED AT A LITTLE LOG HOUSE WITH A MUD-COVERED out-building at mid-morning the next day and George Gaylord and his son, thirteen- year-old Roy, greeted them at their door.

"This here is Jim Howard and Birt Enders, jes' got here from Montana couple weeks ago. Gonna homestead on the same section I'm on," Don began.

"Glad ta meecha' both an' this here's my boy, Roy," George welcomed them.

Don Willey opened the conversation with, "We wanted to get here soon as they arrived, but news came about that Regina Cyclone. Long ways away and ain't much we can do for any of them farmers down there, but we figured we might be needed to go help rebuild things if they was desperate. Don' wanta look like we don' care when folks far away have problems."

The three men talked some about how the country folk around had agreed that a group of them might take a train south to Regina and make a start on putting the city back together. But they had learned that the damage, while serious, had left enough buildings standing that the locals were managing on their own. Don, who loved to gossip, went on.

"Jes' a little over three months ago, that big British ship, the Titanic, that was sposta' be unsinkable , went down off the east coast and now this Cyclone closer to home! Disaster everywhere, it seems. Lotsa people killed on the Titanic, but lots hurt in Regina too! What next?" Don Willey loved to tell a good, tragic story happening near or far. Eventually though, they all got around to discussing business.

"Just like we couldn't do anythin' about that Titanic, I know we can't do anythin' for Regina from here, but is there somethin' I can do fer ya here?" George tried to get the talk back on track.

"Glad ta meecha George. We figure maybe we'll need some black-smith work sooner than later, an' we'd appreciate you showin' us 'roun yer shop." Jim paused and looked around the work space. "Kinda' small ain't it?" he asked.

"It's big as I can afford an' so far, works okay fer folks 'roun here. 'Ain't as big a shop as I had a when I was buildin' wagons fer the Milwaukee Brewin' Company, but it seems ta do fine," allowed George.

"Most smithies try to get the biggest buildin'they can afford. Lotsa blacksmiths tend to gather stuff, an' the more space for 'quip-ment, repairs or holding areas, building supplies, odd bits of scrap an' random storage, the better. I got a sixteen by twenty-foot shop, and 'bout half of it right now's filled with all that. Lots of it's used fer repairs on my shop an' for equipment fer the other things I do. Sixteen feet seems a mite narra after workin' in some of the other shops I been in. My 'quipment gets too spread out in the long direction, and the clutter creeps in from either side." George was clearly thrilled to talk about his business and seemed proud to show it off.

"That there roof's single sided tar paper, nine feet at my forge, runnin' down to six feet or so at the back. I got posts runnin' down the middle and they're a pain in the arse. Got a dirt floor an' I like that 'cause it's easy to clean!" He laughed at his own joke. "I don' hafta worry 'bout losin' a hot chunk a metal under my forge! I'll stick with dirt!" When the other men didn't make a comment at his shop, George went searching for a compliment. "So, watcha fellas think?"

Birt was non-committal but Jim knew a thing or two about blacksmithing. He looked interested. "I ain't no blacksmith, but I know what I'm lookin' fer in one, an' in a blacksmith shop. Why don't ya show us 'roun' an' tell us 'bout it?" Jim asked.

George, silently pleased with the request, began, "Sure thing. First is the forge. Don't like 'em too small. Should be about three-foot square, have a 36-inch bellows and a single nest tuyere iron. Small holes drilled into the top side of the pipe for the blast, and a plug fitted opposite the bellows. If the pipe gets clogged, the plug's pulled out and a strong blast from the bellows'll blow everythin' out. The mos' s'pensive part of the outfit is the anvil. Lotsa folks think the best anvils come from England. Any shop a' mine has to have an American anvil like this one here; I wouldn't bother with a cast iron anvil that won't stand hard pounding." George was clearly knowledgeable about his business and he wanted the others to know it.

"I got a vise here that I can pound on without fear a' breaking. This wrought iron vise has steel jaws an' my machinist's hammer is jes right fer a shop like mine, along with that blacksmith's hand hammer for heavier work." He lifted a strange looking hammer. "Fer sharpenin' plows, I got this here round-faced hammer. I also got a pair a' plain tongs an' a pair a' bolt tongs." He went on, almost without taking a breath.

"See, here's a set a' stocks an' dies fer cuttin' threads on bolts from one-fourth to three-fourths of an inch. Fer me, this is a must. I got one good set for ordinary use, cutting three different numbers of threads and taking bolts or nuts from five-sixteenths to three- fourths of an inch. I also got an upright drill press."

As the three men and the lad walked through the crowded shop, George continued his guided tour. "The shop also needs a supply a' blacksmith's coal and some iron and steel. The best coals's low on sulphur and easy ta pack in the fire. It's free a' dirt an' not much clinker's left after burnin'. I try ta use charcoal 'cause it's not like stove coal. Charcoal has no sulphur an' that makes it better for steel work. But it costs a lot more'n stove coal. I can't use ordinary stove coal, either hard or soft, for blacksmithin'. It's got so much sulphur that iron can't be welded with it an' steel'd be ruined. I take care to keep from gettin' sulphur into my forge."

Jim and Birt gave each other a glance that said they were impressed at the man's knowledge and skill in his craft. This was just the kind of man they wanted to do their work. And he was an American as well, which offered a built in trust level for them. Jim finally got a word in edgewise.

"I can sure tell you came from a place like the Milwaukee Brewin' Company an' operated some good blacksmith shops since then too. You've got one a' the best farm blacksmith shops I've ever seen and I think you really know what yer doin', George Gaylord. The Milwaukee Brewin' Company don't know what they're missin', but, if we can agree on prices, you can do all the blacksmithin' an' repair work we'll need." Jim with an afterthought, concluded with, "But how come you left there?" Jim knew what his own motivation was for leaving his homeland, and wondered if George had a similar one.

"Had 'nuff a' the big city an' went homesteading in Wisconsin for a few years, near a place called Dewhurst. Had a small blacksmith shop there too. We got our mail close by at Merrillan. My two daughters an' my son, Roy, were born there. Their mother died there. Me, my kids an' a few a' my deceased wife's relatives figured we'd come up here an' try homesteading here. So, here we are an' I'm ready ta do whatever blacksmith an' machinery repair work you might need."

"Sounds good to me. But we need ta talk about prices," Birt added. Jim nodded and, taking that as a cue, George Gaylord offered,

"How about when I hand-make new shoes ta fit yer horses, its two dollars a pair. This'll let me make sure I fix any problems yer horses have with their hooves befer they get worse. I do shoeing at twenty five cents a shoe an' we'll look at other jobs at twenty cents an hour. Those prices are fer quiet horses with decent feet. Bad behavior, long hooves an' other hoof problems, leg length and movement problems takes longer and costs more. Workin' on 'quipment is twenty cents an hour. Trimming draft horses' hooves is four dollars, handmade shoes fer draft horses is four dollars a pair an' shoein' em'll be fifty cents a shoe."

Jim nodded. "Seems fair. Whatcha think Birt?"

"If it's good with you, it's good with me," Birt agreed. He was their horse expert, and he knew that a horse needed hoof care continually if it was to be any good.

"Guess we better get back to Don's and start work on our own quarter sections." Jim was impatient to start working, now that the blacksmithing details were looked after. "We got to start breaking land an' see how good that plow and team are that we bought. But before I start that, I wanna get a start on my cabin and get a well dug."

"We might wait on the house 'long's we're stayin' at Don's. Dig yer well and get the pump in so we can have water for the horses and for us. Once we start plowin', how fast will it go?"

"Don Willey tells me that with our team and our sixteen inch, single bottom walking plow, we should be able to do between a half and one acre a day, maybe more if it don't rain," Jim answered.

They soon found out that Don Willey had been right about the work ahead. Farming their homesteads involved many difficult tasks even though much of the power was supplied by horses. It was a good thing the two partners were a team and could share the work, moving from one's quarter to the other. By fall, they had cleared and broken the five acres required on each quarter in the first year.

Jim and Birt developed a comfortable routine together that first summer. A few homesteaders gathered every Saturday morning to visit and drink coffee at Jobson's Store and they had taken to dropping in to chat and listen to the gossip. Jobson still hadn't had his post office approved, but he met the Friday train in Brooksby, picked up a few supplies for his store, picked up copies of the Melfort Journal, the

Prince Albert Daily Herald and the mail for local folks who got their mail that way. On those Saturday mornings, they could pick up fresh supplies and mail.

Over that first summer in 1911, both Jim and Birt forged easy going and trusting relationships with most of their homestead neighbors. They learned to accept advice on sowing oats on their first five acres in the next spring and they looked forward to breaking their next five acres in their first crop year, 1912. For both Jim and Birt, homestead life, though hard and sometimes boring, was quiet and peaceful, unlike the Big Muddy had been. Jim was seen by his neighbors as an effective and respected community organizer as his natural leadership abilities became apparent.

Jim's mind often wandered back to the days after Emancipation and the changes that had occurred on the Samuel Clay County farm. He remembered the struggles he'd lived right from the creation of the Confederacy all the way to his escape to Canada. Now, change was upon him again.

He would later watch with interest as little communities like Brooksby built the grain elevators that would become a common sight on the prairies. They were essential pieces in a growing grain market and demonstrated the rapid settlement and expansion of agriculture that he and Birt had become part of. But he remained cautious. As more settlers arrived and agriculture grew, the chances of his true identity being discovered grew too. He was always on guard, yet he and Birt couldn't resist risking it all with an annual adventure to Moose Mountain, only one week's ride away. They seemed to need a 'fix' of the old days, to rub shoulders with other outlaws and maybe even steal a horse of two.

As Don Willey had warned them, Jim and Birt found life as homesteaders hard. The most difficult experience a homesteader faced lay ahead and that was winter. Cold winds and snow caused difficulties for their neighbors on nearby farms and things often came to a virtual standstill.

In late September of their first year, 1911, with the well dug, logs cut and hauled out of the bush and the pump finally installed, Birt asked Jim, "How ya' think we're gonna make out with this terrible winter these folks talk about an' say they'r gettin' ready fer?"

"Don' know about you, but I'm headin' fer Moose Mountain an' yer welcome to come along or stay here – whatever ya' want. Maybe ya' wanna stay an' see if that Bessie Castle will want ya ta keep her warm. I know you've got yer eye on her, and she knows it too. Don't worry, she'll still be waitin' when we get back from Moose Mountain. Got winter down there too, but folks like John Ryan an' Frank Whitney who used to hang 'roun Culbertson 'n Glasgow have moved up there an' have good, warm ranch houses. They'll feed us an' put up our horses n' us. There also might be some chances to go down south an' west an' do in a few small jobs that can add to our stash an' give us a little cash to pay our way with the ranchers. That'll help 'em keep welcoming us in other years. 'S'only four days from there to Culbertson or to Plentywood an' another two days from Culbertson or one day from Plentywood to Scobey. If we can find the quick 'n easy jobs, should be handy fer both the Willow Bunch guys 'n us to git in 'n outa' Montana. Our homestead entries say we can be off the homestead' fer six months a' the year. This year, we'll make it be back easy in late April or early May, do our seedin,' our next year's breakin' 'n maybe even git our houses near done."

"Think I'll write to Pascal in Willow Bunch and ask him if he an' Indian Jack can meet us in the Culbertson Lone Star saloon around the middle of November. They're only a day's ride from Scobey an' jes two days from Culbertson. That'd give us all a chance to talk 'bout some possible quick an' easy jobs. I'm just interested in a few horses though. No banks or trains. We'll see. If we offer him a good deal, Pascal can give us our cut up front, hide the horses with his Injun friends on the Fort Peck Reservation then sell 'em at Redstone like he done before, or' take em north, sell 'em to a buyer from down east, also like he done before, load 'em on a train an' walk away with his cash.

Jim's eyes lit up as he saw the whole plan come alive in his mind. "We should be able to make a good deal fer them an' fer us. Long as we get twenty five dollars a head for half the horses we get away with, I'll be happy. I don't care how many guys he's got. What ya think?"
Jim looked over at Birt, who was sitting on a stump they had just cleared. Both men had stopped to roll up some tobacco and light it.

"Sounds good to me. As good as we did on our last buncha' horses," Birt agreed.

"Okay, if they show up at the Lone Star, we'll make that deal."

Prospects of those adventures were much more exciting for the two of them than the annual exhibitions that provided opportunities for Saskatchewan farmers to learn about new developments in agriculture. They were much more interested in what their Moose Mountain friends had to say and what opportunities for easy money in the Dakotas and Montana might be.

Two weeks later, feeling that they'd had a successful, productive first summer, they saddled their horses and headed for Moose Mountain on their first homestead winter vacation, telling themselves that it would be a great setting for their second year of planning.

By the middle of October, 1911, their horses were settled into John Calder's barn. That first evening, John's wife had provided a meal of scrumptious stew and biscuits, much better than either of them or Don Willey had prepared all year. Relaxing, they went outside alone and start talking about action over the rest of the winter.

"Think that half-breed an' his Injun friend 'r gonna be at the Lone Star?" Birt said.

"If they think there's a payday comin', they'll be there. They like money just as much's we do. Let's leave here on November eighth. That otta put us in Culbertson on November fourteenth or fifteenth. That's 'nuff time." Birt nodded silently.

They'd arrived in Culbertson on the fourteenth and roomed overnight there, so they put their horses in a Livery barn and were waiting when Pascal and Indian Jack walked into the Lone Star mid-afternoon on the fifteenth.

"Good ta see ya. How're de two homesteaders?" Pascal joked with a teasing grin. "Bored 'nuff yet, you?"

"Good to see you too. We got here ready to find some action." replied Jim, "Got any ideas?"

"Friend a mine tol' me 'bout a horse ranch 'roun 'Opheim, jes west a' Scobey. Der's over t'ree hunnert ranch horses der dat dey're 'spectin' ta sell at auction 'fore January's over. Shouldn' be too hard fer four a us to get in an' run off wit' least two hunnert a'dem dat we can rustle north an' over to Willow Bunch," suggested Pascal.

"Sounds like there might be a deal there, but what do we do with 'em once we get 'em to Willow Bunch?" Jim liked a solid plan before taking any action.

"A guy from Toronto offer me up to fifty dollar a horse plus freight fer good ranch horses. All we gotta' do is get dem to Willow Bunch, load 'em on de train an' when dey get ta Toronto, de cheque'll be in de mail," came the Métis' response.

"What if he don't send the cheque?" replied Jim, always distrustful of those he didn't know.

"Me, I dealt wit dat guy many time before. He always come tru." emphasized Pascal.

"Sounds good fer you, but what 'bout us?" asked Jim, "Do we wait in Willow Bunch 'til the cash gets there?"

"You don' have a post office so I s'pose you don' have a bank eider, up in dat back country where you are," came Pascal's sarcastic response.

"Yeah, we got a bank, but we like cash better. What kinda' deal can we make?" Jim's eyes darkened with anger.

"Sacre blue, I know me dat you gonna be sharin' de risks an' doin' half de work so I was gonna offer half de take, once it got der, but dat don' seem good enuff fer you. How about if I give you your half when we git ta Willow Bunch an' charge ya 20 percent interest fer carryin' you?" Pascal bargained.

"Make it ten percent an' we gotta deal," Jim accepted.

"Bon. If we get two hunnert horses, de total we get will be ten t'ousan. Your share'll be five t'ousan, less ten percent. Means you each go home wit' twenty-two hunnert fifty dollar more'n you came wit'," Pascal responded with a smile and held out his big hand, laughing. "Dat better'n' homesteadin'?"

"For sure, in the short-run," Jim agreed.

As they shook hands, Jim asked, "When do we head west?"

"How 'bout January sevent?" Pascal asked. "We meet at de Livery barn in Scobey?"

"See ya then," Jim smiled again.

Later, when Jim and Birt were back at Moose Mountain after pulling off the Opheim job successfully and being paid for their share, Jim asked Birt, "How 'bout, when we get back to the homesteads, we go into Star City an' buy a set a' them harrows to smooth plowed land fer seedin'?" Their ill-gotten cash would be put to good use.

July 21st, 1928

Dear Mary Susan:

Well, I am writing to you to tell you a bit more about my life in that first year of homesteading. It's unbearably hot in the prison this evening and I can't sleep so writing this letter will cool me off a little, I hope.

Our first year on the homestead was successful, but it cost us a lot of money. We didn't make any on the land, so we decided to ride south a little to stay with some friends on a ranch at Moose Mountain. This made it possible for us to go south and west into Montana to find some jobs that would bring extra cash we needed to live on and continue to keep our homesteads going. As our neighbor, Don Willey, said, "It takes money to keep farming."

But, another friend from England, Bert Jobson, the Teddington storekeeper who is also a homesteader, had some good advice too. He said, "A successful person is one who can lay a firm foundation with the bricks that are thrown at him." I believed that when what Jobson said was combined with I wrote in the letter I sent you about commitment that would lead us to success. The commitment to our homesteads, supported by the cash bricks thrown at us on our trip to Moose Mountain made 1912 a successful year. It meant a brief return to the outlaw lifestyle we thought we had left behind, but truth be told, we hoped it was just a temporary slip to get us past the financial rough spot farming in had put us.

All of that allowed me to hope that I could make a new life here and avoid apprehension by the long arm of American lawmen, but I never forgot about my dear children and always hope one day to be reunited with you. The time just never seemed right. I hope you will forgive me for all the time we lost apart. Just know that I love you.

Papa.

Inmate #1133, Jim Howard, Saskatchewan Penitentiary

Box 166 Prince Albert

CHAPTER XVI

SETTLING IN

HOWARD AND ENDERS GOT TO JOBSON'S PLACE IN TIME FOR COFFEE on the first Saturday in April, 1912.

Bert Jobson spoke for all present when he greeted them.

"How're you two?" He paused to put a wad of chew into his cheek and went on. "Where ya bin? We bin missin' ya." Jobson paused for a few minutes and chewed, then drawled, "See ya each come home with coupla nice new horses. Where're they from?"

"Bin stayin' with some ranchin' friends in Moose Mountain country, they give us a good deal on these ponies," Jim's answer was vague.

"Mus' be nice to have generous friends like that," offered Robert Thompson. "Putcha up all winter an' give ya' a good deal on such nice horses. Mus' be tuff ta come back to ruffin' it up here."

"Naw, its great ta see all of ya agin too," Birt Enders interjected. "An' even if it was good to see ol' friends down there, it's better to see you all up here agin."

"Whacha plannin' to do now?" asked John Scott, one of the ten curious men gathered for coffee in the store on that spring day.

"Well, we each gotta seed the five acres we broke last year an' break our next five acres this year, then we gotta get started on a barn n' house, so we got lots ta do!" Jim smiled.

Later, back at Don Willey's, Jim was thoughtful. "We gotta do a lot better job on the land than last year. We'll have to harrow it before we seed it an' do a good job gettin' ready for seedin' for the next year."

Birt looked over at Don." Don, you can give us some good advice."

"'Fore finishin' last year's work, let's be sure we got 'nuff logs to start a barn. Then we can make sure we each got five acres ready for breaking," insisted Jim. Don agreed.

"It was good that we listened to you, Don. Before clearin' the land, we checked over the hard and soft-woods so we could choose the best logs. Just like you said, a tree can be checked out while still in its roots, and if we pay attention, we can tell if it's straight or twisted an' where the limbs are and if there'r any signs of disease."

"Some say winter's a better time to fell trees 'cause the frozen ground's easier ta haul logs on and cool weather's easier ta work hard in. But I still think Moose Mountain's a better place to spend winter" Birt laughed.

"'That's what I'm thinkin' too so after breakin' our land fer this year and startin' our barns, we'll have time ta do next year's clearin' an' still get ready ta leave fer Moose Mountain," Jim concluded.

"Bes' log-builder roun' here t'advise ya is Robert Thompson," offered Don Willey, before they left to begin their many tasks. The partners agreed to make a request for help.

A trip to Star City yielded a five dollar set of harrows for smoothing the ten acres of breaking in 1912; they negotiated a price of twenty cents an hour with Robert Thompson for his advice and log-building assistance. Building wouldn't start until after breaking and seeding, but they began getting more logs ready for building. Thompson advised that they remove a strip of bark below the crown, to stop the flow of sap from the roots, because a well dried trunk resists insects and fungi, making for better construction.

Thompson explained how a tree must be treated after it falls. "Water's the tree's life, but it threatens the log. Once felled, the tree's limbed up ta the crown and the bark's partly peeled - too much dries the wood too fast and the log will split and twist. Not enough and too much moisture'll be left. That'll bring insects and fungus. So ya don't get decay and rot in the yard, we'll stack 'em on log skids, keepin' 'em outa the sun, wind and rain. Careful drying'll leave straight, smooth logs, easier ta work with."

He concluded, "This is why ya pay me. Experience an' makin' lots a mistakes taught me how ta help ya. I leave no room for mistakes. Once enough logs're cut an' drying, we'll leave 'em 'til early fall. Then we'll start buildin'."

Starting with Birt's land, Jim and Birt began completing their 1912 work on each quarter.

Based on the advice of other homesteaders who met regularly for coffee at Jobson's place, they'd made oats their first crop.

"This here's a temperate region. Better for oats," Don Willey offered,

"An' they stand more heat an' rain than wheat'r barley," added Corny Enns.

"More important, they're an annual plant an' can either be planted in the fall fer harvest in late summer or in the spring fer harvest in early fall," Alf Jensen contributed.

Crop choice settled, Jim agreed they'd start planting Birt's harrowed five acres.

"Since we got an open field, the only choice is what Don Willey calls 'open field broadcastin'." Jim declared. "You go ahead, give it a try. Once you're started, I'll follow with the harrows ta get the seed covered."

A neck-slung sack filled with oats over his shoulder, Birt started walking backwards, reaching into the sack for handfuls of oats, one at a time and methodically casting them left and right. While both men realized it was going to take a lot of practice to plant evenly and at the right speed, the job took longer than they had planned. Finally, Jim suggested, "I'll get my practice here, on yer field, an' tomorra, on my place, you'll get yer turn," adding "We've worked fer four days now, but 'fore we leave an 'go over ta' my place, I better harrow this and be sure the seeds are covered deep 'nuff fer germination."

In another week, they had Jim's five acres seeded and harrowed, but because the logs weren't dried enough yet, they decided building could wait a week and they'd spend the time starting to clear the land that each would be breaking in their third year.

When he arrived, Robert Thompson's first comments were, "I know ya both wanta build a house an' barn, but since the logs're almost dried already an' you're staying with Don Willey, mebbe we should start with barns. What do each a ya' want in a barn?"

"I'll need space fer the two draft horses, my riding horse an' my pack horse so that's four stalls, an' I'll need' a tack room too plus a hay loft," Jim began, "an' I 'pose Birt'll want the same."

"Yup. Right now I only got a ridin' horse an' a pack horse, but I'm hopin' ta git a fast drivin' team so I'll need four stalls an' a tack room too," responded Birt.

After some pondering, Robert asked,

"How 'bout a twenty-four by twenty-four by twenty foot high stable on each place, with two eight foot stalls an' an eight by eight foot tack room on one side an' three eight by eight foot stalls on the other side with a ten feet high hay loft? One of those stalls can be an extra."

"Sounds good, but at twenty cents an hour, what's it gonna 'cost?" Jim wanted the bottom line.

"It'll likely be better if we do both barns an' houses on a per square foot price," Robert was a sharp negotiator.

"Still, how much?" Jim insisted.

"How does a dollar a square foot sound?" Robert, adding, "That's only 'cause ya cut all the logs, got 'em ready an' will also do at least half the construction work. If I did it all, I'd want two dollars a square foot," Robert squinted, knowing he was dealing with some wise men.

"If that's the barn then how much how much fer the house?" responded Birt.

"Each barn's five hundred seventy-six square feet so that's five hundred seventy-six dollars each," came the quick reply," and let's talk about the houses when we get to them," finished Robert. He didn't want to make a final decision until the barns were built.

"One more thing we have to be sure we agree on," Jim insisted. "We all need to understand that, on my place, I'm in charge. Because you know what you're doin', we're hirin' ya to lead the log buldin', an' we won't interfere with that. You'll decide 'how' to build, but I'll decide 'what' an' 'when.' You agree with that?" Jim needed to be in control, just like he had lived his whole life.

"That's the only way I work," Robert responded. "This's yer land an' they're yer buildin's. The same's true fer Birt's place. I'm jest here fer the 'how' an', 'less you ask, I don't want any say in the 'when' or the 'what', Robert emphasized.

"Okay, let's start on mine." Jim wanted to stop talking and start building.

"With roomy floor plans an' space fer four horses, Gable style barns are liked by both horses an' owners. They also have large hay lofts, give lots of choices in arranging stalls, tack room an' doors. How about the stalls, a tack room an' the stall for either a spare or fer washin'? If ya want efficiency, how 'bout an eight by eight foot feed and blanket storage area? Those choices're based on each area bein' eight by eight foot in size, with any arrangement of the spaces ya want. Remember, they're log buildings an' the same kind of buildin' styles, tools and methods used here'll be used with the houses," Robert instructed.

"When we square a log, the first step's hewing. This shaves away the rough outside of the log an' makes it flat where we need it flat. It's done with either a regular axe er broad axe. A smooth log shed waters and cuts down exposure to moisture."

"The next step'll be startin' with log walls. Both the barns and the houses'll have log walls. Ya've likely seen, with houses around here, the walls 're made by lying logs one on top the other. Heaviest wood's fer the sill round - the first row of logs on the bottom." Robert, a good teacher, continued. "We'll make sure ta spread out an' arrange the logs on the ground 'fore we start a wall. This lets us finds the log best matched fer the logs above an' below. They were all picked ta be almost the same size, but they're never 'xactly right - each log has its own bend and shape. Doin' this on the ground makes notchin' the logs fer corner joints easier. Log walls get their strength from locked corners." He paused to let them catch up. "Got it so far or is there more ya want explained?"

"Those corners look pretty difficult ta me," Birt admitted.

"That's only 'til ya've done a few," Robert assured him, "Once ya've finished yer first log building, ya won't believe ya ever thought it was hard to do. Then I'll get ya started on lap notching," laughed Thompson, concluding the first day of log building lessons.

The next morning, just after dawn lit the prairie sky, Robert began the day's next lesson. "Like I said when we started, the sill logs're important to the building's strength an' stability. The whole building rests on these logs so they have ta be strong. That's why I was extra careful pickin' these logs – I chose the hardest an' straightest, an' it's important ta remember, if the sill log's thicker than the rest, the extra few inches of log should lie on the inside 'a the buildin' ta keep from the platform on a sill log that's wider," Thompson concluded.

"Sure lotsa little things ta 'member ain't there?" Birt was getting worried that they wouldn't be able to get the job done to meet Thompson's expectations. A barn and house on the prairies were crucial for a comfortable survival.

"Like I said afore," Robert responded, "seems tough 'til after ya've done a few. After the first one I done, I was scared ta close my eyes to sleep at night." Robert assured him, "you'll git good at it once ya've built yer own."

"And ya say mine's gonna' take six weeks?" Jim was thinking about how much of the winter they would use before they could get down south to Moose Mountain.

"'Bout that an' then we'll move to Birt's place fer six weeks," replied Robert.

"How 'bout the two a ya start over there an' I get the two Skerry brothers an' John Scott to give me a hand with harvestin' the five acres of oats that each of us planted this year?" Jim asked. "They all live close by."

"Ya sure ya don't mind harvestin' yer own an' mine too?" Birt asked.

"We're partners, ain't we, an' 'you jest helped finish my barn. It'll be awhile 'fore I can help on yers so it's fair that I do yer harvestin' an' we share the three-man custom harvesting costs at' twenty four dollars for hired help." Jim answered.

While Birt and Robert headed over to work on Birt's barn, Jim, along with John Scott, Harry and Joe Skerry, looked over Jim's five acres of oats.

"Better be plannin' 'fore the whole harvestin job starts," began Harry.

"You done this afore. How you wanna start?" asked Jim.

"We'll start with the cuttin', then the threshin'," Harry answered, "an' then winnowin', dryin' an' storin'."

"'Fore we start cuttin'," Harry began, " I gotta say, lotsa' folks like ta use a sickle – that's a one-handed tool, but I find a two hand scythe lets me stand up an' go much faster, don't have ta move around so much. I call the curved handled ones 'American style,' an' I like 'em best. Lotsa folks say the scythe was never used to harvest grain. They say it was used fer cutting hay, not grain. But a scythe with a cradle does make it possible ta harvest grain."

"Well, I can see ya know what cher' doin'. Whatcha think we should be doin' here?" Jim struggled to get direction.

"Well, a scythe with a grain cradle's not better'n a sickle," Harry offered. "They're heavy an' dangerous, don't do as neat a job as sickles, so some grain gets wasted." he said. A sickle can leave longer stubble, so it depends on what ya want an' what cha wanna do with the harvest." He continued, "Will ya want grain seed fer feed or bundles a sheaves?"

"We'll want some oats ta feed the horses, but we also need straw fer their bedding," Jim said.

"Then we'll use scythes without a cradle. We'll have Joe an' John gather up the stalks, tie 'em in bundles an' then stand the bundles up in stooks. When they're dry, we'll load 'em in a hay rack ta take 'em inta the barn, lay them on a flat surface an' whack the daylights outta them with a flail ta thresh 'em. Then put the hay in the hay loft." Harry said.

"And 'winnowin's' next?" asked Jim.

"Yep, next step's winnowing – freein' the grain from the chaff, 'fore we put the stooks in the loft. I pour the grain an' chaff from one bucket t'another fer winnowin' outside where a breeze can blow away the chaff. I pour each bucket a grain six ta ten times ta end up with clean seeds, an' we can do that together, one bucket each."

"Okay, let's get started," Jim said as he grabbed one of the two scythes. Harry picked one up too and, before they started on the field of oats, Jim asked, "How long'll it take ta cut these five acres?"

"Shouldn't take long. One man can do two acres a day. If we do that, we can do five acres in one or, at worst, two days easy," Harry estimated.

"Good. How long for threshin', winnowin' an' dryin'?' Jim wanted to know.

""Mebbe two days fer three of us threshin' an' winnowin'," "Once that's done, no reason Birt an' I can't keep an eye on the dryin', lookin' after the storage of hay an' seed by ourselves, is there?" asked Jim.

"No, that should be it," Harry responded.

"Good, we should do it in less'n two weeks. How 'bout I pay ya the twenty four dollars an' we get over to Birt's? Next time we need some custom farm work done, you three wanna have a go?" Jim concluded.

"Too soon to make that commitment," Harry replied, "but, how 'bout we agree to talk when there' somethin' ta' talk 'bout?" Harry asked. Having agreed, they left for Birt's.

By the end of August, with his barn finished, Jim worked with the two Skerry brothers and John Scott while Birt and Robert Thompson got a good start repeating the barn-building procedure at Birt's place.

Once the harvest was finished, Jim got back to help with Birt's barn, and they got it done by the middle of October.

"Now that that's done, ya think we'll be ready ta start on the houses next spring, Jim?" asked Robert.

"Like our farm workers said, "Too early ta decide. How 'bout we talk 'bout it next spring an' decide then?" teased Jim.

"Yeah", Birt demanded, "what're the houses gonna' look like, an' how much'll they cost?"

"How 'bout one room, twenty by twenty-four foot that you can use fer eatin,' visitin,' sleepin', playin' cards an' whatever else goes on for eacha' you? Be room fer table an' chairs, water tank, heater, wood box, wash stand, cupboard an' an extra bed. Room fer one vistor ta' sleep. For more visitors, they'll have ta put bedrolls on the floor. That'd be four hunnret eighty dollars."

"That's only 'bout a hundred dollars less'n the barn, but that's okay 'cause those horses work harder'n we do," laughed Jim.

"Now, we can start getting' ready ta head fer Moose Mountain," Birt rejoiced.

"An' don't forget the fifteen acres a breakin' along with the thirty acres a plantin' we each have ta do next summer," Jim reminded him.

"Leavin' a week later'n we did last year'll mean we ain't gonna' get to Moose Mountain 'til there's only 'bout a week left in October, but I'll let John Ryan know," Jim assured him."

October 5th, 1928

Dear Mary Susan:

It's been a while since my last letter to you. I appreciated your letters to me in this lonely place; it brightens me up, knowing that you are making that connection with your old father. I hope you are doing well, and that my grandchildren are thriving too. Please pass along my love to your brother.

I am going to tell you about our second homestead year after I moved north to Canada with my partner Birt Enders. It was even more successful than the first one. Not only did Birt and I each clear and break five more acres, build two barns, we each seeded and harvested the five acres we had cleared and broke the first year here. As someone that people thought had hit bottom so many times, it was even hard for me to believe.

After living through the Confederacy, the Insurgency, the cattle drives, working as a ranch hand and the Big Muddy days, I thought I had been successful in many ways, but I had a long way to fall. My escape to Canada and the homestead was the bottom of many long falls. But after two years of homesteading, I had bounced a long way up and I was on my way even higher. It feels good to tell you that you should never measure a person's success by how high they've climbed, but rather, by how high they bounce when they hit bottom.

After our harvest and barn building, we made our winter trip down to Moose Mountain, near the US/Canadian border. We spent it with good friends, and were able to make a little cash investing in the business of rustling some horses across the border and reselling them again to ranchers in Canada. It didn't seem dishonest as we only did enough to make a stash to live for the next homestead year. If only I knew then what I know now. Stealing is stealing, no matter how you name it and the good Lord finds ways to teach us what is right. That is why I sit behind prison walls, lonely for my family.

I'll tell you more next time.

Love, Papa.

Inmate #1133, Jim Howard, Saskatchewan Penitentiary

Box 166 Prince Albert, Saskatchewan

CHAPTER XVII

FARMER JIM HOWARD

SETTLED IN AT THE RYAN'S RANCH AT THE BEGINNING OF THE fourth week in October, 1912, Howard and Enders awaited a letter from Pascal Bonneau, replying to a letter written before they'd left Teddington. Jim had let Pascal know that, once in Montana early in 1913, he intended to contact Sam Kelly and ask whether any joint actions were possible. He'd asked Bonneau whether he might be willing to consider such an action and had asked that a reply be sent in care of Ryan. "If he doesn't answer by mid-November, how 'bout we head to Culbertson on our own an' start askin' if anyone's seen Kelly?" Jim asked Birt.

"If we want some action this year, I don't think we'll have any choice," Birt replied, continuing, "Sam's always up to somethin' an' I wouldn't wanna miss out. I'd also like to find someplace to get my hands on a couple of those Standardbreds that I could take back. I don't want to get into any harness racing, but I think, with a team of Standardbreds, I could get from home to Star City and back faster than anyone up there's ever seen."

Pascal's letter arrived at Moose Mountain on the twelfth of November,

"I be in Culbertson on de sevent a December. You guys interested in talkin, I see you den."

"Just like that half-breed, that's what convenient for him an' we can take it or leave it," was Birt's reaction.

"If he's got something worth talking about, I may want it more than I want to worry about changing him," Jim replied.

"Too stuck up to even say where he'll be in Culbertson," Birt observed, continuing, "I don't like that and I don't like him."

"Will you'll feel that way, if he locates some Standardbreds?' teased Jim.

"That's different," responded Birt.

"See? You've each got your own kind of greed. Just need to figure out how to work together and not worry about changing the other guy," Jim observed.

After one more week of doing volunteer chores and visiting with the Ryans before riding their horses to Culbertson, Jim and Birt were waiting when Pascal and Indian Jack strolled into the Lone Star.

"Good ta see ya. Whacha got in mind fer this year?" were Jim's opening remarks.

"Good ta see you too," Pascal said. "Been hearin' 'bout a new horse ranch 'bout half way 'tween der an' Scobey so not too far from Willow Bunch. 'Parently they bin collectin' horses fer a big contract to sell 'roun t'ree hunnert to da army."

"You think that's too many for the army?" Jim speculated.

"Right, me. I had word from my Toronto contact an' dis time he's offerin a hunnert dollar cash per horse. You interested in de same kinda deal 'tween us?"

"Always bin a pleasure doin' business with you Pascal, why change things now?" Jim answered, asking, "What's yer plan an' how'll we git in an' outa' the ranch?"

"Two guys dat useta work fer me're workin' on dat ranch now, but still workin' fer me. I got a deal wit' dem fer ten horse each. "On

January 15, after we meet you two in Glasgow at de Lazy M bar, de four of us'll go into de ranch 'bout ten p.m., t'rough a gate dey'll leave open on de east side. Dey'll herd two hunnert twenty horse into de east-side pasture open to dat east gate an' be waitin' wit' 'em. Dey'll join us in herdin de horses out an head nort' wit' dem, keepin movin 'til we're in Willow Bunch. I'll give each of dem a tousand dollar for his ten horse an after deductin' my ten percent commission, each a you will get forty-five hunnert dollar cash 'fore you leave Willow Bunch. Sound okay to you guys?" asked Pascal.

"It sounds good to me, but Birt can speak for himself," responded Jim.

Birt was quick to answer, "That's good for this job, but I want to talk to you 'bout 'nother thing I'd like your help on."

"Tell me an' we see," said Pascal.

"I'd like to take a team of American Standardbred racers home. I can get a race cart up there," Birt answered.

"I can mebbe have someone go into harness-racers' winter storage barns in Malta, Glasgow an' Williston to get you a nice team, each horse least fifteen hands, but you got to go wit' dem so we know dat you're satisfied wit' what you get," Pascal answered.

"How much're they asking for the team?" Birt asked.

"It's more risk fer more 'pensive horse so I haf to have a tousan' dollar for de team an I'll get dem to de railroad in either Willow Bunch or Coronach an have dem shipped freight collect to you at Star City," continuing, "dat'll leave you tirty five hunnert dollar from dis ranch horse job", Pascal offered.

"You're robbin' me, but I have no choice," Birt concluded.

After having successfully completed both ranch and the Standardbred rustling, providing an additional forty-five and thirty-five hundred dollars to eventually be placed in their Star City bank account 'stashes', Howard and Enders returned to their homesteads, arriving for coffee at Jobson's on the tenth of April 1913. They were dressed once again in the uniform of a prairie homesteader, just like the men already there when they walked in. Overalls, plaid shirts and cowboy hats would be their daily outfits on the homestead.

"I see the ice is already broken up on the river," observed Jim, continuing, "Good to see all of you. How is everyone? Did you all have a good winter?"

"There's no such thing as a good winter here, but this one was no worse'n any of the others," Bert Jobson responded, continuing, "I see ya each brought back another two new horses. Did your rancher friends give you good deals again?"

"Sure did," Jim continued, "and Birt made another good deal of his own that I'll get him to tell you about, Bert,"

"I've always wanted a team of Standardbreds and on this trip I got a chance to get a good deal on a team that will soon be coming into Star City on the train," Birt smiled and continued, "When they do, I'll buy a cart for 'em to pull me an' fer y'all to see what good Standardbreds can do," he concluded.

"But, what'd ya want 'em fer an' what do ya wanna show us?" asked Don Willey.

"I just wanted to tell you all about trotters. They have several speeds, an' can average about eight miles an hour. Fast trot is faster than the gallop of the average ranch horse. Ranch horses can only gallop for a short time and they need to rest. Trotters can do a working trot for hours, travelling quickly from one place to the next. Once I get my cart and my trotters here, you'll see, instead of just listenin' to me, how fast they'll get to Brooksby an' back," Birt finished.

"We'll watch fer that," said Bert Jobson, who didn't believe a word of Birt's bragging so he changed the subject. "Whatcha guys gonna do this summer?"

"Each of us still has to build a house and we each have fifteen acres to finish clearin' and breakin'. Then we each'll have to seed and harvest the ten acres we have from our first two years," responded Jim, adding, "Anybody seen Robert Thompson, the Skerry brothers or John Scott around?"

"They must be at home," Bert Jobson responded, "but if they come 'round, I'll tell them that you wanna see them."

After leaving Jobson's, Jim and Birt rode to the Skerry's and John Scott's. Once all five were gathered, Jim took charge, recommending roles for the work ahead, "Birt, you, the Skerries and John take on our raking and seeding from the last two years. That should take about ten days. I'll start breaking the fifteen acres on my place and that should take about ten days too. Once we've finished, I can shift to your place and the three of you can rake and seed what I've just broke. You should be finished in about five more days when I finish breaking the last five acres on my place." Jim concluded, "Is that okay with you?"

"Means we should be ready to move onto my place by about middle of April and if we make the same time there, we should be done by end of the month, ready to start your house by May," Birt estimated, continuing, "The house'll take about six weeks, and in early August, after we've started it, you guys'll likely have started harvesting. I'll be starting the second house with Robert. After harvest, both of us'll help Robert finish that house. Good thing we stopped at his place and asked him to be at my place around the first of May," Birt finished.

"Before we start anything, we need to get over to George Gaylord's and make sure that horse shoes, tools and equipment are ready to go," Jim said, concluding, "Maybe we can get that young fella of his to come over an' look after horses when we ain't usin' them."

"Yeah, I'm sure the old fella'll 'preciate that and will treat us an' our horses better'n mos'," Birt agreed.

Later, having spotted his two heroes, and riding his own fourteen-hand Bay gelding with his bedroll behind him, fifteen-year-old Roy Gaylord followed Birt and Jim back home.

"Birt and I each have two riding horses and one pack horse. I have two work horses and Birt's soon gonna' have a coupla' trotters. We each gotta' barn with a hayloft an' storage fer oats, but horses ain't in the barns much. Most times we'll be workin' with them horses, but we'll need ya' ta keep an eye on them when they ain't workin'," Jim said to Roy, adding, "A dollar a week ain't much pay, but we'll feed you an' your horse. You can sleep in either my loft or Birt's, an' your horse can stay either here or there. 'Sound all right?"

"Okay," replied Gaylord, who habitually spoke little and quietly. Thus a personal relationship, characterized on the one hand, by Howard's quietness and on the other, by Roy Gaylord's boyhood hero worship, was born. Jim had a need to be seen as selfless and the lad needed to see the strange cowboy as a hero. Roy, in bragging about Jim, was once heard to claim, "Jim Howard's such a good shot he can dehorn a steer at one hundred yards with his .30-30." But on another occasion, when Howard claimed to have shot from the hilltop and killed a moose on the river bank, over one hundred fifty yards away, he asked Roy to ride down and dress the carcass for him.

When Roy returned, Jim asked, "Did you bring back any meat?"

"No, Jim. That ain't a moose. It's a horse so I didn't dress it."

The incident concluded without further discussion about Jim's sharpshooting and Roy's discretion, and they kept knowledge of the incident between the two of them.

From the beginning, this helped Howard to appreciate Roy Gaylord's discretion and he said, "Look young fella, while Birt, Robert Thompson and I are working on my house, we'll need you to be tending our horses and planting our gardens. Once we're finished mine and started on Birt's will be a good time for you to be picking some blueberries for canning along with some garden stuff. I'll talk to your sister, Jessie, and maybe if we pay her something, give her some vegetables and berries, she'll can some for Birt and me, too" Jim suggested.

As their friendship grew, Jim began to fulfill his inexplicable need to justify his past to someone. He thought to himself, *After all, who was young Gaylord going to tell and who would believe a kid anyway? And, I won't tell him the whole story. Just a bit about the Big Muddy and the escape to Canada.'* The story that Jim told was limited to a horse-stealing episode by him, Birt and Curt Armstrong.

In Jim's story, Curt simply fell off his horse in the wild current of the Missouri and, because the posse was shooting at them, he and

Birt had to leave him there. In the telling, Birt and Jim escaped with over thirty horses, making their way past Plentywood and north across the border. He told of selling the horses before heading farther north to the homestead office in Prince Albert to select homesteads. Comments about the Big Muddy outlaw days, the Oklahoma insurgency and the Civil War were conveniently left out. That didn't matter to Roy Gaylord. The picture of his cowboy-bad guy hero was complete. All that remained for him was to tell his own secret-hero version with his four-year-old nephew, Allie Hammerschmidt, son of his sister, Jessie. Allie was very impressed that his uncle Roy was such a good friend and trusted confidante as Jim Howard and quickly agreed to be very secretive about any Howard and Enders information that Roy shared. Those secrets lasted a lifetime, until he shared them with his own son many years later.

As was agreed when they started building Jim's house, Robert Thompson shared initial information regarding building log houses with Jim and Birt. "In log houses, just like in the barns, we want to close gaps, to keep heat in and to keep moisture, bugs and pests out", he instructed, continuing, "We'll fill the gaps with either moss or chinking that we make by mixing mud, clay, grass and moss."

"If we're ambitious and take time, we can use a tongue-and-groove system, insetting splines between the logs to fill in the gaps, but these are your first log buildings so I think that we'll stick with round notching with locked and dovetail notching as we try to get a tight fit at the corners," Robert suggested. "Lap Keying is still the easiest. It allows for free movement of the logs and for water to enter the joint. This type of joint (and the round notch joint) needs to have a tie-log put high up on the wall to keep the whole thing from pulling apart if the soil shifts during freezing and thawing. We'll place these along the front and back walls. A problem with Lap joints is that they can make the wall need treenails or tendons for extra support. One good thing though is the tiny gaps in between the logs," Robert almost finished, but "we still have to look at Round/Saddle notching. It's the oldest method and there's not much drainage for rain and snow.

The round notches work better than laying the logs flat on top of one another, but it's hard to get the notches to fit perfectly because they are concave. These loose joints act like a saucepan for collecting water. In a few years, they are quick to rot.

As they listened, Robert lectured on. " Another problem is that the log-ends twist as the wood shrinks with seasons changing. The twisting increases the gaps in the joints, so more water collects. This weakens the building. In dovetailing, the inter-locking of each log in the wall keeps the two walls from pulling apart, shifting sideways, or twisting away from the building. It's impressive, but I don't think we have time to get into it" he concluded, before adding, "There will always be settling of the log work after construction - more so inside the walls than at the notched joints. Room for settling needs to be remembered while building so that loose-fitting joints won't become secure and tight,"

When Jim's house and barn were completed, Robert and Birt moved over to begin Birt's house in mid August while Jim, the Skerry brothers and John Scott tackled the 1914 harvesting.

In mid-September, with the shells of all four buildings done, Robert said, "If you still want to finish by the end of October, now's the time to do the finishing touches. Since we're on Jim's place, want to start here doin' roofs and then windows and doors?"

"Let's get at it right here, right now," Birt's insisted.

"Good," responded Robert, "looks more complicated than it really is. Let's get started with ceiling joists. They'll be spaced sixteen inches apart for ceiling's made with thick planks. Both barn and house will have a stove, but the house will have a wood cook stove and the barn a wood-burning barrel heater. The chimneys will be stove pipes and these will need openings in the roofs," instructed Robert. "Then, to finish up, windows and doors need to be cut in. For this, we'll use and axe, auger, and cross-cut saw. We'll make doors and window frames on the spot, but you'll have to buy windows in Star City or they might even have some in Brooksby".

"Should get the places all closed up in a couple days so wild animals don't get in," Robert warned and concluded with, "Most folks use double hung sash windows. Can get them in Star City and they are more weatherproof than casement windows. The window frame should be about an inch thick, secured into the building with squared toenails driven into round drill holes in the log. Casement windows are for homes that are more high class than homestead homes.

Robert's lessons were never ending.

November 10th, 1928

Dear Mary Susan:

I hope this letter finds you and the children well and healthy. I know you are passing along my letters to your brother and your uncle so I will say a hello to them as well. There isn't much news on my end here. Prison is still prison, and things don't change much from day to day. I am able to keep fairly well, though my old bones are not up to the tasks as they used to be. It's easy to forget that there was ever a life outside these walls. I will tell you a little more of my lost years in this letter.

During our third year on our homesteads, Birt and I each finished our houses, and seeded and harvested the ten acres we'd already cleared and broken. We each also cleared and broke our third year's fifteen acres. When we asked, we received advice from and we worked together with neighbors to do this. The respect for each other reminded me of the South, of the Insurgency, of the cattle drives, of the ranch and of the Big Muddy years. I guess good people are the same the whole world over.

Bert Jobson said that in the Teddington area people respect each other. When it's time to work together, they do that and when it's time to respect the individual's right to do things the way he wants, they respect that, if he isn't harming other folks or the community. That makes this a great place to be.

Many times, as I sit here in my cell, I think of how much your mother would have loved the homestead life. I wish I could have offered her that instead of a marriage to an outlaw who had to disappear to survive. Life is full of regrets.

I'll write more next time.

Love, Papa.

Inmate 1133, Jim Howard, Saskatchewan Penitentiary,

Box 166, Prince Albert, Saskatchewan

CHAPTER XVIII

COMMUNITY LEADERSHIP

JIM LAY ON HIS COT ONE SPRING SUNDAY AND LET A RARE RAY OF sunshine fall on his face as he slipped into a daydream state. He smiled as he recalled the days of his middle age when his body was still strong and healthy. He touched the palms of his old, arthritic hands and remembered what they had felt like when they were powerful and calloused with good, hard work. He could almost smell the strong coffee and bread coming from the counter of Bert Jobson's little store back in Teddington.

• • •

Jobson and the eight people gathered in his store for morning coffee on the last Saturday of April, 1913 were surprised, when Birt Enders and Jim Howard arrived for their Saturday coffee, They'd been expecting them to show up, but were amazed at how they arrived. They had become used to the two men driving fine-looking new horses, but this time Jim pulled up in a Model T Ford, something that most of them had heard about, but never seen. Not far behind him was Birt, driving the two Standard bred horses that they had only seen a few times last summer. The surprise was that neither of them had a new working ranch horse.

The first response came from Bert Jobson. "What've you two been up ta? No new ranch horses? We jest got used ta your trotters, Birt, but what's that noisy black thing-on- wheels machine that's brought yer partner here taday? Where'd cha' get that? And what in tarnation are ya plannin' ta do with it, Howard?"

"First one that come into Star City an' I got it, figurin' it can git me back an' forth even faster than Birt's Standard breds can do fer him," smiled Jim "It can travel a rocky or muddy farm road, cross a shallow stream, climb a steep hill an' if one of its tires loses air, it can be taken off an' fixed right there," he finished.

"Looks too fancy fer me an' probably costs too much too! Think I'll stick to horses," exclaimed Don Willey. Jim Howard smiled, feeling secret elation at how impressed they all were by his new Model T.

Later that April morning, as soon as Howard and Enders had departed, discussion among the Teddington homesteaders returned to habitual speculation concerning Jim Howard, who was now entering his fourth year of Teddington area residency. Beyond the hero worship of young boys, Howard had become thought of by many of his neighbors as somewhat wealthy. No one else had such impressive horses; no one else had a well with a pump. No one even knew anybody, other than Jim Howard, who owned a gasoline driven vehicle. Obviously, this was either a wealthy man or a crook.

Because, he was so quick to help out in any way he could before even being asked, Jim Howard was seen as one who put community first. In the estimation of local leaders like Bert Jobson, Howard Thompson and Don Willey, Jim Howard had become someone who often took on more than his share of responsibilities.

One Saturday morning, Don Willey observed, "He seems satisfied giving, and being needed, but he sometimes lets himself be drained by taking care of other people instead of himself."

"From working with him," Howard Thompson pondered, "I noticed that he seems attached to his habits and sometimes he has a problem making even small changes," he concluded. The three of them agreed that Howard seemed to hold back his feelings and never opened up about a past they didn't know anything about. Collectively, they agreed that Howard's strengths included patience, and generosity, but they hoped he would be more open to change and a stronger sense of self.

Young Roy Gaylord, not ever having heard of a car of any kind, was impressed and couldn't hold himself back from crawling through the Model T and inspecting the entire creation. He was fascinated by the gas-burning engine, the magneto, the spark plugs, the generator; the whole ignition system, but especially by the three speed transmission and the engine in front that transmitted its power through the rear wheels and drove the vehicle forward. Especially fascinating for him was the magic of the three foot pedals and the two levers close to the driver that controlled the transmission and speed of the car The whole thing was amazing and, just like Jim's well with a pump, there wasn't another one anywhere that they'd ever heard of. Even though his horses and lariat had made him a hero, Howard's status with Roy was dramatically elevated by the car.

For Roy Gaylord, and later, for young Allie Hammerschmidt, Roy's nephew, the mystique of Howard continued to grow after Roy had cautioned Jim about the gun that he always carried in his car. For Roy, Jim Howard's heroics had long been focused on his outstanding abilities with a horse, lariat and gun. He described his hero when on horseback, as *ridin' like the wind. He can ride, holdin' the reins in his mouth, shootin' with either hand at a target, moving or still, an hit it. He never misses.*

However, he still warned Jim, "My dad told me that a person should never carry a loaded gun in a car an, even if they do, they should never have a live shell in the breach."

To which Jim Howard replied, "If I was gonna carry a gun with no live shell in the breach; I might as well just carry a stick."

The Teddington rural community, at the urging of several rate payers whose families were growing, and who had school aged children, had agreed on July twenty second, 1914 to petition the provincial Department of Education for the declaration of a Teddington School District. The petition was granted and the first school meeting was held on July thirteenth, 1915. The first trustees elected were Carl Hendricks, George Reodiger and Jim Howard, with Jim Howard subsequently elected Chairman of the School Board by his colleagues. Jim was seen by all as a stand-up man who was responsible and dedicated to his community.

A tragedy in late August of 1915, while it frightened everyone, made another major contribution to the hero worship, leadership status and mystique of Jim Howard. The Dexters, a homesteader couple living just east of Don Willey, and south east of Jim Howard, as a matter of habit, had always used kerosene to ready the wood in their woodstove for easy igniting. The kerosene was kept in a small container just outside the house. Unfortunately, an identical container was also used for the high-test gas which they kept to refuel the lanterns used for evening lighting in the house. On this day, Dexter, who had always looked after the woodstove and the lanterns, was in the bush cutting logs. The two containers had small and unclear identification marks on them to distinguish between them, and Dexter, not having seen reason to make his wife aware of these marks, never thought to advise her about their different contents.

Mrs. Dexter, wanting to have a meal ready for her husband when he came home, and needing to enhance the slow burning wood fire in the cook stove to do this, had inadvertently picked up the wrong container and poured the high test gas directly into the fire box. The explosion not only set the house on fire, but also threw burning high test gas all over Mrs. Dexter and her clothes, blowing her back out the door. People who heard the explosion immediately shouted, "Someone get Jim Howard! He'll know what to do."

Mrs. Dexter, clothes on fire, and screaming in pain had begun to run frantically in circles in the yard, spreading the raging flames from her clothing into the bushes. Recalling the words of the guerrilla fighters who had ridden with Bloody Bill Anderson, Jim knew that he needed to get her to stop running and waving her arms, fall to the ground and roll around to smother the flames. "Lie down and roll, Mrs. Dexter," Jim shouted, but his words were not heard over the horrible screams of the burning woman.

Jim realized that before he could help her, he'd have to lasso her. This he did with dispatch, mounting his horse and twirling his lariat, while galloping after Mrs. Dexter as she ran. He was able to rope her and after tethering his horse, he ran up with his horse blanket and threw her to the ground. Knowing he had to smother the flames, he grabbed the horse blanket and then, deafening himself to her screaming, used his awesome strength to hold her while he wrapped her in it and tightened it around her with the lariat. His horse stood perfectly still throughout, staring with stoic obedience at the scene without moving. Once secured, Jim galloped home and got his Model T Ford and took Dexter and the burned Mrs. Dexter to the hospital in Star City, where she died of her burns shortly thereafter. In spite of her passing, everyone admired Howard for his quick thinking and his amazing effort to save her.

Dexter eventually repaired his burned house and hired a housekeeper to look after it and his two children. When Teddington School opened the next year, he retained his housekeeper. Because of this, he was able to provide room and board for little eight year old Allie Hammerschmidt and a Baumgartner boy, who would attend the new school. The parents of the Hammerschmidt and Baumgartner boys lived too far from the school to make the daily walk back and forth possible so they arranged that the boys be accommodated for a small cost.

The first teacher hired for the school year was the young and lovely Miss Bessie Castle. Birt Enders' homestead was on the quarter section immediately northwest of the school and he frequently dropped by.

"Miss Castle, if there's anythin' I can do, I'd sure be glad ta. I can keep the school and the teacherage supplied with wood fer the heaters and whatever repairs an' maintenance the school or teacherage needs." Hoping to build a relationship with her, Birt was willing to do anything for her. He was smitten.

Don Willey's homestead was immediately north of the quarter section on which the school was located and Howard's homestead was the next one north. Water from the school's well had to be accessed with a pail suspended by a rope over a pulley. Schoolboys assigned to keep the school's drinking water urn filled preferred to walk a half mile, carrying the pail, to Jim Howard's well which was the only one with a pump that they'd ever seen. The children knew Howard as an honest and friendly, but strict man who laughed and joked whenever they saw him. They loved to get him to show and talk about his horses, but they were especially impressed when, during visits to his place, he showed them tricks with the lariat. They were always amazed when Jim pumped water into his big Stetson hat, then held it up, tipped it back and drank water from it. They all wished they could do that, but none of them had a large enough hat.

Schoolboys, while watching Jim with his water pump, lariat, and horses and drinking from his hat, were fascinated when they noticed that the middle finger on his left hand was missing. Finally, one of them had the courage to ask him what had happened to it.

"Once I was tryin' to clean my pistol an' I pulled the trigger by mistake. Shot this finger clean off my left hand. What a *dingus* I was. Let that be a lesson to you kids. Be careful around guns." Howard, the good citizen, wanted to make sure that the children would learn not to be careless.

Besides helping the Teddington school community as it began its school and teacherage construction, Howard and Enders finished their 1915 harvest and prepared for another Moose Mountain winter.

Contacts made through the Teddington Mennonites with one Abe Friesen in a Manitoba Mennonite community, had established a relationship that Howard hoped might lead to sale of his homestead once he had title. His Homestead Entry agreement committed him to avoid negotiating any conditional sale prior to having met the legal requirements for securing title. However, it was in Howard's nature to always be thinking of the future, and he and Friesen had agreed privately that until the time came to consider sale, Howard would continue to reside on the homestead, making the required improvements on it and paying the municipal and school taxes. To Jim Howard, a verbal hand shake agreement was more credible than a signed, written document. Even so, Howard began to look for land that might provide a relocation option if and when his land was sold. One piece of land that he'd had his eye on was the homestead of a John Wachniak that he and Birt often passed on their way to Brooksby and Star City. He began to stop by there occasionally to water his horses and to discuss possible options and timing.

As the fall of 1915 approached and it was time to head for Moose Mountain, Jim Howard took time to appreciate anew the Saskatchewan River bank area that, over four years had become his home. His Moose Mountain trips had always brought a longing to return to his Teddington homestead. He felt safe and comfortable there for the first time in his life.

These thoughts filled his mind as he waited for Birt to come over to discuss their plans for their approaching annual trip. When Birt arrived and polite greetings had been exchanged, Jim began with, "You'll remember that the Ryans told us last spring that they were hopin' to sell their ranch. I jest got a letter that they've sold it this past summer."

"Who'd they sell to?" When Jim was slow to answer, Birt went on. "What'll that mean fer us?" Birt was worried that they'd lose the many opportunities they had enjoyed in Moose Mountain, an outlaw's mecca.

"They sold to a guy from Plentywood called 'Ross'. He's a self-righteous bachelor that says he don't want any Big Muddy bandits livin' with him, so the Ryans have talked with Tap an Shirley Duncan. You remember them. They've had a ranch close to Kipling fer 'bout three years. They came up there from between Poplar and Culbertson so they know about Valley County and the Big Muddy. They'll be happy to put us up." Jim paused. "What do ya think?"

"If they're okay with the Ryans an' with you, it's ok with me. Does Pascal have anythin' to say 'bout action fer this year?"

"He says there are so many more a those Mounties in that Wood Mountain and Willow Bunch area that he doesn't want to test them. He says they've even spooked Jasper Huntley into givin' up his rain barrel warnin's. Pascal figures if Jasper's being careful, the rest of us better be too," Jim continued, "and I figure if we're gonna bring horses north, we better only bring em through North Dakota along the Souris. Fer a ten percent cut, Pascal can convince his Toronto contact to deal with us." As he spoke out loud, Jim's mind quickly formulated a plan. "Tap Duncan's convinced the railway folks in Kipling ta take on a shipment a horses if we have one, an get it ta Toronto. We'll have to wait a couple months for a cheque that'll have Pascal's cut deducted first, but I think we'll be ok."

"Sounds okay ta me. How long ya figure we can keep that up?" asked Birt.

"Seems like a good thing may be getting close to ending an we better think 'bout folding our little business down there ourselves an looking ta other things 'fore it's too late," Jim cautioned. "I'm thinkin of becomin' a full-time farmer an school board chairman. Maybe I'll even expand my farm holdins. You got anythin in mind?" Jim shuffled his feet and looked away, indicating a desire to conclude the discussion.

"I been thinkin of gettin married an becomin an honest, hard-working citizen-farmer with a wife who's a hard-working citizen-school teacher," Birt laughed, and they both changed the subject about their life of crime.

"Let's do our Moose Mountain trip this time and when we get back next spring, we'll begin ta live like good Teddington citizens."

On the third day of the six day trip to Moose Mountain, during their short noon-hour break, Jim, sipped his black coffee and thoughtfully commented, "It's nice to sit back fer awhile. At sixty-eight, I'm gettin a little old for this kind a life," "Sixty-eight! What do ya mean old? I'm just thirty-eight and I have a tough time keepin up to ya," responded Birt with a laugh.

Jim replied thoughtfully, "I no longer get the same kinda thrill outta that feelin of risk that I used to. It isn't that I wasn't afraid. It was jest a thrill to defy the fear'n still get away. Its jest not that much of a thrill anymore. I'm feelin more satisfied to face the unpredictable weather an climate, finish the season with a good crop that makes enough money to pay my way. Sure, it's a lot less money, but it's a lot lower risk an a much more satisfying return."

"I git what you're saying. I'm feeling, even at my age, I'd be a lot more comfortable jest riskin things like the weather an' the grain prices, married ta someone like my Bessie, an' not needin ta run an' hide from sheriffs an' posses anymore," Birt agreed, adding, "If we're gonna become full-time farmers, we'll have ta start hirin a lot more custom work an' git a lot a help from neighbors. But we got a lot of good neighbors around Teddington an we git along pretty good with them."

"So, it'll be okay with you to write Pascal an' tell him that we're only interested in grabbin some horses from between Culbertson an' Medicine Lake, taking them east through North Dakota an' then north? He'd be welcome to join us, but he'll be on his own with his share of the horses to take west an' then north."

And so the stage was set for a final trip to Moose Mountain and the real beginning of the new life they'd been seeking when they had decided four years earlier to escape to Canada and become Canadians by homesteading.

March 29th, 1929

Dear Mary Susan:

Well my girl, another year has passed and I'm still sitting in this cement prison cell, waiting to tell you the rest of my story. Christmas here was the same as any other day, except we had some tough old turkey and gravy for supper, and an extra cup of coffee. I am sure you had a much more tasty dinner and festive celebration with your family.

As I look back at it, 1914 was a year full of challenge, tragedy, excitement, change and acceptance to say the least. Both Birt and I had nearly completed our houses and barns; we've each cleared and broken twenty-five acres. Just twenty-five more acres each to get to the total of fifty we'll need to get title.

Teddington had just formed a new school district and we helped build a new school. Birt Enders hoped to marry the teacher. I was finally becoming a full-time farmer and had been elected school board chairman, thinking more about the community and its future than about myself. I hoped to do some things for kids there that I never did for you. It was a new challenge for me. There was also a tragedy when a neighbor woman had a stove blow up and set her on fire. Even though I tried to save her by lassoing her,(she was running around so much in pain that we couldn't catch here on foot), she died, leaving her husband and two kids.

I finally admitted that, at sixty-eight years old, I was ready to stop being chased by possees, whether in Missouri or Montana. The civil war, the insurgency, the cattle drives, the ranch and the Big Muddy may have been more exciting than homesteading and developing a farm, but the lesson I've finally learned is that you can never bring back the past; you can only plan for the future and let the past slip away. I also accepted that the winter of 1915–16 would be our last trip down to Moose Mountain and over to the Big Muddy Valley to make extra money.

I hope you have been advised by my lawyer about a possible parole to Montana. I dream of seeing you again soon.

Love, Papa

Inmate 1133, Jim Howard, Saskatchewan Penitentiary,

Box 166, Prince Albert, Saskatchewan

CHAPTER XIX

FARMER, SPECULATOR

AS HAD HAPPENED OVER MORNING COFFEE IN BERT JOBSON'S STORE on an early Saturday in April in each of the past four years, Jim Howard and Birt Enders made an unannounced appearance. "Good to see you back again." All the coffee drinkers turned to the open door of the store and smiled. "Did you guys have another good winter? What are the plans for this year," was Bert Jobson's greeting.

"It was a good enough winter, but we missed you fellas an' this place, so it's good to be back," was Jim's quick response. He continued, "If I remember right, we need to help finish building the school an' teacherage so it can be open in September."

Birt Enders grinned. "Before we get jawing, we should let you know that we've decided to finally become full time, year-round farmers." Everybody clapped and offered handshakes all around. Birt went on, "To start with, I figure we're still going to need a lot of help and since we still don't have much machinery we'll have to hire some custom work."

"Both of ya have been good to all of us an' good to an' for the community so we're glad to hear that ya're going to make this yer year-round home. Ya won't have any problem getting all the help you'll need," was Robert Thompson's warm response.

"How much do ya think that kind of assistance'll cost," asked Jim with a wry grin.

"It seems, from what I hear, farm workers 'round here get one to two dollar a day." responded Don Willey. "Ya know that custom costs are different fer different kinds'a work a' ya'll have ta work that out with the person providin' the work."

"We all hired help at different times, a course. Some of us've hired immigrant workers from Eastern Europe an' some, not me, call 'em 'bohunks'. I don't like that word an' I don't like hearin' it. Like the rest of us, them Polish, Serbian an Ukrainian immigrants jus' came here ta work hard an' try ta make a better life fer themselves. We oughta respect them an' I'm sure you an' Birt will."

"Well, like most folks, we came here from the U.S. of A. and as long as they're good workers, we respect 'em all, no matter where they come from," Jim replied.

"In Missouri, and South Dakota, some of our first jobs when we were kids were farm jobs. Every spring, we 'picked stone'. We'd take turns going through the fields between the rows, while scanning for rocks larger than our fists. We'd pick 'em up and chuck 'em in an open wagon. Those stones were later dropped in piles along the fence rows. I recollect, one year my Dad bought me my own little five dollar pony as payment for helping out." Jim looked out the window as he remembered his early and happier years with his family.

"When I got a little older, I went through a Clay County right-of-passage my dad called corn-detasseling. Every June or early July, the corn tassels had to be taken off the plants to hurry up cross fertilization. Detasseling's a hot, sweaty job. Wrapped in a canvas bag to keep the dew off my clothes, I hustled along rows of corn, pulling the tassels off and throwing them on the ground. Needless to say, I didn't last too long doing that."

"By the time I was fourteen, I even supervised cotton picking. I had to start by being a cotton picker long before that until my daddy thought I was able to be a supervisor. People who've known me here are surprised to hear these stories. Maybe I spent my adult life mainly in the military and cattle ranching, but I definitely grew up farming."

"I settled here in Canada with my feet firmly planted in this sandy, loamy soil. After our side lost the war in the U.S., I couldn't get a homestead and I couldn't get a loan to buy a farm to start over. It was only by coming up here and agreeing to become a Canadian that I was able to get the rights to own a quarter section of land. I respect others who do the same thing, no matter where they come from. Moose Mountain's been good to me, but Teddington has been better and this is where I want to live," Jim concluded.

"Startin' this year, we'll work with ya both ta do yer spring work, plowin' or cultivatin', seedin', fertilizin', hayin', harvestin', grain storage, haulin' an' sellin' yer grain," Don Willey listed off the many tasks until he was out of breath. "Ya already got the work horses, plow an' harrows. I can let ya use my cultivator an' seed drill if you'll use yer horses ta pull the drill an' seed my land. I can help ya make that same kinda deal with others, be it a mower, rake, hay wagon, binder or threshin' machine. But here's some things to remember."

"It's a little different than Missouri up here. We got some new methods ta help us get better crops, but we still use the power of yer work horses. The first thing is plowin', cultivatin' or discin'. Since yer land was plowed last year an' don't have any hard sod or plant growth, I'd recommend we jus' work it with the disc this spring. That'll cut up an' smooth out the soil an' make it ready for plantin'. Then, we'll harrow to smooth out the furrows an break up the sod into smaller pieces. Sometimes the packer's used jus' before seedin' oats or hay grasses ta leave an even field surface fer the seeds to be spread on or fer rows to be made. Then the soil's ready ta seed an', instead a broad-casting like ya did fer your first couple years, we'll use my horse-pulled seed drill. Last step after seedin' is ta use the packer. It has a large roller with small grooves along its full length an' presses the seeds into the ground ta help 'em germinate better."

"That'll finish yer spring work an' by summer, ya'll need to get busy with hay making," Here in Teddington, we put hay up loose in barn lofts or in stacks. A hay or straw stack's a stack a six, ten or fifteen small square bales, seventy to ninety pounds each, that can be picked up by one person an stacked in the field. Carl Hendricks said if you use your horses an' help him put up his hay this summer, he'll lend ya his mower, dump rake an' hay wagon."

"Now, with the shell a that new school built an' only the inside finishin' plus the teacherage left ta do, Bert Jobson has organized a community box-social dance to celebrate. I figure Birt Enders is gonna bid on an' buy the lunch box that Bessie prepares."

Everyone stood up and got ready to head out. Don Willey, as usual, had the last word. "In the meantime, I think that Birt has an appointment with Bessie Castle ta go on a picnic down by the river. Best let him get to it."

The harvesting meeting got delayed by another week when Birt Enders and Bessie Castle decided to go to Star City the day after the dance and have a local Presbyterian Minister marry them. One week later, at his place, Don began his farming lecture again.

"First thigs first, congratulations ta Bert an' Bessie on their marriage. Now, on with plannin' yer farmin'. Each of ya each have fifty acres broken an' are breakin' more, so we can't do that much by hand. We'll use Binders ta cut the grain, tyin' it into sheaves, then stooke or bundle em by hand in bunches a eight to ten sheaves in an upright position to dry. After three, four days, when they're dry, we'll pick em up by hand an' take em by horse-drawn 'rack' wagons to threshin' machines ta thresh the grain. Seats on the binders are pretty hard an' hot for sittin' on fer 12-hour days!"

It was break time and the men never liked to miss a snack and a coffee, so Don suggested, "Well, let's go have a coffee an' a visit."

Later, when they got back to talking farming again, Birt asked, "Where are we goin' ta get one of those threshing machines?"

Don answered, "Brother-in law of that young Roy Gaylord, Charlie Hammerschmidt.

He's the father a that young Allie Hammerschmidt. He has one an' he does custom threshing fer people fer a share a the crop. People who get their own threshin' done in exchange show up with their teams an' wagons ta pick up sheaves an' take them to the threshing machine. Their wives come ta help prepare an' serve food fer the threshing crew. It's jus' everybody helpin' everybody, one farm at a time. All together they're called 'a threshing crew," Don concluded.

The wives who lived on the farms being threshed reminded Jim of the chuck wagon cooks he'd known on cattle drives and Montana ranches. Helped by other threshing crew wives who had come along, they assured good meals at haying time where they were a very important part of the crew. A good cook, like a good farm wife, helped keep the ranch or threshing crew hands productive. The farm wives supervised helpers in the preparation of meals, dispensing of needed medicines and sometimes assurance that bedrolls were stored. At the end of the day, they provided coffee to the crew as they sat around the farm house discussing the day, plans for the next day and just 'shootin' the breeze'. They would even supply sandwiches or cookies for an evening snack. Between seasons, threshing crews often talked about which farmer's wives provided 'the best eatin'.

In July 1916, having already agreed by handshake with Abe Friesen to sell his homestead at a price of fifteen hundred dollars once he had title to it, Jim arranged to stop at John Wachniak's on his way to Star City. He and Wachniak were able to make a handshake agreement that, once Jim had sold his own homestead, Wachniak would sell his homestead to Howard in August 1919 at a price of two thousand dollars.

From 1916 through July of 1919, Howard continued to farm his homestead, working cooperatively with Birt Enders, Don Willey, Bert Jobson and others in the Teddington area. In August of 1919, he moved to the newly purchased Wachniak homestead and continued to farm there, following the same annual seeding, haying and harvest routines like those that he had followed at Teddington, but now he was working with new neighbors. Fortunately, he was able to convince Howard Thompson and Birt Enders to come up from Teddington to help build a new log cabin. He also managed to hire young Roy Gaylord, who lived not far from what had been Wachniak's homestead, to help with log building and gardening as well as picking berries. Howard carved his name into one of the interior log walls. He wanted to be sure that any visitors had a clear idea about who owned this property now.

A happily married Enders, driving his Standardbreds on his way to or from Brooksby or Star City, dropped by occasionally to share recollections about the Valley County, Big Muddy and Moose Mountain days. In the fall of that year, he informed Jim that he had finally sold his homestead quarter, like Howard had done with Abe Friesen. He had received three thousand dollars from R.J. Reiger for it and Enders intended to move with his wife on to the homestead quarter he had taken out in Meade County, South Dakota in 1910.

Howard always picked up his mail and a few groceries at the Ratner store and post office just a few miles north and east. He now had another well with a pump, but the new Taelman School was two miles north and another two miles east, so no children came by for their daily supply of water. However, he still managed to get Charlie Hammerschmidt to do his threshing, but with a different crew made up of his new Ratner neighbors.

One day, as he crossed the east/west road just north of his place, on his way for a Teddington visit, he happened to see young Allie Hammerschmidt walking west on his way home from Taelman School and Jim asked him if he'd like a ride.

"Sure, thank you Mr. Howard. I never been in a car before."

Jim had Allie give him directions to his place. Through the easy smile that Teddington school boys had become familiar with, he asked, "What do you think of your new school?"

"Pretty good," Allie answered, "But we have desks that seat two a us so if both are right-handed, it's hard fer one of em to write. Lucky

I'm left-handed an' this one right-handed kid, Steve Sleipic, asked me ta sit with him so its easy fer both a us to write. One thing that's not so good is there's no one close by the school with a well an' a pump like you had at yer old place, so we have ta pull water up by hand an' there's nobody 'round with the nice horses you always had." Little Allie never talked much but he was fascinated by Jim Howard and by his Model T Ford. "I like yer car an' I'm really glad you're givin' me a ride home. My uncle Roy misses workin' for you, but sometimes he gets to work for Birt." The lad had a bad case of hero worship.

Another day on a trip to Star City, Howard happened to meet a Half Breed man named Thomas Halcro who said he had a homestead north west of Melfort in the Bagley area and was interested in selling it. Howard indicated possible interest that resulted in another handshake deal to be formalized in the summer of 1922, this one between Howard and Halcro for fifteen hundred dollars. Halcro gave Howard the land description, South East -23-47-19-W2nd, one mile west and one mile north of the Bagley community hall in the Brockington area and Howard agreed to provide a deposit of five hundred dollars in July or August of 1922, with final payment of one thousand dollars and transfer of title scheduled for the summer of 1923.

Between 1919 and 1922, Howard occasionally saw Halcro in Star City when they met up on trips there. Each time they met, they renewed their informal handshake deal and in August of 1922, Howard gave Halcro a cheque for the five hundred dollar deposit and agreed to pay the remaining one thousand dollars in August of 1923. However, unable to make the one thousand dollar final payment, Howard had paid two hundred fifty dollars, making his total payment to Halcro, to that date, seven hundred fifty dollars, or half their fifteen hundred dollars agreed upon. They had shaken hands on that and Howard believed this entitled him to title to eighty acres or half the quarter section. Halcro tried to say Howard had defaulted when the final payment wasn't paid in full and in late 1923, he claimed foreclosure and renewal of full ownership of the land.

Neither of them could have predicted the impasse that resulted in the violent confrontation that would occur in October of 1924.

April 26th, 1929

Dear Mary Susan

It'll soon be Spring up here in Canada. I miss the smell of the ground at my homestead as the snow melts and the buds start to form on the bushes. My life out here on the prairies has been good to me since 1915 when Birt and I decided we would become full-time citizen-farmers in the Teddington district. We needed lots of help from our neighbors to succeed, and luckily, that help was there and we quickly learned to be successful farmers.

Once I had finished my homestead requirements and had title to my land in 1919, I was able to sell my Teddington land for enough money to buy another homesteader's land in a nearby district called 'Ratner' that I liked better. I built a log cabin there and moved into it. It felt like home right way.

Farming was good from 1919 on and I got along well with my new Ratner neighbors who also helped me a lot. I ran into a half breed man who owned a farm about fifteen miles west of mine and he said he wanted to sell it. We talked about it a lot and because his land was in another good area, I thought about maybe buying it. I was becoming a gentleman farmer!

Well enough story telling. Things are getting busy up here as we get ready to prepare and plant the prison gardens and flower beds. I hope I can write again soon and tell you a bit more about my efforts to get that farmland from old Tom Halcro. I didn't trust that old man, but my own greed led me to dealing with him against my best judgement.

Love,

Papa

Inmate 1133, Jim Howard, Saskatchewan Penitentiary,

Box 166, Prince Albert, Saskatchewan

CHAPTER XX

HALCRO CONFRONTATION

ALTHOUGH HE WAS UNCONVINCED, HOWARD HOPED THAT BY VISiting Thomas Halcro personally, he could amicably resolve the longstanding dispute between them. Before driving the fifteen miles west to the Halcro land that was the focus of their dispute, he had agreed that Felix Rozmarniewich could accompany him, as long as Felix, a Polish immigrant, agreed to stay out of the discussion with Halcro. Impressed with Howard's knowledge of and ability with horses, as well as his apparent success as a land speculator, Felix had expressed strong interest in seeing Howard's new farm and agreed to that condition. He knew a little about the background to Howard's apparent animosity, which appeared to be, not so much toward Halcro as toward Halcro's Métis ancestry. He had been the victim of discrimination himself many times since coming to Western Canada from Europe. Felix cautiously asked,

"Why you have a hard time getting' along wit' the guy you bought your new farm from?"

"I don't have a hard time, but he hasn't been honest with me and I need to settle up with him before we do have a hard time and get mad at each other," Jim replied.

"Mebbe it's because he one of dose people called a 'half-breed' dat you don' like him?" Felix asked.

"Nope. But his attitude puts me in mind of those black slaves we used to own on our farm down south, wanting to gain favor because they weren't white. We fed em, gave em shelter, looked after their health and took good care of them and their kids, but it was never enough. Other folks, 'Yankees,' in the north of our country decided to 'free the slaves' and tell us how to run our farms and our lives.

Howard paused and looked up at the blue sky, lost in memory. After a long moment, he narrowed his eyes, and went on. "Those times remind me of that other Half Breed guy, Louis Riel, who almost started a civil war in Canada forty years ago. He even wanted the Métis to be have their own government. That's what Halcro is like. He must have been a follower of that Riel guy. He's got some of that Half-breed Scrip land that he's claiming is his homestead and he wants to sell it. It's just a handout from the government and he wants to turn it into quick, easy cash. I've already paid him half the total and now he claims that I didn't so he wants the land back. Since I paid him half, eighty acres of it should be my land and I just want him to go into the Land Titles Office and sign the papers."

Rozmarniewich noticed Howard's face become very red and his eyes flashed with anger as he talked about the Halcro's Script land. It was apparent to him that Howard's racism, left over from the American Civil War days, was alive and well. Although their discussion eventually ended, he saw that Howard's anger still hadn't subsided by the time he pulled up to Oscar Person's Bagley store. Oscar came out and asked,

"Need gasoline?"

"Not yet. I'm going up to Halcro's place to straighten things out. Might get some when I come back, before I go home." He turned to Felix and said, "Halcro's place is just a mile west and another north from here. I'll just drop you off on the road before I go there and pick you up after I settle up with him, before we come back here and get some gas. Then we'll go back to Ratner."

Rozmarniewich sat in the car when they drove up to Halcro's lane, then Howard said, "You get out here and wait for me on the road." Rozmarniewich wondered why Howard wanted to make the visit alone, but abided by his wishes.

Howard rolled up to the front of the house in Halcro's yard and when Halcro came out, Howard growled, "When are you going to get that land transfer signed, Halcro?'

"Soon's I get the money from ya," smirked Halcro. He was sure he could intimidate Howard into giving up his claim on the homestead.

Howard's steely voice trembled with control as he squinted away from the sun. "The money was in the Star City bank when I gave you the cheque for seven hundred fifty dollars last year and we shook on me giving you the final seven hundred fifty this year." His blue eyes turned to grey and he struggled to control his breathing as he leaned into Halcro's words.

"That's a lie. I was in Star City right after you gave me that cheque and the money wasn't there so your cheque bounced and I don't want another bad cheque." Halcro hooked one thumb into his suspenders and grinned at Howard's obvious anger.

"You're the liar. The money was there and the money for this year is there and I've got the cancelled cheques proving that you cashed them. For you, getting to Star City means going through Melfort. You could've easily gone to the Melfort Land Titles Office and signed the transfer." As he spoke, he leaned further out the window of his Model T Ford and pointed a gnarly old finger as if it was the old Colt 44 pistol he had used during the Civil war.

"This is Half-Breed Scrip land. You didn't even pay for it in the first place. I've already paid you seven hundred fifty dollars. That's half of what you agreed was your total selling price so I own at least half this land. Half the crop, after expenses, is mine and you owe me for that. Now you want me to pay for the land twice and you don't want to give me my share of the crop so cough up the cash for the crop and I've got a cheque here for the seven hundred fifty still owing when you're ready to sign the land title transfer."

Halcro raised his voice and sneered, "Don't ya try ta give me another rubber cheque. You get off this place an stay off."

Calmer now, in the face of Halcro's defiance, Howard replied quietly, "I don't have to get off for you and you can't put me off either."

After a few more minutes of quarreling, Howard started his car and drove off few feet. The he turned around and returned. He and Halcro immediately began quarreling again.

Halcro came over to the car, and grabbed Howard's shirt front. "Don't mouth off ta me, Howard, ya old windbag. I'll haul ya out of that car, crutches an' all, an' give ya a beatin' ya won't forget."

Howard, conditioned by his years of fighting as a guerilla, insurgent and bandit, instantly recalled that the best resolution for conflict was either the threat of violence or actual violence. "I've handled Indians and half-breeds tougher than you before from all the way down in U.S. Indian Territory and up to Montana and the Dakotas. Even on crutches, I'm not afraid of you."

"Don't talk about how tough Jim Howard was back in the old days. Ya weren't on crutches then an ya didn't have a twisted old arm." Younger and stronger, Halcro strutted aggressively back toward the car window.

"Stay back Halcro or you'll get it. I brought this gun to protect myself from you if I had to. I'm not afraid to shoot, and if you don't stay away from my car, I'll blow your head off," warned Howard.

"Ya don' scare me Howard. It's not the first time I looked down the barrel of a gun." Halcro laughed loudly and boldly dared Howard to make the next move. The birds chattered in the summer trees and a prairie dog stuck his head out of his hole to see what all the noise was about.

"Well, it's the last time," Howard said quietly and then pulled the trigger. In that instant, the birds stopped their song and the prairie dog dived for his hole. The warm afternoon silence was filled with the echo of the gunshot and the smell of gunpowder. Howard watched as Halcro slowly fell to his knees, then keeled over on his side, bleeding from the hole in his chest.

Out on the road, Felix had heard the discussion coming from the direction of the Halcro house and, although he recognized Howard's voice, he couldn't recall any details of the argument; but he did remember hearing a shot. Filled with fear, he started walking hurriedly down the road and back the way they had driven from the Bagley store.

Before long, Howard's car pulled up alongside him, and Jim Howard, leaning out the driver's window, politely said, "Jump in."

As he was coming around the front of the car to the passenger's side, Felix noticed blood on the left front fender and as soon as he got in, Howard simply said, "I shot him." They drove in total silence back to the Bagley store.

When they got there, Howard walked in and said to Oscar Person, "Oscar, I want you to call the Provincial Police in Melfort right away and tell them to come out here as soon as possible. Halcro and I had a real chewin' match and I killed him. I'm going east to my farm and I want you to tell the police that if they want me, they can come out to my place."

Corporal George Watson, in charge of the Melfort Saskatchewan Provincial Police (SPP) detachment, accompanied by Constables M. Smith and J.A. Mestdagh, all in uniform, soon arrived at Howard's farm in the Ratner district. When his dog barked, Howard shouted out who was there. The police identified themselves and Howard, undressed and in his night attire, opened the door and invited them in. When he calmly started to talk about the Halcro incident, the police warned him that they were there to arrest him for killing Thomas Halcro and that anything he said might be taken down in writing and used against him. They then arrested him, in the name of the King, for the murder of Thomas Halcro.

Howard showed the police his blood-stained car, his twelve gauge Winchester Repeater, a Model 1897 shotgun No. 48332, admitting that it was the gun he used to shoot Halcro after they'd quarreled. The police found five loaded shells in the magazine and one discharged shell in the breach, with a little blood on the barrel of the gun. They then conveyed him to Melfort and locked him up in the town jail.

The Corporal later said, "Mr. Howard was quite cool and did not appear to be very excited. I have always found him to be a quiet fellow. He did not appear any different from what I usually knew him to be. He was just talking about his trouble with Halcro. I have always found him quite honest".

After Howard was taken into the local jail, the charge laid against him was, '*That James Marion Howard did murder Thomas Halcro by shooting him with a shot-gun, contrary to section 263 of the Criminal Code of Canada*'.

Once charged and asked if he had anything to say in response to the evidence presented against him, Jim Howard quietly and politely replied, "I have nothing to say at the present."

May 23rd, 1929

Dear Mary Susan

In my last letter, I said I would tell you how things turned out when I tried to negotiate an amicable resolution to the argument over the land that I thought I had purchased from a local Metis man, Thomas Halcro. I thought we had made a deal for me to pay over a two-year period when we shook hands. A gentleman's handshake was all I had ever needed to make a deal in my lifetime.

I was not able to make the final payment on time, as agreed, so we shook hands again to delay that overdue payment for one year. However, when I went to his place to talk about it, instead of honoring our agreement, Halcro foreclosed on me and denied ever cashing my cheques. I figured I owned at least half the land and half the proceeds from the crops he took off. Instead, he threatened me, an old man on crutches and ordered me off 'his land'. I knew I couldn't win that fight, so I shot him. I gave him fair warning, but he kept coming so I did what I had to do. It was ugly.

I knew I had to call the police, but never expected them to arrest me and charge me with murder. I am ashamed that my actions landed me in prison, but I don't know how I could have done anything different. The judge didn't see it that way so here I sit in a grey cement cell, writing to you. I hope you can forgive me.

My lawyer is still very hopeful that he can negotiate my release if I can go back to the United States. I dream about that every night in my cell.

Love, your Papa

Inmate # 1133, Jim Howard, Saskatchewan Penitentiary

Box 166, Prince Albert, Saskatchewan, Canada

CHAPTER XXI

SASKATCHEWAN PENITENTIARY

JIM HOWARD HUNCHED OVER HIS LITTLE TABLE IN HIS CELL AND tried to start his monthly letter to Mary Susan. For some reason, on that Sunday, he kept recalling his first days after being incarcerated in the prison. He had been sure he would not survive his sentence, yet there he was, nearly five years later, still breathing in the stale air of the place and trying to make it just one more day. He had spent every day of that time, reflecting on his trial and commitment to prison. His letter lay unwritten as he stared at the cement wall and went back in time.

• • •

As ordered by Judge MacDonald, the Saskatchewan Provincial Police on November 5th 1924, Melfort Detachment delivered James Marion Howard to the Saskatchewan Penitentiary in Prince Albert, Sask. As they approached the prison, Jim stared at the huge red brick and cement building. It was surrounded by twenty-foot-high walls, eight observation towers, and five strands of barbed wire. This would be his new home. He had heard from other prisoner in the Melfort holding cells that the inside of this sprawling facility smelled like formaldehyde on hot days.

Once Jim was admitted and assigned his federal penitentiary number, he was given a prison uniform of plain denim and work boots and then taken to his cell. Desperate thoughts soon overtook him. *Even when I was on the run from a posse, I never thought I'd end up in a jail,* he thought as he speculated his situation at the new Saskatchewan Penitentiary and those who lived there.

The vast majority of those, about 300 prisoners, lived in a world strangled by monotony, violence, and strict routines, where barred doors and barbed wire etched the horizon and the sole purpose was punishment. Corrections officers and other staff checked the new "fish" for contraband, (even the seventy eight-year olds like Jim Howard), conducted medical evaluations, and advised them that bad behavior could affect whether they were classified to maximum or medium-security. New inmates were strip searched with every orifice checked and they then were given the starchy gray work clothes, ill-fitting canvas boots without laces and a paper bag with essentials, including soap, a dull razor, several pairs of underwear, and a pencil. Any possessions, including their street clothes, were either destroyed or were mailed home.

Most of the prisoners were on edge, especially when it was hot. Their food was only marginally edible and they lived in cramped cells with a bucket for a toilet. They were expected to stand for inmate counts several times every day, allegedly to make sure they had not escaped. It occurred to Jim Howard that it may also have been a tactic to remind prisoners that they had to submit to any order by guards to reinforce the feelings of powerlessness.

As he sat in his cell, Jim became very depressed and wondered if he could ever adapt to life behind bars. "It's a terrible place to be," he thought. "They call it the King's Hotel, but it isn't a hotel for sure."

He sat on his narrow bunk, a rough plank of wood with a thin pad of mattress. It hung from the cement wall by two heavy chains and was folded up in the day time because the cell was only six feet by nine. A grown man could reach out both ways and touch the walls on either side of him. Across from the bed was a small wooden table that served as a place to write his letters, or to drink a cup of warm water in the evening.

He held his head on his hands, trying to reflect on how long he would be in this place that some called a hell hole. His trial had ended November 5th, 1924 and the provincial police had deposited him in the Penitentiary in Prince Albert the next day. As he had shuffled through those big wooden gates and heard them slam behind him, Jim had felt a chill through him.

A Corrections Officer had explained the routines that lay before him. It had sounded like every day would be just like the one before and like the one to follow. Three times a day, beginning at 5:30 am, a guard would come by the row of cells in the range. In the morning, he would drag the tip of his Billy club along every bar of every cell. This would mean it was time to wake up. Jim soon realized that his arthritis would make it hard for him to sleep and he wouldn't need a wake-up call.

Once up, inmates would be required to "stand for count" in front of their cells and wait for a guard to slowly walk by and count each one. The guard would be followed by a water boy, pulling a trolley that carried a small tank of hot water. Each cell would get a can for a quick sponge bath and shave. The warden required that each inmate wear his hair short and his face clean of whiskers, just like the army the warden had come from. All had their heads shaved every three weeks because bugs were a problem here and long hair could be a disguise.

Each meal time, they had fifteen minutes to be standing at their cell door when the keeper turned the big wheel at the end of the range opening all the doors so they could line up for their trip to the mess hall. Jim would have four sets of stairs to go down to get to the dome floor and then march to the mess hall and while it was difficult to make it down, let alone up again, the warden insisted that Jim would not get moved to a ground floor range. Maybe just as well, as there he would have to make a stand with new range mates. That could be dangerous as he would have to try to prove himself.

The dome was a huge central area into which all the ranges fed, like six spokes of a wheel. Some fool had decided to paint the ceiling yellow, like it was the ceiling of a cathedral. The result was not a heavenly effect, but rather an illusion of distant sunshine – enough to remind all who lived there that the real sun, warmer and kinder, was not to be found in this place. As each range was let out to do the slow march to the mess hall, their heads had to be down and no man was allowed to talk. This was the silent system and its purpose was twofold: It made it hard for prisoners to plan any kind of misbehavior and it suppressed any self-esteem a man might have. An inmate was just a thing, an object; livestock to be shuffled and herded around.

The mess hall was dark and gloomy. Long tables lay in rigid rows, with benches on either side. Each man brought his tin cup and bowl to the hall, along with his 'tools' – a large spoon. To prevent stabbings or even a riot, no other cutlery like a knife or fork was allowed. As inmates walked through the narrow passage past the serving trays, a kitchen worker slopped the meal into their bowls. Breakfast was usually some gray gruel flecked with bits of husk. This was followed by a large pot of tepid tea waiting at the end of the line. No milk or sugar like he'd been used to on his homestead. Once seated, the men had fifteen minutes to eat their silent meal and then they all rose and formed a line to the wash stand where the bowl, spoon and cup were washed and put back into their little grub bags to be taken back up the four flights of stairs and into their cells. Whether he admitted it or not, old age and injury had slowed him down for sure.

First call for lunch was usually at eleven o'clock. The inmates had no pocket watches so a bell rang out the call to meals. All the work crews had returned to their cells to get ready for lunch. Then, once again, it was stand for count, march down the stairs they'd just came up and line up for a bowl of thin soup and one piece of bread. "Hardly enough to live on," Jim often thought as he recalled the sumptuous game and livestock roasts and vegetables he had cooked for himself back on the farm. Then, after fifteen minutes, a repeat of the after-breakfast routine of washing the tools followed and the prisoners lined up to go back to range. Once again it was lock down until standing for count again at 12:45, then off to the work crew for the afternoon.

Work was seen as required to keep the men busy, so again every able-bodied man stood in front of his cell for count and then was released to his work place. The trouble makers were sent to work on a rock pile, or to dig a hole only to be assigned to move it or fill it in the next day. The chain gang was not the place for a handicapped old man like Jim. Nor was the kitchen where he would have to stand on his sore legs for long periods of time. Jim was assigned to work on his range as a cleaner; he swept and mopped the floor and generally tidied up, though there was never much to clean. A bunch of silent men locked in cages most of the time didn't make much mess.

Four o'clock was return to the cell block to rest or lie down and think until 4:45 pm when once again, they all stood for count, lined up and trudged down to the mess hall all over again. Supper might be a boiled potato, bread and tea with a piece of meat - pork or beef that tasted like it had been boiled. Tough as it was, Jim knew he had to chew it and get it down or he would lose his strength.

The rules were many and most seemed made just to antagonize the inmates. Each man could earn 'good time' every month – two days off for good behavior. But if you broke one of the many rules, or got on the wrong side of one of the guards, he could write you up, and get his friends to do so, and you might not get any good time for months.

One day, during his second month in the prison, he was in the dome when the guards brought a young fellow up from the basement where they had carried out punishment with the paddle. Jim was so appalled at what he saw that he could hardly keep himself' from swearing under his breath, for the boy's bare back was drilled with little holes that bled slowly out onto the floor. The paddle was an instrument of torture; made of quarter inch leather that had many small holes cut into it to better cut and pull the tender flesh through them. Any man looking at the result of ten strokes could hardly keep his mouth shut.

It was barbaric; almost as barbaric as a week in the segregation unit or 'hole'. Other inmates informed him that the segregation unit was a place where no one wants to go. The shower floors were scarred from the blades of sharpened shanks made from an old razor handle or toothbrush. Sometimes prisoners played chess by calling out their moves on separate boards in separate cells, where prisoners were required to spend twenty three hours a day.

Peter Grubavich, who was serving up to fifteen years for armed robbery, was in the segregation unit, or hole, for his third time after being accused of verbally assaulting a staff member. "Everything is hard about being in there; you have to be mentally strong," he said to Jim through the wires of the fence that formed a cage-like outdoor space for his daily hour of fresh air. "I read so much that my eyes start to twitch to the point that tears comes out."

Jim's determination to avoid the horrors of the hole intensified as Peter's description went on, "The cell there has no bars, just solid steel walls with a cage door in the front and one bare light bulb in a cage in the ceiling. The 'hole' is much smaller than my cell."

Jim had panicked when imagining how the claustrophobia that had been his partner since he first came to prison would react to the hole. At least he could see out of his cell bars, but he imagined the hole to be horrible and endless. Peter told him that all he had had to eat in the hole was Bean cake and water. Bean cake was made from the left-overs from the kitchen, pressed into cakes, sliced cold and served with a slice of bread. Jim was sure he couldn't survive on that so he was determined to keep his eyes down and his mouth shut in the presence of guards.

Jim had first tried to get on the crew working at the tailor shop. It would allow him to sit and sew the denim pants, shirts and coats the men wore, but he had been given a job as a cleaner and that was okay too. He didn't have to walk those stairs as often. When he first came to prison, he had hopes of working in the tailor shop so he might steal a scissor or some kind of cutting tool that he could use as a weapon, but that dream had burst when he learned that only the sewing machines and not the tools were used by the inmates. As a result, he had become content to stay where he was, like an old woman doing housework.

Once back in their cells, the men could lie on their bunks and think about better days or read the bible if they had not been able to get a book from the little library located just off the dome. Sometimes the Salvation Army people came and left pamphlets to read as well. They were wonderful people who came to minister and in later years, stayed on to act as parole supervisors, because the prison did not have enough staff or money to do that. Because of their presence, they saw a lot of the abuse that took place too, and they were good folks to have on your side.

By eight o'clock, the last stand for count arrived and the water boy followed, handing out a little jug of warm water to clean up with or to save for drinking in the night. If there was any left in the morning, you could brush your teeth with it, using a piece of a shirt tail or your finger. Jim often lay down after that and dreamed of better days when he had been a wild young fellow with a cause. He dreamed of the family he had left behind in Missouri and he dreamed of the homestead he had worked alongside young Birt Enders from South Dakota and Don Willey from Iowa. How had he ended up in this place? He dreamed of his wife, Zee, long dead, and the children who had grown up without their father. He wondered about the school whose board he'd chaired. He couldn't even cover his tears with his rough grey army blanket because it was against the rules to cover your head. They feared it might prevent the guard from seeing your face. Your head always had to be nearest the bars so that the guard could see you when he came by for count. The drumming of the billy club on the whole range of bars would almost make a man deaf before it made him crazy.

Not long after arriving at Saskatchewan Penitentiary, toilets were put in every cell. Although just a hole in the cement, it was definite improvement from the smelly bucket that was only emptied once a day. With the advent of toilets in the cells, new problems arrived to curse inmates. The sewer was connected to the river nearby, and nocturnal visitors were common.

The last chore before going to sleep at night was to cover the open hole with an old piece of wood or cardboard and your heavy work shoes on top so a sewer rat didn't climb out and nibble on your toes. Then you could pull the covers up and pray you didn't wake up tomorrow.

Every day was the same except Sunday, when there was no work and the men could choose to go to church. Born to a Baptist pastor-father and an evangelizing Baptist mother, Jim had been baptized in their faith. There was no Baptist Chaplain in this place, but an Anglican Priest, J.I. Strong, welcomed all Protestant inmates to a service he held each Sunday. The chapel was built of the same concrete and brick, but somehow, the wooden cross and several bright windows made it seem more welcome. Rev. Strong also found a bit of time for short visits with inmates who wanted to talk with him. The rest of Sunday was spent in the cell. There was one monthly piece of paper that an inmate could use to write letters, if he had anyone to write to.

In the first month of his fifteen-year sentence, Reverend Strong's counsel had convinced Jim that he needed to write to Mary Susan even if it was only one letter a month. Chaplain Strong had told him that he should write to Mary Susan and that he should let his lawyer know about Mary Susan and give him her address so he could keep her informed of her father's legal status.

If he didn't write, Jim knew he wouldn't last through the boredom of this place. Following the excitement of his life, this fifteen year sentence, with no outside contact would kill him. Besides monthly visits from the chaplain, he had regular monthly visits, as well as occasional extra visits by appointment, from his lawyer. Fortunately, his lawyer had processed the necessary legal documentation that had enabled him to leave his "stash" in the Star City bank within the authority of his lawyer, A.E. Cairns. This not only made it possible to pay his legal fees for the Halcro case, but also to engage the Cairns, Hill & Cairns legal firm in continuing the procedures for seeking parole and also for keeping both Birt Enders and Mary Susan informed and involved in the preparation for his life after parole.

During a mid-1925 visit, Attorney Olin Hill of Cairns, Hill and Cairns, began to involve Chaplain Strong and representatives from both the Salvation Army and the John Howard Society in their discussions of options with Jim Howard. Hill outlined recent Government of Canada provisions such as Ticket of Leave, Parole by Exception and Parole by Deportation'. This policy provided guidance to Parole Board members to assist them in making decisions with regard to full parole applications for exceptional parole cases. Offenders could apply for parole by exception if they met any of the criteria. Hill read them out loud to Jim.

"Parole by exception may be granted to an offender:

- whose health is likely to suffer if the offender continues to be confined;
- for whom confinement would be hardship not foreseeable at time of sentencing; or
- has applied for an order of surrender, agreeing to be kept in prison until paroled."

He read on.

- "The Ticket of Leave Act makes similar provisions and in each case, regulations require that the inmate be deported from Canada and that there be written concurrence to receive the deportee by the administration of the jurisdiction to which he is being deported."

"You certainly should be eligible under each of these," Hill pointed out, "because you are an offender whose health is likely to suffer if you continue to be confined and for whom confinement would be hardship not foreseeable at time of sentencing; and you have applied for an order of surrender, agreeing to be kept in prison until paroled."

Howard wanted to return to his birthplace, the State of Missouri, so Hill recommended that Mary Susan, a resident of that State, seek concurrence from Governor Henry S. Caulfield. Jim agreed, giving Hill authority to apply for all of Ticket of Leave, Parole by Exception and/or Parole by Deportation, as well as an order for surrender under the Extradition Act and to have Mary Susan proceed.

"You know how slow government works", Hill responded, "but I'll get the applications and I'll contact both Mary Susan and Birt Enders. I will also arrange to come in from Melfort to meet with you regularly so there you are aware of the process of getting ready for parole, even if it takes a long time."

A tall woman at five feet, 8 inches, Mary Susan (Howard/James) Barr was strong physically, emotionally and spiritually. She was attractive and willowy with shoulder length brown hair, often tucked up into a prim upsweep. Her features were soft and gentle, and she was quick to smile. Her speech, like her smile, was soft and gentle, yet assertive and not given to aggression. Much like her mother, she prided herself in speaking only when she had something to say rather than speaking when she wanted to say something.

Like the father she hadn't known growing up, she had high cheekbones and an erect posture that was the envy of many. Also like her father, she had large, blue eyes that were very clear and penetrating within the frame of her dark hair. She, like him, had a discerning glance that saw through most with whom she met. People often said her eyes snapped as she carried on a conversation.

Born into the Baptist faith, she had, with her mother, Zee, become a strong Methodist after her father's alleged assassination and had maintained that faith throughout her adulthood, raising her three sons within it. Her faith convinced her that it was more important to do the right thing than to do things right.

Like her mother, Zee, Mary Susan was not only a strong woman, but had become a gentle, loving wife and mother; fiercely loyal, and always trustworthy, without interfering in whatever her husband's chosen career might be.

After years of settling her mind about receiving letters from the father she hadn't seen for 42 years and was only just beginning to know, she opened a letter one day from her father's lawyer, sent from an unheard-of place called Melfort, Saskatchewan in Canada. The letter surprised, shocked and frightened her. If she was surprised to have received such a letter, she was shocked by its contents and amazed at the audacity of its request.

October 12th,1928

Cairns Hill and Cairns

Barristers and Solicitors

Melfort, SK

Dear Mrs. Mary Susan Barr

My name is Olin D. Hill with the law firm of Cairns, Hill and Cairns in Melfort, Saskatchewan, Canada. I obtained your address from your father, James Marion Howard and I informed him that, with his approval, I would be contacting you. He has told me that you were born with the last name, Howard, a surname he and your mother had assumed to avoid legal apprehension. For reasons that he has explained in letters to you, he returned to that surname fourteen years ago and that is the name he has been known by here since 1911.

As you are aware from his letters, he is serving a fifteen year sentence for manslaughter in the Saskatchewan Penitentiary in Prince Albert, Saskatchewan. My law firm represented him at trial, and we have continued to represent him. Recently, we have been working at having him paroled. Your father is not a bad person. Yes, like many of us, he has done some bad things that he is sorry for. He has admitted to and apologized for the wrongs that he has done, wanting sincerely to make up for them and, where possible, make restitution. That is why I am personally and my law firm is professionally committed to helping him achieve that.

We agree with your father that you could also be helpful, so I am asking for your cooperation in facilitating his release.

Sincerely yours,

Olin C. Hill, *Esq.*

Mary Susan spent almost a week in daily prayer seeking what action to take to this strange request by a lawyer she didn't know, from a place she didn't know and from a father she barely remembered from her childhood. But in the end, she knew she had to do all she could to set free the man she had got to know through his many 'prison' letters.

She replied in a letter to Orin Hill with a vigorous agreement to do all she could to make Jim Howard's return to Montana possible.

June 12th, 1929

Dear Mary Susan

I wish you a very merry new June, my dear. This week, I have spent some time remembering my days as a young child on my parents' farm, just as your children will one day. My best memories are picking cotton for my daddy and feeling like a little man, but those days soon passed as the big war broke out. Only last month, I read in the newspaper about a mill built after the great Civil War by big merchants in South Carolina It was built from the ruination of poor cotton farmers like we were. In May of this year, those poor workers, who had lost their farms and were forced to work in the hardest conditions of the big Loray Mill at Gastonia, South Carolina, went on strike when the greedy owners enforced work conditions impossible to work under. I reckon the world will keep repeating its mistakes until we get it right. That seems to be what I have had to learn through all the mistakes of my life. Things will keep repeating themselves until I figure out how to do them right.

My life certainly hasn't been easy since I came to this place. Thinking back on when I was delivered here to begin my sentence on November 26th, 1924, I remember being impressed by something said to me on my second day by a 'fellow' inmate. He said

'Everything is hard about being in here. You have to be mentally strong." He was so right.

I hope by now you have received the letter from my lawyer, Mr. Olin Hill. He is trying very hard to find a way to get me released before I die, and he has made a plan that might just work. If you can find it in your heart to participate in that plan, write him back and let him know. I will accept whatever role you will play.

You are ever in my thoughts and dreams.

Love, Papa.

Inmate 1133, Jim Howard, Saskatchewan Penitentiary,

Box 166, Prince Albert, Saskatchewan

CHAPTER XXII

PREPARING FOR PAROLE

ON A VISIT TO THE PRISON, LAWYER OLIN HILL INFORMED HOWARD that he had written to both Birt Enders and Mary Susan, confirming that Mary Susan was going to contact Governor Caulfield of Missouri. Following her contact with the Governor and the exchange of letters between Mary Susan and him, Hill had to inform Howard that Governor Caulfield had replied that, as far as he and the Missouri State Legislature were concerned, they had had enough of outlaws over fifty years ago and would not provide refuge to anyone who was a convicted killer, parole or no parole. The Governor and the State said that they didn't want any reminders of those outlaw days so, 'No, they would not accept Jim Howard in their State.'

"No surprise! What did we expect from those Republicans anyway? What's next? You're the lawyer so what do you recommend now?" Jim asked Olin Hill.

"Well, remembering that you came to Canada, not from Missouri, but from Montana, I'm thinking that we might ask the Governor of

Montana if they would consider having you deported to that State and ask him to write me, stating acceptance."

"If he knows that I caused more trouble there than I ever did in in Missouri, he'll never welcome me!" Jim expressed with certainty.

"But in Montana, you were never a Missouri outlaw and Black Jim Howard was an outlaw who, along with John Allen was wanted, dead or alive by the State of Montana, before you came to Canada to homestead. Black Jim Howard is long dead. John Allen, like many other Big Muddy outlaws, has disappeared and I have evidence that the State of Montana paid a reward for Black Jim Howard's death. You're just an unrelated white Saskatchewan homesteader who happens to have the same name. You are a Canadian citizen from a province neighboring Montana where, although you were highly regarded by your community you were sent to prison under a questionable conviction. We will have successfully appealed that conviction and you will have been granted Parole by Deportation. Also, I'm told that John Erickson, the newly elected Democratic Governor there, is a very progressive, forgiving Christian. Will you give me authority to contact him?"

"Yes, by all means, particularly since he, like me, is a Democrat. I'm giving you direction to contact him as soon as you can get a letter in the mail."

A month later, Hill was back at the prison with news of Erickson's response and informed Jim that, "Governor Erickson says that he, with the State Legislature's approval, has both the authority and the inclination to support your request, but to get the approval of the State Legislature, they will insist on having written evidence that you have 'Fee Simple', or mortgage-free ownership of your own place of residence in Montana and that you have sufficient funds to support your own livelihood so you won't become a burden on the State."

"Can we get Birt Enders to help set this up?" Jim's eyes lit up with real hope for the first time.

"After we settle for my legal fees, you'll still have thirty-five thousand dollars in trust with our firm and that will be more than enough, but we'll have to assure moving of that money to get some of it legally transferred into ownership of a Montana residence as well as some more in a Montana bank account in your name," replied Hill, continuing, "How about I get Birt to temporarily relocate from South Dakota to Great Falls where he can establish a General Delivery address under the name of your fictitious cousin *Charles* Howard, and open a bank account in that name?" Then he continued, "Do you feel comfortable trusting Birt with your stash?"

"Birt's a sharp businessman, but his word is good. I don't want to insult lawyers, but a hand shake agreement with Birt is better than any legal document" Jim responded, concluding,

"Offer him ten percent plus up to five hundred dollars for expenses that he has written receipts for. I'm a sharp businessman too. Now, what's your proposal?"

"First, Birt comes up here, meets with me, signs a receipt for thirty-five thousand dollars from your trust account with us and then goes to Great Falls, first deducting his thirty-five-hundred-dollar fee and then getting established as Charles Howard, General Delivery, Great Falls. He will, as Charles Howard, open a bank account with ninety percent of the thirty-five thousand, that is, thirty-one thousand five hundred dollars. Charles will then use that bank account to establish second bank account with five hundred dollars to be held in trust for documented expenses that Birt may eventually claim.

Charles, (Birt) will then purchase your Saskatchewan property for twenty thousand dollars and, upon receipt of that amount, my firm will sell it back to Charles for the same price of twenty thousand dollars, thus leaving a free and clear ownership for my firm for our own profit. Charles will then purchase a thirty-five-hundred-dollar house in Great Falls for you to live in.

That will leave you, Jim Howard, with legally documented twenty-eight thousand dollars in Montana-based assets, made up of a thirty-five-hundred-dollar house, twenty-three thousand five hundred dollars in one bank account and five hundred dollars in another, and my firm with the Fee-Simple title to a property to be disposed of, to either an individual or corporation seeking to develop homesteader land."

"That all sounds pretty good, but when I do get paroled? The conditions of parole will be if I can't look after myself and my health is likely to be damaged if I'm kept here, and because being here will be more of a hardship than could have been seen when I was sentenced, then how am I going to physically take care of myself and look after a house in Great Falls?" Jim asked.

"Good question. I've already written to Mary Susan and talked with Chaplain Strong about that. Chaplain Strong has contacted the American Baptist Church in Great Falls. They're prepared to have someone do your shopping, cooking, laundry and housekeeping as well as yard and home maintenance. One member of their congregation is a nurse who offered to check on you regularly. A doctor from their congregation volunteered to be available as needed."

"I really appreciate that, but make sure they know that I won't be a bum. I know churches aren't rich and I insist on giving something to the congregation if not to the individuals. Tell them that, if they are providing all that, I insist on tithing the church at least one hundred dollars a year," Jim demanded.

"I'll do that, but remember, it's likely to be a while before we see any real movement from these prison folks up here, especially since it involves parole. Mary Susan offered to help you get packed and moved and wanted to come up by train right away. I told her that it would be best to wait until we had definite word from the Canadian government," advised Hill, continuing, "I think the Chaplain here should have the folks in Great Falls wait until things progress further before they start getting ready. They can be started before Mary Susan comes north, but if she can come through Great Falls, stopping there to meet those Baptist folks, she can help them get the house ready and go with you when you get there to introduce you to them and help you get settled."

For the remainder of 1928, all of 1929 and most of 1930, activity on the Howard case was taken up by letter-writing and meetings. Olin

Hill, Rev. Strong, Mary Susan, Birt Enders, Great Falls American Baptist congregation, Jim Howard himself and even the warden at Saskatchewan Penitentiary spent much time preparing for a pending parole hearing. There was Great Falls housing, bank accounts, medical and home care, disposition of Saskatchewan property, Mary Susan travel, federal, provincial and municipal political questions, legal surprises, as well as unpredictable and uncounted minor contingencies to be confronted.

It was early 1928 by the time Birt managed to get all the Charles Howard Great Falls banking and housing matters looked after. In September 1928, Attorney Hill arranged a meeting with Jim Howard to begin the process of dealing with issues surrounding Howard's Ratner property. He brought with him legal documents he had prepared that required Howard's signature to sell the Ratner property to Howard's 'cousin,' Charles, General Delivery in Great Falls, Montana, and have 'Charles' subsequently 'sell' the property back to Attorney Hill. He also brought the receipt for thirty-five thousand dollars that Birt Enders had signed after coming to Melfort from South Dakota.

Jim wondered, "How do we buy and sell all this property in Saskatchewan and Montana from here without anybody even seeing, never mind touching, any money?"

Hill responded, "At this point, all the money is in your Star City bank account and you have signed a document that gives me legal authority over that money, but the document says that each time any movement of cash is made, I have to bring a legal document signed by you that authorizes that movement of your cash."

Hill agreed with Howard that he would return with documentation to show Jim after Birt had made Charles Howard's banking arrangements and house purchase in Great Falls. A month later Chaplain Strong visited to inform Jim of the arrangements he had made with Great Falls American Baptists for Jim's care when he was in Great Falls.

Even though Jim knew the prayers and efforts of these supporters outside the prison were ongoing, Jim still had difficulty staying optimistic. This was a difficult place for anyone, but even more so for an old man over eighty years of age. While he waited for the parole process to unfold, Jim had to accept a meaningless prison life. There were no goals to set, no challenges to meet and no satisfaction from productivity. The only times of interest came in meetings with either his lawyer or with Chaplain Strong and in letters to and from Mary Susan.

Jim had attempted to become a well-behaved prisoner and finally a transfer to a ground floor cell became available allowing him easier access to the mess hall. One Sunday, lying back on his cot, he chuckled to himself. "Had to wait all this time to finally get a ground floor room in the King's Hotel. Just when I'm getting ready to leave, things are getting a little more tolerable."

Old prisoners did have more free time to read and relax. In the mess hall, still a tinderbox where sitting in the wrong place could be a provocation, there were separate tables where old men, among others, could segregate themselves. It seemed a little safer.

Following a series of visits and discussions each had had with Jim Howard during their parole-planning meetings, Attorney Hill and Chaplain Strong agreed that "society needs to examine this culture that keeps people imprisoned under what can only be deemed inhumane conditions". Although most of Jim's information was anecdotal, he told them about policies regarding solitary confinement that were inhuman. Some prisoners were locked up for as long as twenty three hours a day in a small single cell, without windows or direct access to natural light, and without meaningful activities of any kind. These discussions and perspectives influenced both Hill and Strong to become even more committed to successfully achieving parole for Howard.

Their commitment was further intensified as they observed Jim gradually being whittled away by age as he shuffled more slowly, took longer to get up from a chair and saw his memory begin to slip. Strong wondered aloud about Jim and at one of the meetings with Hill, asked, "How much longer will he be able to climb in and out of an upper bunk bed? How much longer will he remember where his cell is? How much longer will his brittle bones cope with a thin mattress and blanket in a cold cell in winter, or his weakening heart with the summer heat. If he had a 'toilet,' accident, who would help him clean up? Would he be seen as one of those older inmates that, having committed violent crimes, are prisoners who should only leave prison in a pine box?"

Hill added, "As a lawyer, I know that anger, grief and the desire for retribution are understandable, and we can all agree that people who commit serious crimes should be held accountable. But retribution can shade into vengeance. While being old should not be an automatic get-out-of-jail-free card, infirmity and illness can change the calculation of what justice requires. What do we, as a society, get from keeping these people in prison? People like an old guy who has an "L" painted on his left shoe and an "R" on his right so he knows which is which and who doesn't even seem to know he's in prison."

Reverend Strong, deferring to the lawyer, asked "So what can be done? I know that the Ticket of Leave, Exceptional Parole and Parole by Deportation programs were recently introduced but they are poorly used and often exclude people who have committed violent crimes, even if those people are no longer able to repeat such crimes," adding, "and many Corrections staff are strongly opposed to those programs."

Hill was adamant." If the programs were properly devised and used, some aging prisoners could go back to their families. Others could be released to boarding homes — although it is difficult to find homes that will take former prisoners. If we aren't willing to change or make more use of these releases, we'll need to pour money into prisons to provide for increasing numbers of old prisoners and that could mean special training for correction officers and renovating buildings; units with lower bunks and no stairs. There an increasing number of people in prisons who are frail, old, and sick. They're not going to jump off of their beds and commit new crimes. They are no longer a threat to public safety."

Strong commented, "A lawyer's perspective is enlightening. As Chaplain, I get to meet most of the inmates, at least the Protestants; because so many inmates have mobility problems, I try to convince staff to bring them meals and let me provide religious services in their cells. Many inmates are too ill to cause much trouble, and Jim Howard is one of those. I tell prison staff that they must balance care with security."

Hill added, "Although he's a long way from terminal, Jim is ill enough that his time remaining will be much more fulfilling outside than it would be to have him live out his days in prison. That's how he met the criteria for "Parole by Deportation. Requests for Exceptional Parole or Patrol by Deportation release are rarely granted, but as Chaplain, I'm sure you agree that everybody should have the opportunity to die with dignity."

Jim Howard's case had brought a new perspective to their thinking about prisons and for the rest of their careers, Olin Hill and Reverend Strong would spend endless hours taking on the Herculean task of attempting to bring change to the Canadian Correctional system.

October 12th, 1929

Dear Mary Susan

My lawyer, Olin Hill has told me about Exceptional Parole, Parole by Deportation and Ticket of Leave changes in Canadian Parole Low. He says that both he and Chaplain Strong have been keeping you and Birt Enders informed about the steps involved in seeking a parole for me. Strong and Hill have also managed to get the support of the Salvation Army and the John Howard Society in each of Prince Albert, Saskatchewan and Great Falls, Montana. For all three of the parole categories, guidelines are just that: They can apply for parole for me because I meet the following criteria, but the Parole Board doesn't have to grant it to me.

-My health is likely to suffer if they continue to be confine me,

-Confinement would be a hardship not foreseeable at time I was sentenced,

-And I have applied for a parole, agreeing to be kept in prison until paroled.

Hill says he has shown that I meet all three of these criteria as well as having made arrangements to be deported from Canada, with written concurrence from the administration of the State of Montana, to receive me. Lawyer Hill pointed out that I am certainly eligible under these criteria. Now we just have to wait for the decision of the Parole Board and the powers that be to make a favorable decision on my case. I thank you for agreeing to help your old father. I certainly don't deserve all you have done, but will be eternally grateful for it.

Your Papa

Inmate 1133, Jim Howard

Saskatchewan Penitentiary,

Box 166, Prince Albert, Saskatchewan

CHAPTER XXIII

JIM'S RELEASE FROM JAIL

THE PROCESS OF OVERCOMING HER INITIAL SURPRISE TOOK MARY Susan some time. She contemplated the absence of a father/daughter relationship and struggled with the request to assist in his parole some forty-two years later.

She opened her mail one day to find letter from Rev. J.I. Strong, Protestant Chaplain at the penitentiary that currently housed her father. In it she learned that parole had been requested by Hill.

January 15th, 1929

Dear Mrs. Barr

I have been your father's spiritual adviser since November 1924. Attorney Hill has suggested that I write you, telling you about the impressions your father has left on many of us.

First I want to comment on your father's relationship with your mother. He has told me of the commitments made between your mother and him. They each promised to never have another love. Your father wants you to know that he's kept his pledge of love for only her.

The area where your father had his homestead is called "Teddington" and that is the name of the school for which he was the first chairman of the board. I've talked with people from the Teddington area and they have told me their impressions of him. They all said he was a quiet, strong gentleman surrounded by neighbors who respected him deeply. They also said he loved to help others, no matter what the situation.

These are among the many reasons I am supporting your father's application for parole and, like Attorney Hill, I hope that you will be willing to forgive him and help in this process.

Sincerely yours,

Rev. J. I Strong

Rev. J.I. Strong, Protestant Chaplain, Saskatchewan Penitentiary

And so, Mary Susan began the process of overcoming the confusion and hurt that had been with her since 1882. She felt a great deal of comfort in assisting in her father's attempt for parole.

By October, 1929, letters flew between Attorney Olin D. Hill, Birt Enders, Rev. J. Strong, Bert Jobson, Governor Erickson of Montana, and the Baptist Pastor Joseph Anderson and the American Baptist Church Congregation in Great Falls, Montana. She also corresponded with the Salvation Army in Prince Albert, the Warden of Saskatchewan Penitentiary and Corporal Watson of the Saskatchewan Provincial Police in Melfort, Saskatchewan.

Attorney Hill, after receiving a positive response from Mary Susan and Chaplain Strong's initial correspondence with her, laid out in a letter the proposed strategy for her father's release.

For the remainder of 1929 and 1930, much of the activity on the Howard case was taken up by letter-writing and meetings. There were housing issues, bank accounts, medical and home care; disposition of Saskatchewan property, Mary Susan's travel, federal, provincial, municipal and international political questions, legal surprises, as well as unpredictable and uncounted minor contingencies to be confronted.

By late-1929, most of the logistics, save looking after Jim once he was in Great Falls, seemed to be in place. Since Chaplain Strong had good relations with both the Salvation Army and the John Howard Society in Prince Albert, it was agreed that he should start the process of readying those stakeholders for Jim's transfer. This would be best facilitated by the Baptist Prison Ministry.

Letters between Attorney Hill, Chaplain Strong, Birt Enders, the American Baptists in Great Falls and Mary Susan assured that all were prepared, once a release date had been set and known. Mary Susan would come by train from Kansas City to Great Falls, meet with the American Baptist Congregation, the Salvation Army and the John Howard Society. Once she was comfortable with the setting, she could travel by train to Prince Albert for Jim's release. A peace officer was required to accompany the parolee as far as the U.S. border, then Reverend Strong and Mary Susan would take him to Great Falls. With the assistance of the American Baptist Congregation, the Salvation Army and the John Howard Society, Jim could settle in to his new home. Once he was settled in, Mary Susan would be free to return home.

In June 1930, arrangements were made for Mary Susan to travel by train from Kansas City to Great Falls. She met with the various partners in Jim's care, and at that first meeting, Mary Susan was introduced to each of the individuals who would be responsible for her father's shopping; cooking; laundry; housekeeping; as well as yard and home maintenance. A nurse would check on him regularly and a doctor would be available as needed.

Mary Susan then travelled by train from Great Falls to Prince Albert where she was met by Chaplain Strong and Attorney Hill. She would wait there until her father's parole date while final details were attended to.

On October 8th, 1930, Mary Susan met with a reporter from the Ratner District where Jim Howard had lived before going to prison. She said she was writing a 'Ratner News' column for the Melfort Journal and was interested in the reasons for his release. Mary Susan told the reporter, "My father is being released for three main reasons; because, as an old man with arthritis and a crippled arm, his health is likely to suffer if he's kept in prison. For him, being in prison is a hardship that couldn't be seen when he was sentenced. And finally, he has applied for deportation, agreeing to be kept in this prison until he is paroled." Then, "The State of Montana has agreed to accept him as a resident in a house he has there and I have agreed to escort him to Montana and to look after him."

An October 10th meeting of Attorney Hill, the Prince Albert Salvation Army, the Prince Albert John Howard Society, Chaplain Strong, Mary Susan and Jim Howard, chaired by the Warden provided opportunity for the Warden to announce, on behalf of the Secretary of State and the Government of Canada that James Marion Howard was granted Parole by Deportation to begin on October 11th, 1930.

Jim Howard, Mary Susan, Chaplain Strong and Attorney Hill were met at the large wooden prison gate by an RCMP officer who escorted them to the Prince Albert train station and accompanied them by train to Regina where he left them to board an overnight train to Great Falls.

Jim gazed out the train window as it snaked through the newly harvested, snow-covered farm fields from Prince Albert to Regina. He thought about how much more quickly they slipped past the window now than they had when he and Birt crossed them on horseback just nineteen years ago He realized that in those 19 years he'd been able to discover that this country is one of patience. To understand the beauty of this place, one had to understand, as he'd come to, why this land is seen as 'next year country'. In deep contemplation, he regretted his role in helping merge this land in the northeast with other prairie lands that been conquered by the breaking plow and overcrowded by man. He regretted being part of this course of destruction of free lands. His years in prison had given him a new appreciation of this land's vastness, romance, awe and sometimes it's heart-breaking loneliness. He knew, free or not, he'd miss all that forever.

It would take Jim many months of freedom to feel comfortable in his new home, especially after existing within a system of silence and deprivation. But after a few weeks of adjustment and settling into a routine, it was time for Jim to send Mary Susan home to Kansas City to her family once more. She promised to carry greetings to her brother and their uncle Frank from the man who had 'survived' his own assassination.

So late one autumn day, as the falling leaves spoke of the coming winter, Jim and Mary Susan went to the train station to say a final farewell before the train left for Kansas City.

The station was only a block from Jim's house, and they strolled slowly as Mary Susan held Jim's arm, more to offer him support than for him to support her. Fallen leaves blew around their feet and whispered softly with each step. Knowing that it was unlikely he'd ever see her again, he was unable to hold his tears back.

"I'm so happy that you came to fetch me from that jail. I didn't deserve your forgiveness, especially after so many years of abandoning you. Your mother and I were sure that life would be much better for you children and her without me in your lives. I had a price on my head, and was running and hiding from the law." Jim paused to wipe a tear away and swallowed twice before he could go on. His voice broke. "You have your mother's beauty. You look just like her. My going away and avoiding contact with you all was an act of love but I never stopped loving you. That's why Chaplain Strong thought I should write. Even if you hadn't come, I'd still always be glad that I wrote you," Jim said.

"I never stopped loving you either, Papa," Mary Susan responded. "I never stopped loving you and never stopped thinking about you. I missed you terribly at first when I thought you were dead, but I was just a little girl and finally got used to it. Your first letter shocked and surprised me, but after each letter, I could hardly wait for the next one. They gave me the past I'd missed, and they told me you'd been missing us too. I know it now. I'm glad I came and we that we got to spend this time together."

"I have to go back to Kansas City now, but I'll take your love with me and leave mine with you. I want my family to see you before you're gone." Mary Susan became quiet and a shadow of her childhood grief passed through her eyes before she went on. "Please take care of yourself, Papa."

"Don't worry. I'm only 83 and my mother lived 'til she was 86 so I expect to be here for a while yet."

"Please look after yourself and write often. We all want to see you again."

"Take my love to your three boys and your husband. Your brother and his family too. Even if I've never met many of them, I love them all because they are part of you." Jim had never been one to show his love openly, but he quickly straightened up and leaned into Mary Susan. He put his good arm around her shoulders and looked into her eyes.

"Before you get on the train, let me give you a big hug and a kiss. This is farewell, but not good bye." They embraced in a hug and shared a tender kiss before Mary Susan reluctantly climbed onto the train.

James Marion Howard's life was born yet again. This time, he would make it a good one.

AFTERWORD

A RECORD OF SASKATCHEWAN HISTORY SHOWS THAT, AFTER AN altercation with and the shooting of Thomas Halcro on October 24, 1924, James Marion (Jim) Howard was charged with murder and convicted of manslaughter, in Melfort Court of King's Bench. He was sentenced on Nov. 5th 1924 to 15 years in the Saskatchewan Penitentiary in Prince Albert. Judge H.V. MacDonald presided with Attorney General's Agent F.B. Goodwill, prosecuting and A.E. Cairns, of Cairns, Hill & Cairns as counsel for Howard who pleaded not guilty. The jury was called by C. Hatton, clerk of the court; In my records search, Representatives from Archives stated that there is <u>absolutely no way</u> to recover <u>any</u> record of this Court of King's Bench trial. Why? I've established from various records that:

1. The Protestant Chaplain's (J.I. Strong) register, (the original which I now possess after it was discovered in a pile of junk about to be thrown out), states that upon being received at the Saskatchewan Penitentiary on Nov. 6th, 1924, Howard

was recorded as a baptized Baptist, came from Missouri, and moved in and out of the Moose Mountain area often. He was given the # 1133;

2. The Protestant Chaplain's register records Howard as being discharged by parole on November 10, 1930. Could this have been either a Ticket of Leave and/or a Parole by Exception?

3. Could Howard have been born Jesse James, a farm boy in Missouri in the U.S.A.? James' family had been slave owners and he had been a Confederate guerilla fighter in the American Civil War. Carrying on the fighting after the war, he'd been an infamous outlaw. Wanted dead or alive, with a price on his head, my story claims that he'd agreed to a fraudulent assassination and escaped to Montana. There, I claim that after working for a couple years as a ranch hand, he'd returned to the outlaw life. Not wanting the danger anymore, he'd escaped to Canada where successful homesteading could earn his

Canadian citizenship and an escape from being a wanted outlaw.

1. Though I have created a story line that is fictitious, I have used facts supported by evidence in court reports, local newspaper accounts, American Census, Canadian prison records from a Chaplain in the Saskatchewan Penitentiary where Howard was incarcerated, and local lore as given by living witnesses and handed down legends.

2. Based on Max McCoy's book, Jesse, A Novel of the Outlaw, Jesse James, I surmised that the Matrilineal DNA gathered from James' grave established that the body was the child of Zeralda. It could have come from a brother or half-brother who had the same mother as James. Jesse's half-brother, in my story, could have been the body buried in that grave.

3. I'm not sure the mystery will ever be solved, but I was convinced that Jim Howard was Jesse James when I showed an old photo from a history book to my father without telling him who it was, and he smiled in recollection. He looked back into his childhood and identified it as his childhood hero, James Marian Howard.

ACKNOWLEDGEMENTS

JENNIFER MAHLBERG – my step daughter, who so kindly, created my cover page.

ALVIN (ALLIE) HAMMERSMITH (1910 - 2010) in 2002, discussions with my father - convinced me that the Jim Howard story could drive a historical fiction novel.

MOLLY (BYERS) HAMMERSMITH (1910-2000) – my mother's patience, encouraging focus through years of false-starts, contributed greatly to this work.

KAREN BOOTH – My sister, telling me in 2002, "Somebody better write that story,"

JOAN M. HAMMERSMITH – my loving wife, without whose support, editorial and IT advice, this work couldn't have been completed

TAMMY AND MICHAEL BURGESS – Big Muddy ranchers, writers and artists. They told us about Joseph "Jasper" Huntley, who'd lived on their land in 1901 and also told us much about the Big Muddy outlaw history. They gave us the name of Robert Mann as a potential reference in Plentywood, Montana.

PENNY MARKLAND -Branch Librarian of the Wapiti of the Melfort Public Library found 1924 Melfort Journal newspaper accounts from which the story began to unfold.

BILL BARRY – a Saskatchewan historian who directed me to resources for the history of the Teddington School District and Saskatchewan homesteads

CLIFF MOORE – Chief, Education, Saskatchewan Penitentiary - Moore found Anglican Chaplain J.I. Strong's Register containing entries showing that James Howard had indeed been there.

CARILYN SCHWARTZ and **CATHERINE HOLMES** supported by Saskatoon staff of the SASKATCHEWAN ARCHIVES BOARD were very helpful in my search for facts.

TIM NOVAK - Archivist, SASKATCHEWAN ARCHIVES BOARD was very helpful in the search for written records of the Jim Howard trial and conviction

CELESTE HANNANT - Information Services Corporation, Prince Albert, SK. provided useful information regarding homesteads and early land transactions.

JAMIE BENSON - Prince Albert Historical Museum provided helpful information concerning homesteading, the 1911 Prince Albert streetscape and the 1911 Dominion Land Titles Office.

KIRK WALLACE - Researcher, Western Development Museum, Saskatoon provided helpful information regarding Saskatchewan pioneer history and R.M. of Willow Creek history details.

STEVE SMITH & **KATE REILLY** – in Nelson, New Zealand, provided friendship, lodging, sustenance, IT and cooking magic nurturing what passes for my creativity.

R.M. of NIPAWIN at **CODETTE** and **R.M. of WILLOW CREEK** at **BROOKSBY** – provided helpful homestead information as hard evidence of Howard's Saskatchewan presence.

ROBERT MANN - Plentywood. MT druggist and historian – provided historical discussion and many references.

RESOURCES

Bennie J. McRae Jr. (1996) "*Black Cowboys*" in January 1996 edition of "Lest We Forget," LWF Publications, http://www.historynet.com/

Cordley, Richard, *(1895) A History of Lawrence, KA, E.P. Coldwell, Lawrence, Kansas.*

Edwards, John N. (1877) *The Making of a Confederate Guerilla* by, Bryan, Brand and Company, Chicago. Edwards, John N (1877) Noted Guerillas, Bryan Brand and Company, original from Oxford Press.

Hansen, Ron (1983) *The Assassination of Jesse James* by the Coward Robert Ford.

Lewis, Margaret L. (1999-2000) "*Murder on a Beautiful Afternoon, 'Portneuf Canyon Stage Robbery,*" P.31, December Issue of *Treasure Cache Magazine,* Lost Treasure Inc.

Marley, Brant (1998), *Jesse James: The Man and The Myth,* Berkley Trade.

Max McCoy (1999), *JESSE, A NOVEL OF THE OUTLAW JESSE JAMES,* Bantam Books, New York.

McCorkle, John, (1998) *Three Years with Quantrill: A True Story,* University of Oklahoma Press.

Settle William A. Jr. (1977) *Jesse James Was His Name,* University of Nebraska Press.

Steele, Phillip (2003) *Jesse and Frank James: The Family History.*

Stiles, (2002) T.J. *Jesse James: The Last Rebel of the Civil War,* Alfred A. Knopf

Washington Post, (1911), *Obituary of Zerelda (James) Samuel*

Yeatman, Ted P (2001). *Frank and Jesse James: The Story Behind the Legend,* Cumberland House.

ONLINE REFERENCES

1. http://www.legendsofamerica.com/

2. http://www.legendsofamerica.com/we-cowboys.html

3. http://www.legendsofamerica.com/we-ponyexpress.html

4. https://www.losttreasure.com/Home/Archives

5. https://www.amazon.com/Mystery-Jesse-James-Investigating-History/dp/B000RJ6MOW

6. http://www.ericfoner.com/reviews/092202latimes.html

7. http://www.truewestmagazine.com/was-jesse-james-a-terrorist/

CPSIA information can be obtained
at www.ICGtesting.com
Printed in the USA
LVOW11s0252020118
561474LV00001B/1/P

9 781773 702810